BODIES IN WINTER

A New York mystery from a talented new writer

On a cold winter's morning in New York, NYPD detective Harry Corbin and his partner Adele Bentibi arrive at the scene of a murder. It looks like a cut-and-dried case but, as Corbin and Bentibi investigate, they uncover a murky world of bent cops and cover-ups that puts both of their careers (and their lives) in serious danger...

BODIES IN WINTER

Robert Knightly

Severn House Large Print
London & New York

This first large print edition published 2013
in Great Britain and the USA by
SEVERN HOUSE PUBLISHERS LTD of
9-15 High Street, Sutton, Surrey, SM1 1DF.
First world regular print edition published 2009 by
Severn House Publishers Ltd., London and New York.

British Library Cataloguing in Publication Data

Knightly, Robert.
  Bodies in winter. -- (A Corbin and Bentibi mystery ; 1)
  1. New York (N.Y.). Police Dept--Fiction. 2. Ex-police
  officers--Crimes against--Fiction. 3. Police corruption--
  Fiction. 4. Detective and mystery stories. 5. Large type
  books.
  I. Title II. Series
  813.6-dc23

  ISBN-13: 978-0-7278-9996-5

Severn House Publishers support The Forest Stewardship Council
[FSC], the leading international forest certification organisation. All
our titles that are printed on Greenpeace-approved FSC-certified paper
carry the FSC logo.

Printed and bound in Great Britain by the
MPG Books Group, Bodmin, Cornwall.

PROLOGUE

Officer David Lodge stumbles when he attempts to enter the blue and white patrol car double-parked in front of the 83rd Precinct, dropping first to one knee, then to the seat of his pants. His nightstick, which he failed to pull from the ring attached to his belt, is the most immediate cause of his fall. When it jams between the door and the frame, Lodge has one leg in the vehicle with the other just coming up. From that point, there's nowhere to go but down.

Lodge ignores his colleague's hearty chuckle. For a moment, as he struggles to gather himself, he stares at a full moon hanging over Wilson Avenue. He wonders if the moon's bloated appearance is due to the brown haze and drenching humidity trapped in the atmosphere. Or if it's just that his eyes won't focus because he passed the hours prior to his tour at the local cop bar, the B&G on Stockholm Street. Lodge has reached that stage of inebriation characterized by powerful emotions and he stares at the moon as if prepared to cradle it in his arms, to embrace a truth he is certain it embodies.

'Yo, spaceman, you comin' or what?'

The voice belongs to David Lodge's partner, Dante Russo. He who must be obeyed. Lodge

5

works his way to his feet, then yanks his nightstick free before getting into the car. He is about
to address his partner, to offer some sort of half-
hearted apology, when the radio crackles to life.

Eighty-three George, K.

Russo starts the vehicle, shifts into gear and
pulls away from the curb. 'That's us, Dave,' he
reminds his partner.

Lodge brings the microphone to his mouth.
'Eighty-three George.'

*George, we have a 10:54 at four-three-seven
Wyckoff Avenue. A woman unconscious in the
lobby.*

'That's in Boy's sector, Central.'

Eighty-three Boy is on a job, K.

'Ten-four.'

Russo proceeds along Wilson Avenue, passing
beneath the Myrtle Avenue El before turning
onto Himrod Street. The job on Wyckoff Avenue
is now behind them.

'Where we goin', Dante?' Lodge suddenly
asks, the fog having lifted from his brain
momentarily. He adjusts the louvers on the air-
conditioning vents, directing the flow to his
crotch. 'The job's in the other direction,' he says,
craning his neck to peer out the window at the
street signs slipping by.

'We're goin' where we always go.'

'For coffee? You serious?'

Lodge steals a glance at his partner when his
questions go unanswered. Dante's thin nose is in
the air, his jaw thrust forward, his lips pinched
into a thin disapproving line. Not for the first
time, Lodge feels an urge to drive his fist into

6

that chin, to flatten that nose, bloody that mouth. Instead, he settles his weight against the backrest and faces the truth. Without Dante Russo, David Lodge wouldn't make it through his tours, not since he started having blackouts. Plus, nobody else wants to work with him. 'Shitkicker' is what his peers call him. As in, 'You hear what the Shitkicker did last night?'

'What about the job?' he finally says. 'What do I tell Central if they wanna know where we are?'

Russo sighs, another irritating habit. 'C'mon, Dave, wise up. We both know it's gonna be some junkie so overdosed her buddies dumped her in the lobby like yesterday's garbage. Now maybe you wanna go mouth-to-mouth, suck up that good HIV spit, but me, I'm gonna let the paramedics worry about catchin' a dreaded disease. They got a better health plan.'

When Lodge and Russo finally roll up on the scene twenty minutes later, two Fire Department paramedics are loading a gurney into an ambulance. A woman strapped to the gurney attempts to sit up, despite the restraints.

'You see what I'm saying?' Dante Russo washes down the last of a frosted doughnut with the last of his coffee. 'Things worked out alright. No harm, no foul.'

Three hours later, Russo breaks a long silence with an appreciative whistle. 'Well, lookee here, just the man I wanna see.'

Lodge brings a soda bottle to his mouth and takes a quick sip. The one-to-one mix of 7-UP and vodka lifts his spirits. He is on the verge of a blackout now, and predictably reckless.

'What's up?'

'The Beemer.' Russo jerks his chin at a white BMW trimmed with gold chrome.

'What about it?'

'That's our boy.'

'Which boy?'

'David, that there car belongs to Mr Clarence Spott.'

'Who?'

'Spott's picture is hangin' in the muster room. He's one of the bad guys.' Dante's mouth expands into a humorless smile. 'Whatta ya say we bust his balls a little?'

'Fine with me.'

When Russo momentarily lights up the roof rack and the BMW pulls to the curb, both cops immediately exit their patrol car. They are on Knickerbocker Avenue, the main commercial drag in the Brooklyn neighborhood of Bushwick. The small retail stores lining both sides of the avenue are long closed, their graffiti-covered shutters drawn and padlocked.

After a quick glance in both directions, Lodge joins Russo who stands a few feet from the BMW's open window. Lodge knows he should approach the vehicle from the passenger side, that his job here is to cover his partner. But David Lodge has never been a by-the-book police officer, far from it, and when his partner doesn't object, he settles down to enjoy the show.

'Why you stoppin' me, man?' Clarence Spott's full mouth is twisted into a pained grimace. 'I

8

ain't done nothin'.'

'Step outta the car,' Russo orders. 'And that's *officer*, not man.'

'I ain' goin' no place till I find out why you stopped me. This here is racial profilin'. It's unconstitutional.'

Russo slaps his nightstick against the palm of his hand. 'Clarence, you don't come out, and I mean right this fuckin' minute, I'm gonna crack your windshield.'

The door opens and Spott emerges. A short, heavily muscled black man, his expression – eyes wide, brows raised, big mouth already moving – reeks of outrage. Lodge can smell the stink from where he stands. And it's not as if Spott, who keeps his hands in view at all times, isn't familiar with the rules of the game. There's just something in him that doesn't know when to shut up.

'Ah'm still axin' the same question. Why you pull me over when I'm drivin' down a public street, mindin' my own damn business?'

Russo ignores the inquiry. 'I want you to put your hands on top of the vehicle and spread your legs. I want you to do it right now.'

Spott finally crosses the line, as Lodge knew he would, by adding the word *pig* to his next sentence. Lodge slaps him in the face, a mild reprimand from Lodge's point of view, but Spott sees it differently. His eyes close for a moment as he draws a long breath through his nose. Then he uncoils, quick as a snake, and drives his fist into the left side of David Lodge's face.

Taken by surprise, Lodge staggers backward,

9

leaving Spott to Dante Russo, who assumes a two-handed grip on his nightstick before cracking it into Spott's unprotected shins. When Spott drops to his knees on the pavement, Russo slides the nightstick beneath his throat and pulls back, choking off a howl of pain.

'How you wanna do this, Clarence? Easy or hard?'

As Spott cannot speak, he indicates compliance by going limp and crossing his hands behind his back.

Russo eases up slightly, then pushes Spott forward onto his chest. 'You alright?' he asks his partner.

'Never better.'

David Lodge brings his hand to the blood running from a deep cut along his cheekbone. Suddenly, he feels sharp, even purposeful. As he watches his partner cuff and search the prisoner before loading him into the back seat, he thinks: *OK, this is where it gets good.* His hand goes almost of itself to the soda bottle stuffed beneath the seat when he enters the vehicle. He barely tastes the vodka as it slides down his throat.

'You got any particular place in mind?' his partner asks as he shifts the patrol car into gear.

'Not as long as it's private. One thing I hate, it's bein' interrupted when I'm kickin' some nigger's ass.'

Lieutenant Justin Whitlock sets the precinct log aside when David Lodge and Dante Russo lead Clarence Spott into the 83rd Precinct, universally called the 'Eight-Three' by those who toil

10

within its walls. Both sides of Spott's face are bruised and he leans to the left with his arm pressed to his ribs. His right eye, already crusting, is swollen shut.

Whitlock is seated at a desk behind a wooden railing that runs the width of the Precinct reception area, serving to keep the public at a safe distance from their protectors. He glances from the prisoner to Russo, then notices the blood on David Lodge's face and Lodge's blood-soaked collar.

'That your blood, Lodge?'

'Yeah. The mutt caught me a good one and we hadda subdue him.'

Whitlock nods twice. The injury is something he can work with.

'I want you to go over to the emergency room at Wyckoff Heights and have that wound sewn up. Count the stitches and make sure you obtain a copy of the medical report. Better yet, insist that a micro-surgeon do the job. Tell 'em you don't wanna spoil your good looks.'

'What about the paperwork on the arrest, lou? Shouldn't I get started?'

'No, secure the prisoner, then get your ass over to Wyckoff. Your partner will handle the paperwork.' Whitlock's expression softens as he turns to Russo. 'How 'bout you, Dante? You hurt?'

Russo flicks out a left jab. 'Not me, lou, I'm too quick.'

'I see.' Whitlock glances at the prisoner. 'Did the mutt use a weapon?'

'Yeah, lou, that ring. That's what cut Dave's cheek.' Russo lifts Spott's right hand to display a pinkie ring with a single large diamond at its center. 'You know what woulda happened if Dave had gotten hit in the eye?'

'He'd be out on the street with a cane.' Whitlock's smile broadens. He and Russo are on the same track. 'Charge the hump with aggravated assault on a police officer. That should keep the asshole busy. And make sure you take that ring. That ring is evidence.'

Spott finally speaks up. 'I wanna call my lawyer,' he mumbles through swollen lips.

'What'd he say?' Whitlock asks.

'I think he said something about your mother, lieutenant,' Russo declares.

Russo leads Spott through a gate in the railing, then shoves him toward the cells at the rear of the building. 'Hi ho, hi ho,' he sings, 'it's off to jail we go.'

Smiling at his partner's little joke, David Lodge trails behind.

Five minutes later, Dante Russo emerges to announce, 'The prisoner is secure and Officer Lodge is off to the hospital.'

'You think he's sober enough to find his way?'

Russo starts to defend his partner, then suddenly changes tack with a shrug of his shoulders. 'Dave's out of control,' he admits. 'If I wasn't there tonight, who knows what would've happened. I mean, I been tryin' to straighten the guy out, but he just won't listen.'

'I coulda told you that when you took him on as your partner.'

'What was I supposed to do? I was told that

12

nobody wanted to work with him. I'm the union delegate, remember? Helping cops in trouble is part of my job.'

The conversation drifts for a bit, away from David Lodge, finally settling on the precinct commander, Captain Joe Hagerty. Crime is up in the precinct for the second straight year and Hagerty is on the way out. Though his replacement has yet to be named, the veterans fear a wholesale shake-up. Dante Russo, of course, at age twenty-five, is far from a veteran. But he's definitely a rising star within the cop union, the Patrolman's Benevolent Association – a rising star with serious connections. Dante's uncle is the Trustee for Brooklyn North and sits on the PBA's Board of Directors.

They are still at it thirty minutes later when Officers Daryl Johnson and Hector Arias waltz an adolescent prisoner into the building. Dwarfed by the two cops, the boy is weeping.

'He done the crime,' Arias observes, 'but he don't wanna do the time.'

'Found him comin' out a window of the Sung Ri warehouse on Gratton Street,' Daryl Johnson adds. 'He had this TV in his arms; the thing was bigger than he was.' Johnson gives his prisoner an affectionate cuff on the back of the head. 'What were ya gonna do, jerk, carry it all the way back to the Bushwick Projects?'

'Put him in a cell,' Whitlock says, 'and notify the detectives. They'll wanna talk to him in the morning.'

'Ten-four, lou.'

Not more than two minutes later, Daryl

13

Johnson returns. Johnson is a short overweight black man long renowned for his deadpan expression. This time, however, his heavy jowls are lifted by an extension of his lips unrelated to a smile. 'That mope locked up back there? I mean it's none of my business, but who does he belong to?'

'Me,' Russo responds. 'Why?'

'Because he's dead is why. Because somebody caved in his fucking skull.'

The evidence implicating David Lodge in the death of Clarence Spott is compelling, as Ted Savio explains in the course of a fateful meeting at a Rikers Island jail several months later. Ted Savio is Lodge's attorney, provided gratis by the PBA.

Although Savio's advice is perfectly reasonable, Lodge is nevertheless reluctant to accept it. Lodge has been ninety days without a drink and the ordeal of cold turkey withdrawal has produced in him an almost feral sense of caution. Alone in his cell day after day, he has become as untrusting as an animal caught in a snare. At times, especially at night, the urge to escape the inescapable pushes him to the brink of uncontrolled panic. At other times, he drops into a black hole of despair that leaves him barely able to respond to the demands of his keepers.

'You gotta face the facts here, Dave,' Savio patiently explains. 'Which, I note, are lined up against you. You can't even account for your movements.'

'I had a blackout. It wasn't the first time.'

14

'You say that like you maybe lost your concentration for a minute. Meanwhile, they found you passed out in the basement, the empty vodka bottle at your feet.'

'I knew that's where it was kept,' Lodge admits. 'But just because I was drunk doesn't mean I killed Spott.'

'You had the victim's blood on your uniform and your blood was found on the victim.'

'That could've happened when we subdued the mutt.'

'We?'

'Me and my partner.'

'Dave, your partner didn't have a drop of blood on him.' Savio makes an unsuccessful attempt at eye contact with his client, then continues. 'What you need to do here is see the big picture. Dante Russo told Lieutenant Whitlock that he had to pull you off Clarence Spott. He said this before the body was found, he repeated it to a Grand Jury, he'll testify to it in open court. That's enough to bury you all by itself, even without Officer Anthony Szarek's testimony.'

'The Broom,' Lodge moans. 'I'm being done in by the fucking Broom.'

'The Broom?'

'Szarek, he's a couple years short of a thirty-year pension and the job's carrying him. He spends most of his tour sweeping the precinct. That bottle they found me with? That was his.'

'Well, Broom or not, Szarek's gonna say that he was present when you and Russo brought Spott to the holding cells, that he heard Russo tell you to go to the hospital, that he watched

15

Russo walk away...'

'Stop sayin' his name.' Lodge raises a fist to his shoulder as if about to deliver a punch. 'Fucking Dante Russo. If I could just get to him, just for a minute.'

'What'd you think? That you and your partner would go down with the ship together? Maybe holding hands? Well, Dave, it's time for you to start using your head.'

Lodge draws a deep breath, then glances around the room. Gray concrete floor, green cinder-block walls, a table bolted to the floor, plastic chairs on aluminum legs. And that's it. The room where he confers with his attorney is as barren as his cell, as barren as the message his attorney delivers.

'Face the facts, Dave. Take the plea. It's not gonna get any better and it could be withdrawn.'

'Man One?'

'That's right, Manslaughter First Degree. You take the deal, you'll be out in seven years. On the other hand, you go to trial, find yourself convicted of Murder Second Degree, you could be lookin' at twenty-five to life. Right now you're thirty-seven years old. You can do the seven years and still have a life left when you're paroled.'

Though Lodge believes his lawyer, he still can't bring himself to accept Savio's counsel. At times over the past months, he's literally banged his head against the wall in an effort to jog his memory. Drunk or sober, he feels no guilt about the parts he can vaguely recall. Yeah, he tuned-up Spott. He must have, because he remembers

16

Russo driving to a heavily industrial section of Bushwick north of Flushing Avenue; remembers turning onto Bogart Street where it dead-ends against the railroad tracks, remembers yanking Spott out of the back seat. Spott had resisted despite the cuffs.

But Spott deserved his punishment. He'd committed a crime familiar to every member of every police force in the world: Contempt of Cop. You didn't run from cops, you didn't disrespect them with your big mouth, and you never, under any circumstances, hit them. If you did, you paid a price.

That was it, though, as much as Lodge remembered. To the best of his recollection he'd never entertained the possibility of murdering a prisoner. Never.

'What if I'm innocent?' he finally asks his lawyer.

'What if there's a million black people residing in Brooklyn who already think you're guilty?' his lawyer replies.

ONE

There's something about bodies in winter that gets to me. I'm referring to bodies found out of doors on weekday mornings when an ambient temperature of twenty-one degrees is reinforced by a wind cold enough to crack the porcelain on your teeth. Mornings when a malevolent sun glares down from the bluest of innocent blue skies, when blood congeals into greasy black balls that resemble nothing so much as rabbit droppings on a suburban lawn.

When I first saw David Lodge I wanted to cover him with a blanket, to comfort him, to preserve the heat of his body. I wanted to compensate him for having the misfortune to be murdered in January. He was lying at an angle in a tiny yard, his feet pointing out towards a low railing dividing yard from sidewalk, his head nearly touching the foundation of a modest, two-family house. The house was on Palmetto Street in the Queens neighborhood of Ridgewood.

'He tried to crawl away. You see that, Corbin? The wall stopped him.'

The voice belonged to my partner, Detective

18

Adele Bentibi. Adele always called me by my last name. Not Harry, as I was generally known to my peers, but simply Corbin, with a heavy emphasis on the first syllable.

'Show me.'

Adele gestured to parallel smears of blood running across the brown grass. 'He got hit, went to his knees and tried to crawl away. The head shot finished him.'

We were standing on the street side of the railing, having made our way through and around an army of little paper flags that marked the resting positions of spent 9mm cartridges. The paper flags were numbered, one to thirty-three, and most had already blown over. Ahead of us, David Lodge was lying on his left side, one leg curled nearly into his chest. His left arm was bent beneath him, his right splayed out with the wrist twisted into a position so unnatural it could only have been produced by violent death.

There was blood everywhere. On the sidewalk, the railing, the grass and especially on David Lodge. His wool trousers were saturated with blood, from mid-thigh to the tops of his black engineer boots. But it wasn't blood loss that killed him, or at least I didn't think so. Lodge had a small bullet wound in his right temple, a little forward of his hair line. Though I couldn't see an exit wound from where I stood, a halo of spatter extending outward to stain the concrete foundation of the house guaranteed its presence.

'How close was the shooter?'

'Within a few inches of the vic's temple.' She pointed to a small object next to Lodge's right ear. 'You see the brass? The shooter had to be leaning down with the gun twisted to the right for the brass to end up that close to the body.'

I think Adele would have liked nothing better than to jump the railing and examine each of Lodge's many bullet wounds. But the yard enclosing Lodge's body was no more than eight-by-ten feet and there was blood all through it. I could see a half-dozen shoe impressions from where I stood. Had they been left by Lodge's killer? Or by the first cops on the scene who'd checked for a pulse and ID on the victim? Whichever the case, there was nothing to be gained by adding to the chaos.

'Are we done here?' I asked Adele. My toes were numb, as were the tips of my fingers, the tip of my nose and both ear lobes.

Adele shrugged, the gesture without sympathy. For her, foul weather was something you ignored in your quest for excellence. Adele often spoke about excellence, about bringing excellence to life's mundane tasks, and I could see it in her meticulous approach to small details. The larger tasks, on the other hand, the big picture, sometimes escaped her. Adele and her husband, Mel, for instance, were perpetually on the verge of separation. And then there was the simple fact that when it came to interviews and interrogations, she didn't have a clue.

A Crime Scene Unit step-van pulled up behind the cordon of vehicles on the north end of Palmetto Street, luring Adele's attention away from the crime scene. She shielded her eyes from the sun, then announced, 'Ray Gutierrez.'

For a moment, I was caught up in the miniature suns reflected in her perfectly manicured fingernails. They formed shimmering white circles in the clear polish. But then her hand dropped to her side and she began to work her way toward the van, placing her feet carefully to avoid the scattered brass. I think she would have committed hari-kari before moving one of those casings so much as a millimeter.

Sergeant Ramon Gutierrez was a short balding man with a round belly that strained the front of his white jumpsuit. His perpetually sour expression (or so he once told me over drinks) had been honed by years of trying to extract physical evidence from scenes contaminated by the very cops charged with protecting them.

'Anybody approach the body?' he asked.

'The first uniforms on the scene.' I gestured to Officers Pearlman and Aveda. They were standing just inside a yellow streamer that extended all the way across the street, talking to their boss, Sgt Vinny Murrano.

'Anybody else?' Gutierrez asked.

A blaring horn drowned out Adele's response. Thirty yards away, my own boss, Detective Lieutenant Bill Sarney, was parked at the curb. Impatient as always, he waved us over.

'Bad news,' I told my partner as we hastened to obey. Sarney was a hands-off supervisor who only showed up when a particular job was likely to attract the attention of the bosses.

'Why bad?' For Adele, the bosses' scrutiny was an opportunity to prove her worth. For me,

21

the facts on the ground told another, much sadder story. If the investigation produced results, the bosses took the credit. If the investigation went bad, the rank-and-file caught the blame. Given that my promotion to detective, second grade, along with a transfer to Homicide Division, was almost a done deal, I'd just as soon have passed under the radar screen.

I glanced back at David Lodge as I approached the unmarked Caprice. He didn't look any warmer at a distance than he did up close.

The inside of Sarney's car was toasty-warm and I opened my coat to let in the heat. Sarney was sitting behind the wheel, alongside Adele. 'Tell me what you've got so far,' he demanded.

'We put out an alert,' Adele explained, 'for a late model, four-door sedan, dark red.'

The *we* part wasn't strictly true. Sgt Murrano had put out the alert after interviewing a pair of eyewitnesses. That was before we arrived.

'That mean you got witnesses?'

'Two so far. They live upstairs.'

'Did you speak to them?'

'Lou,' I interrupted, 'we arrived all of twenty minutes ago, but if you want an evaluation, here it is. The vic, David Lodge, was murdered by persons unknown who subsequently fled the scene. And what we're doing, me and my partner, is investigating.'

Sarney flashed a grim smile. 'The victim, David Lodge, you know who he is?'

'*That* David Lodge?' Adele asked. 'The cop? I thought he was in jail.'

22

'Apparently not.'

By this time, I'd realized who they were talking about. David Lodge was an obscure street cop working out of the Eight-Three who'd killed a pimp named Clarence Spott in a precinct holding cell. This was six or seven years ago, when I was a street cop myself, working out of the 34th in northern Manhattan. Needless to say, Lodge was the hot topic of conversation at the house, as he was in every precinct throughout the five boroughs. The way I remember it, he had few defenders because the killing was obviously deliberate. The consensus was that he'd crossed a line when he drove the sap into the back of Spott's head and paid the price.

But there was another consensus, this one in the community at large, that drew a different line when Lodge was allowed to plead to Man-One instead of murder. Encouraged by self-righteous editorials in New York's three major newspapers, a coalition of civil rights groups had conducted a massive protest in the park fronting City Hall. I'd worked that protest, assigned to temporary crowd-control by a desk lieutenant who didn't like me all that much anyway. I was cursed at and taunted for three and a half hours. All the things that no mutt on the street would dare to say to a cop's face were said to me. Though I was able to control my actions, my emotions ran wild, relentless as army ants. By the time it was over, I hated the faces on the other side of the barricades as much as they hated mine.

Score one for Lieutenant Sarney. He'd per-

23

ceived the threat. Now he was here to protect his interests.

Adele broke the silence. 'There were two shooters,' she announced. 'They drove down the block, jumped out of the car, and began to fire as they approached the victim. The brass is 9mm, laid down in a pair of converging tracks, and the casings are evenly spaced, at least for the most part. Given the number of rounds fired, the shooters probably used something exotic, a TEC-9, maybe, or an Uzi. A pair of ordinary handguns won't hold enough rounds to leave that much brass.' She paused long enough to gesture at the crime scene, then continued. 'The victim was on the sidewalk when the first bullets hit him. There's blood on the concrete and more blood on the railing where he jumped the fence. By this time, his thighs were pumping blood and his pressure must have been dropping because the best he could do was crawl toward the house. At least one of the shooters followed him into the yard. The fatal shot was fired into his head from no more than a few inches away.'

At the other end of the block, a woman burst from a house and began to run toward the crime scene. She was intercepted by a pair of newly arrived officers bearing paper bags that displayed the Dunkin Donuts logo. The cops spoke to the woman briefly, then waved to Vinny Murrano who walked over to join them. It was time to get moving again.

I opened the door and set a foot on the street. 'Thanks for the warning, lou,' I said. 'We appreciate it.'

Though Sarney was barely into his forties, his noticeably rounded skull was entirely bald on top. When he was being serious, he liked to lower his chin, to present his subordinates with that shiny dome. He did it now, at the same time cocking his head to the right.

'Don't fuck around with this,' he warned. 'Cross the *t*'s, dot the *i*'s. And if anything unusual comes up – and I mean *anything* – I wanna know about it right away.'

Sarney was looking directly at me as he spoke, and I had the feeling that he was asking for a commitment. Certainly, he had the right. Sarney was my mentor, my rabbi. If not for his personal efforts, neither my promotion, nor my transfer to Homicide – an assignment I'd coveted from my earliest days on the job – would be in the works.

I smiled reassuringly and winked. 'Ten-four, lou. Message received.'

TWO

We made a pair of stops before interviewing the witnesses. The idea was to alert the two sergeants on the scene, Murrano and Gutierrez, to the victim's celebrity. Gutierrez thanked us for the tip, then went back to supervising his workers, one of whom was photographing the shoe impressions leading to the victim's body.

Vinny Murrano was more informative. 'That

woman who ran down the block,' he told us before we could deliver our message, 'is Ellen Lodge, the vic's spouse.'

'You put her on ice?' Adele asked.

'I told her you'd be wantin' an interview. Seems like she runs a day-care center out of her house and won't be going anywhere until the parents come by to fetch the kiddies.'

A flurry of movement drew my attention away from the conversation. I turned just in time to see a cardinal land on a telephone wire across the street. The bird's red feathers were puffed out against the cold, lending it an almost round profile, like an escaped Christmas ornament. It sang once, a complex song that seemed expectant to me, as though it anticipated a response. But when the only response was a gray morgue wagon turning onto the street, the bird flew into the upper branches of a sycamore thirty feet away.

When I looked back, Adele was explaining the significance of Lieutenant Sarney's arrival. Murrano listened closely, then said, 'So that's what the wife meant when she told me her husband just got out of jail yesterday morning.' He ran his fingers through his hair as though checking to make sure he hadn't lost his most precious asset. In his mid-thirties, Murrano's wavy brown hair was thick enough to be fur. 'Anyway, I appreciate the heads-up. If there is something I can do...'

'As a matter of fact,' I quickly responded, 'you could lend us Officer Aveda over there to start a canvas of the neighborhood. Sarney asked us to

26

get back to him as soon as possible and it would definitely speed things up. Of course, I could always phone the lieutenant and ask for help. If you can't spare anyone.'

Murrano's narrow lips expanded into a wry smile. He should never have opened his big mouth and he knew it. 'Anything else?' he foolishly asked.

'Yeah,' I said. 'The way it looks right now, the shooters were waiting for the victim. That means they had to be within sight of Lodge's house. Two men sitting in car? On a block like this? The locals would most likely notice, especially if the shooters were Black or Hispanic.'

'Fine.' Murrano waved us away before we could voice another request. 'I'll make sure the question is asked.'

The witnesses lived on the second floor of the two-family home Lodge had been crawling toward when the *coup de grace* was administered. They were Otto and Eva Hinckle, in their early seventies and retired from the work force. The story they told was simple. They'd been watching television in their living room when they heard a series of small explosions. Eva described these sounds as similar to popcorn in a microwave. Oscar suspected kids setting off fire crackers.

Foolishly, as both admitted, they went to the front window and looked out just in time to see a man wearing a ski mask and gloves fire a single shot into David Lodge's skull.

'The guy, the one who got shot, was trying to

turn his head away,' Oscar explained, 'and the other guy was leaning way over with his gun turned around like this.'

Oscar twisted his wrist to the right, exactly as Adele had done twenty minutes before. I glanced at her and she flashed me a quick smile. Adele loved to be right.

'The gun was gigantic,' Oscar continued. 'It looked like a machine gun, only without the...' He tapped his shoulder several times, then said, 'The wood part.'

'The stock?'

'That's right. And the other thing, the thing that holds the bullets?'

'The magazine?'

'Yeah, it was a foot long and it was in front of the trigger. And believe me, it caught my full attention. I was concentrating so hard on the guy with the gun that I didn't even notice the other guy who was with him until the first guy ran back to the car. The second guy was also wearing a mask and gloves. And he had the same kind of gun.'

'Describe the men,' I said. 'Were they short, tall, slim, heavy...?'

Although the initial image the Hinckles carried, of cold-blooded murder, was indelibly imprinted in their memories, they disagreed on most of the smaller details. Height, weight, who got into the car first, who was driving, what the men wore besides gloves and masks. They didn't remember any of these things clearly and their hesitant answers reflected their confusion. But they did agree on the dark-red color of the getaway vehicle, which was why Murrano had put out an alert.

'Did you notice anything else about the car?' Adele asked. 'Maybe a logo?'

Oscar shook his head. 'When I was a kid, I could tell you the year, make and model of any car drivin' down the street. Now they all look alike.'

'How about damage to the exterior. Dents or rust?'

Oscar and Eva stared at Adele for a moment, then shrugged. They just didn't remember. Myself, I would have let it go at that point. In my experience, when you push friendly witnesses, they fill the blank spaces in their memory with false details simply because they want to please. Better to leave a business card, or come back a few days later, when stray recollections surface on their own.

But Adele had other ideas. 'Think hard,' she told her witnesses. 'Is there anything else you remember? I don't care how insignificant.'

The Hinckles exchanged the sort of pregnant look only possible between long-married couples. Then Eva crossed her arms over her chest before turning to Adele. A decision had been made.

'I think they were black.' Eva again looked at her husband, her expression this time defiant. 'The way that gun was twisted around, it's how black gangsters hold their guns. You know, in the movies.' She gave her husband a poke. 'And the way they walked back to the car, with that shoulder thing they do, and bouncing up and down?

29

That swagger? That's a black thing.'

Oscar Hinckle was quick to reply. 'I didn't see nothin' like that.' He ran a finger across his snow-white mustache, the wiry hairs rippling beneath his touch like an animal seeking affection. 'Those two guys, they were all business. They didn't say one word to each other. They just got in that car and peeled the hell outta there.'

THREE

Ellen Lodge met us at the door of her single-family home and quickly ushered us through the living and dining rooms. Our progress was followed by eight, very silent children. Adele and I had been able to hear the children as we approached the front door, a muffled din we expected to become raucous when the door was opened. Instead, everything stopped the minute we came into view. The kids were toddlers, old enough to walk, old enough to have minds of their own. They pinned us with unwavering stares. Who were we? What were we doing here? Was something bad about to happen?

A second woman, not introduced to us, knelt beside a bench covered with little bowls of paint. She was staring at us, too.

We were finally led into a large kitchen and the door closed behind us. Like the outer rooms, the

30

kitchen had been pressed into service. Two trays stacked with sandwiches on paper plates rested on a table in the center of the room. A bubbling crock pot on a chipped counter was flanked by packages of Oreo cookies.

'I haven't said anything to the kids, but they know somethin's wrong. No sense makin' it any worse than what it is.' Ellen Lodge was a small, bony woman just entering middle-age. She had a noticeably slender neck, a droopy nose and lobeless ears set very close to the side of her head. Thick and wiry, her graying hair was cut short enough to be termed butch, especially in a conservative neighborhood like Ridgewood.

'I'm sorry about your loss,' I said. 'But we need to ask you some questions.'

Ellen walked over to a cabinet, pulled down eight plastic tumblers and set them on the counter. The tumblers came with spill-proof caps and she began to speak as she removed them. Her movements were quick and precise, a counter to her weary gray eyes and the smudged pouches beneath them. 'I gotta keep workin',' she explained. 'You got questions, fire away.'

'We understand you told Sgt Murrano that your husband was released from prison yesterday.'

'Yeah, from Attica.'

'Did you pick him up?'

'Does it look like I have time to drive upstate?'

'So you didn't pick him up?'

Ellen Lodge paused long enough to wipe her hands on her apron. When she spoke again, her tone was a little softer. 'I'm a cop's wife,' she

31

told us, 'and I know where you're goin' with this. So, let's just cut to the chase. I didn't love my husband. I admit it. The only reason I didn't divorce him was because I couldn't afford a lawyer.'

'Mrs Lodge, I only asked...'

She threw up her hands. 'Alright, already. I don't know how Dave got here. The bus, probably, or a train.'

'You're sure nobody else gave him a ride.'

'If they did, he never mentioned it.'

Though Mrs Lodge's tone was challenging, I refused to respond in kind. I wanted her help, if she had help to give, and I wanted to get her on the record. Those were my immediate priorities.

'But he didn't just show up, right? You did invite him to stay with you?'

'I felt sorry for him, OK?' She opened the refrigerator, removed a gallon container of apple juice and began to empty it into the plastic tumblers. 'Look, there's something you gotta understand. When Dave killed that pimp it turned my life upside down. You see what I do here five days a week? Well, on weekends, I'm a telemarketer for Time Warner. That's right, I'm the one you curse at before you slam down the phone. So if I sound bitter, it's most probably because I am.'

'I understand, Mrs Lodge, believe me. I'll try to keep this as brief as possible.'

But Ellen Lodge was having none of my sympathy. 'Ya know, after it happened, me and Dave were tossed out of the family. You're cops and I don't have to tell you that I'm talkin' about

32

the Great Cop Family. Me, I don't see what I did to deserve that, but I been scrambling to survive ever since. Now, you want the story, it goes like this. I wrote to Dave from time to time and I went to see him maybe twice a year. About three months ago, he mails me a letter sayin' he's gonna be released soon and could he stay with me until he gets back on his feet? It's either that or a homeless shelter. Nice, right?'

'He didn't have any family? Mother, father, siblings?'

'His mother's dead and his father lives some-where out west.' She turned away from me, lifting the lid on the crock pot to release the fragrance of simmering vegetables.

'Mrs Lodge,' I asked, 'do you know any reason why somebody would want to kill your husband?'

She laughed out loud. 'How about one of the monkeys who spit on us whenever we came in or out of the courthouse?'

'You mean the protesters?'

'Yeah, the protesters.'

'Anybody else? Anybody specific?'

'No, but Dave was worried about the possibility of revenge. Definitely. He mentioned it to me a number of times in his letters and—'

'We'll need to see those letters.'

Ellen stopped short, her eyes rising to mine, then jumping away. 'I didn't keep them,' she admitted after a long moment. 'I mean, they weren't love letters or anything like that.'

'Can you remember what he wrote?'

'Besides how he was worried?'

33

'Yeah, besides.'

Ellen shrugged. 'The usual stuff. How tough the screws were. How bad the food was. How he was trying to stay positive.'

'But you don't remember anything specific?'

'Hey, you're not listening. Me and Dave weren't all that close, not after seven years. In fact, we were on the outs before he ever went away.'

'Then what did he say that led you to believe he felt threatened?'

'He said there were prison rumors that Clarence Spott's old crew had a contract out on him. Personally, I didn't take it all that serious, but the guy you wanna talk to is Pete Jarazelsky. You know who I'm talking about?'

'I don't.'

'Pete Jarazelsky was stationed at the Eight-Three, same time as Dave. He got sent upstate a few years back for knockin' over a warehouse. What I understand, they were pals. They told each other everything.'

'And Jarazelsky's still in prison?'

'That's what Dave told me last night. Dave said he was worried about Pete. You know, now that he wouldn't be there to watch Pete's back.'

From outside, a chorus of small sharp voices rose in song: *I'm a little teapot, short and stout* ... Ellen Lodge took another look at the soup, then shut off the crock pot.

'Gotta let it cool,' she said. 'Some of these kids, they don't even know how to use a spoon. They stick their whole face in the bowl. One of them gets burned, I'll never hear the end of it.'

34

I think she meant the remark as an exit line, but I wasn't taking the hint. Over the years, I've mastered the art of passive-aggression. I'm the Rock of Gibraltar and the only way to move me is to answer my questions.

'Now, you said your husband asked to live here until he got on his feet. Did he have a job lined up? Any prospects?'

'Not that I know of. He told me he was gonna look up his old buddies at the Eight-Three, see if they'd help him find something.'

'So the stay was open-ended?'

'The stay?'

'You told me your husband was going to stay with you until he got back on his feet. If he didn't have a job lined up, he might have been with you for months.'

Outside, the children broke into widely varying renditions of 'Frere Jacques'. Ellen listened for a moment, then said, 'Lemme take out these sandwiches and the juice, get the kids started. If you don't mind.'

'Hey, children have to eat. I understand. But just so it won't be a total loss, would it be alright if my partner and I look through your husband's room? In case there's something up there we need to ask you about.'

I watched Ellen Lodge's reaction closely. In my experience, even cooperative citizens don't want cops roaming through their homes unaccompanied. But Ellen continued to replace the caps on the children's tumblers. 'It's the bedroom in the back,' she told us without raising her eyes from her work. 'Look anywhere you want.'

35

Adele and I took Ellen Lodge at her word, exploring every inch of the room, even checking beneath the mattress. In a bureau drawer, three pairs of newly purchased socks and an unopened three-pack of Jockey briefs nestled in a corner. On the floor, a plastic bag held a pair of jeans, a T-shirt and a pair of dirty socks. On the night table, a few toilet articles – razor, shaving cream, toothbrush, deodorant, nail clippers – were scattered next to the lamp. Beyond those items, we found nothing.

We came downstairs just in time to make the acquaintance of Ellen's helper, Sonia Ramirov. She told us that she hadn't known her boss was even married until Lodge had made his appearance that morning. Then she rushed back to her charges.

For the next ten minutes, I studied Ellen Lodge at work. Though she was patient throughout, cajoling here, firm there, it was obvious to me that she needed more help. What was equally obvious was that she was running an unlicensed, shoestring operation, providing a service to working-class couples who couldn't afford the real thing. I might have used that against her – Adele would already have done so – but I tend to hoard my ammunition.

Eventually, Ellen left the children in the care of her helper, then returned to the kitchen. Her timing, as far as I could tell, was arbitrary. After closing the door, she went to the sink and rinsed her hands.

'You're very good with the kids,' I told her.

'They respond to you.'

She threw me a sharp look, and for a moment I thought she was going to become angry. Then her look softened, the weariness flooding back into her eyes. 'Me and Dave,' she told us, 'we wanted to have kids, but I never got pregnant. A year before he went away, I practically begged him to go with me to a fertility clinic. Big mistake. Dave broke appointments, showed up drunk, threatened the doctors. It was a nightmare.' She shook her head. 'So, where were we?'

'Well, there's a question that occurred to me while I watched you with the kids out there.' I smiled sincerely as I hit Lodge with the sharpest arrow in my quiver. 'You told us your husband had been threatened, that he believed somebody was out to kill him.'

'That's right.'

'So why weren't you worried about having him in your house? What with the kids and all.'

FOUR

Ellen Lodge never did answer the question. Instead, she began by insisting that she hadn't taken the threat seriously, then shifted, without prompting, to a pair of grudging admissions. Beneath her genuine and justified anger, she did have some feelings for her husband. And maybe

37

she was just a little bit lonely.

I let her explanations stand, turning her to Lodge's movements from the time he arrived at her home. Her responses were vague. He'd come in around four o'clock, while she was still burdened with the kids, and had gone directly to his room upstairs. After the kids left, she and Sonia had begun the clean-up and the preparations for the following day, which included shopping for supplies and for the meal they would prepare. It wasn't until eight o'clock that she finally got around to her husband and a Chinese take-out dinner. By that time, she was so tired she could hardly think.

Over dinner, Dave had talked about old friends neither of them now had, about Ellen's raw deal, about how he'd turned things around in prison, about his intention to live a good and sober life, a life of atonement. Ellen had listened, perhaps sympathetically, but if she'd expressed any opinions of her own, she couldn't remember them.

They'd finally retired to separate bedrooms at ten o'clock. Ellen had fallen asleep immediately, then risen at six-thirty to get ready for the children. What with all the rush, she'd barely remembered that Davy, as she called him, was sleeping upstairs until the phone rang at nine o'clock. The call was for her husband, from a man whose voice she didn't recognize, and she'd summoned Davy to the phone without giving the matter a lot of thought. A few minutes later, Davy had gone back upstairs to fetch his coat before leaving the house.

'Look for me,' he'd told her, 'around five.'

Or maybe it was four-thirty, or six-fifteen, or eight minutes past seven. Ellen wasn't absolutely positive. What with the kids and all.

The Crime Scene Unit was still going strong when Adele and I walked out onto the street. They were measuring the distance between David Lodge's body and each of the shell casings on the street.

'You know, Corbin,' Adele said, 'the merry widow seemed very unsure of the details. In fact, she was only certain about one thing.'

'That we simply must see Pete Jarazelsky?'

Adele tossed me one of those sharp unamused smiles she's so good at, then said, 'Got it on the first try.'

We split up at that point, Adele to check on the progress of the Crime Scene Unit. I watched her walk away, then drove off to look for Paolo 'Wonder Boy' Aveda, the uniformed officer who was canvassing the neighborhood. Wonder Boy was what his brother officers called him, though not to his face. They were jealous, of course, as people of little talent always are in the presence of the gifted. Three years into the job, Aveda knew everybody in the precinct, from the priests and the merchants to the mutts and the mopes. He had more snitches than I had friends, a rabbi in high places and a hundred credits toward a college degree. Soon he would be called to better things, by Narcotics, Organized Crime or even the vaunted Detective Bureau. That's why I'd picked him in the first place.

I found Aveda two blocks to the south, the

direction from which Lodge's assassins had come. Glad to see me, he jumped into the Ford I was driving and stuck his hands into the flow of tepid air coming from the defroster.

'I think,' he told me, 'if I touched my ears, they'd crack.'

After giving the car and himself a chance to warm up, Aveda went on to admit that the canvas wasn't going particularly well. That was because most of the houses and apartments along Palmetto were empty, the parents off to work, the children either in school or day care.

But Aveda's partial canvas hadn't been entirely without results. Three elderly women had walked up Palmetto around nine, on their way back from the eight o'clock mass at St. Catherine's. They'd seen nothing amiss.

'These kind of old ladies,' Aveda told me, 'you find 'em all through Ridgewood. They're the alarm system for their blocks. I couldn't tell ya how many times I been called out because one of 'em saw something out of place.'

'Something with the wrong color skin?'

'You got it.' Though Aveda was Puerto Rican and fairly dark, his tone was matter-of-fact. This was an issue he'd dealt with long before. 'I also talked to three other people, a disabled guy with an aide who pushed him around the block in a wheelchair, and a woman who went shopping. Nobody saw anything out of place.'

We were parked before a line of modest row houses that stretched the length of the block. The houses were of brick and flat-roofed, with bow windows on the upper and lower floors. Under a

40

noon sun, the yellow brick appeared warm to the touch, an illusion dispelled by the icicles dangling from cornices so uniform they might have been part of a single structure.

I was gathering the courage to suggest that Aveda and I face the cold implied by those icicles when my cell phone began to ring. Though I was hoping for rescue, I was nevertheless surprised when my partner told me that a pair of Bushwick cops had located the red sedan beneath the El on Broadway.

'There was a handgun inside, a TEC-9,' she explained. 'We better get over there.' Then she hung up.

Delray Webber, a patrol sergeant from the Eight-Three, was waiting for us at the intersection of Broadway and Linden Street when we arrived ten minutes later, along with a pair of uniforms who had the good sense to remain in their cruiser. Adele went off to get the names of those officers, along with a few details, in case they were needed to testify at some later date. Across the street, on the south side of Broadway, a maroon Toyota Camry was double-parked beneath the elevated tracks carrying the J line. Surrounded by ribbons of yellow tape fixed to the girders of the El, it looked to me like the featured vehicle on a used car lot. The one I couldn't afford.

'The officers noticed the car double-parked and ran a check,' Webber explained. 'When the vehicle came up stolen, they moved in for a closer look and found the gun. Then they

41

called me.'

'You know when the car was stolen?'

'Last week, on the eighth.'

Webber led me to his patrol car, then pointed through the window. A TEC-9 was lying on the front seat next to Webber's driver. In appearance, it was nothing short of ferocious. The fifty-round magazine was a foot long and the barrel was surrounded by a stainless-steel baffle. You couldn't look at the weapon without imagining a gangster spraying bullets in all directions. But appearances are deceiving. Relatively cheap, the TEC-9 is a triumph of style over substance. It fires ordinary 9mm cartridges, one round at a time, just like the Glock parked at my hip, the main difference being that my Glock is far more accurate. True, the TEC-9's magazine holds thirty-two rounds to the Glock's fifteen, an advantage for street criminals with no training and no opportunity to practice. But that's not why the mutts love them. No, mutts are attracted to TEC-9s because their own lives are a triumph of style over substance.

'What I'm gonna do here,' Webber explained, 'is take this to the house, voucher it and send it on to the lab. Meanwhile, I called for a tow. They should be here in about fifteen minutes.'

'I appreciate that, sarge.'

'Good, because I got a rape on Troutman Street that needs lookin' after, so if you'll excuse me...'

For a moment, after Webber left, I stood where I was. The sun was still high enough to filter through the tracks above me, to throw bars of light over the red car across the street. Broadway

42

is the dividing line between the neighborhoods of Bedford-Stuyvesant and Bushwick. Not only was the TEC-9 a weapon of choice in both, the J Train running above my head would carry you to any number of similar communities.

FIVE

I spent the next half-hour, until the tow truck arrived, making careful notes of the Ellen Lodge interview while a succession of J Trains contributed to the layer of greasy soot coating every object beneath the El. As a rule, I don't take notes in the course of an interview. Writing not only distracts the subject, it draws attention to those elements of the subject's story that most interest me. Forewarned is forearmed, as they say.

With cooperating witnesses, like the Hinckles, it doesn't matter all that much. With Ellen Lodge? Let's just say that I wanted to get her story on paper in case a few inconsistencies turned up at some later date. Of course, I might have asked her to sign a statement, as I had with the Hinckles, but I had no desire to telegraph my suspicions.

Adele was looking over my shoulder, adding a generally critical comment from time to time. As she couldn't do this without our bodies coming into contact, I didn't mind the back-seat driving.

43

My physical attraction to Adele had begun on the day we became partners, long before I really got to know her. I could invent any number of reasons to justify this attraction: her confidence and poise, her clear indifference to the opinions of her peers, her advanced policing skills. But that's all in retrospect, more justification than explanation. I only knew that my desire for her, even a year later, was intense and immediate, and that the closer I got, the stronger it became.

The sad part was that I still hadn't dredged up the courage to put a move on her, though there were times when I sensed that she was ready. I told myself that I was waiting until she and her husband finally split up, but I think it was more likely that I feared the consequences if my overtures were rejected. Adele's tongue was rough enough to grind glass.

There was a second reason for my timidity as well, a compelling reason that played in my head with the intensity of a police siren. Without ever intending to, I'd made a career of short-term relationships, enduring a string of failures so long I'd managed to convince myself that short-term was the best I could do. Adele, on the other hand, was all about commitment.

David Lodge was right where we'd left him, on his back, staring up at the wide blue sky. The Crime Scene Unit was through with him, the morgue wagon still waiting. I walked through the open gate, squatted down and went through his pockets, gathering his personal effects. They didn't amount to much: a watch, a comb, a

44

wallet and thirty-eight cents in miscellaneous coins.

Adele was standing alongside me, her hands on her hips. 'A contact wound, Corbin. You see the pattern?'

The skin around the entrance wound on Lodge's right temple was split into lines that radiated outward from the wound. This star-shaped pattern could only have resulted from the barrel of the gun being in contact with Lodge's temple when the fatal shot was fired. The chain of events was simple and easily recognized. When the trigger was pulled, heated gases had poured from the barrel. These gases had bounced off the bony plates of Lodge's skull, then ricocheted back to split his flesh from the inside.

'So what?' I asked.

Adele's hand swept over the street behind us. 'All that brass, it's too extravagant. You close your eyes, you see a pair of coked-up kids pulling the trigger with their eyes closed. You see *gang* kids. But from in here, it looks like a professional hit. It looks like the perps were cool, calm and collected.'

'That mean you think the TEC-9s were overkill?'

She nodded twice, then squatted down beside me. 'Like the Toyota double-parked beneath the El, the weapon left behind, Lodge's nice clean room and the car being stolen a week in advance.' She paused briefly before adding, 'And the widow's tale.'

Like I've already said, Adele was nothing if not meticulous.

45

In quick succession, we released the body and conferred with Officer Aveda and Sgt Gutierrez. Aveda's diligent efforts had turned up two additional witnesses. Each of them, attracted by the gunfire, had seen the red car as the shooters made their escape. But no identifications were forthcoming. The men in the car were still wearing their ski masks.

We found Gutierrez inside the CSU van, along with his assistants. They were chomping on slices of pizza.

'Same old same old,' Gutierrez told me. 'We'll put the evidence in the pipe, see what shakes out.'

'That mean you didn't find the perps' wallets while we were gone?'

''Fraid not, but we collected enough blood to keep the lab rats busy for the next two months.'

Gutierrez was referring to the very faint hope that some of the blood evidence had been contributed by one or both of the perps.

'I'm not holdin' my breath,' I told him, 'any more than I'm expecting fingerprints to show up when you dust that Toyota. But I do appreciate the effort.'

To my left, the morgue attendants were hoisting David Lodge onto an unzipped body bag. Protected by the cold from the onset of rigor mortis, his limbs were surprisingly supple. Lodge was a big man, well over six feet, and at first I was sure the attendants were going to drop him. But they finally made an effort that brought his sagging butt off the ground far enough to

46

clear the edges of the body bag.

Both men sighed audibly when they let the body down. The three minutes of work they'd done for their three hours of pay had exhausted them. Nevertheless, their timing was exquisite. The first reporters arrived as they zipped up the body bag. The reporters were met by Aveda and his partner, Jake Pearlman, who kept them at bay long enough for David Lodge to be loaded into the morgue wagon. And long enough for me and my partner to get away without so much as a 'No comment.'

There were chores to be done. The first of these was accomplished by Adele who examined the contents of Lodge's wallet on the ride back to the house. She found twenty-two dollars in bills, a photo ID issued by the Department of Correctional Services, an appointment card for a one o'clock meeting with Parole Officer Paris Blake. She also found a photo of Ellen Lodge taken at least fifteen years before. Ellen was posed on a strip of sand, her back to a roiling ocean, an attractive young woman with a sassy smile.

Our basic plan was to complete as much paperwork as possible before we returned in the evening to re-canvas the neighborhood. A numbered complaint, called a UF-61, would have to be generated first, then each of the interviews written up on supplementary complaint forms, called DD-5s. The complaint number on the UF-61 would forever identify the case file. This was important because it had become clear that Adele and I were going to need the case file for

47

the homicide Lodge committed almost seven years before. Though the file had long ago been swept from the Eight-Three to an archive maintained by the Property Clerk Division in Long Island City, it wouldn't be difficult to retrieve once we had the file number in hand. Adele was about that task, calling up Lodge's rap sheet on a squad computer, when Lieutenant Sarney walked into the room.

'My office,' he said to me without so much as nodding to Joe Mangone, who was pecking away at a keyboard three feet to Adele's left, or to Lemuel Henderson who was at his desk, taking a victim's statement from an elderly woman who'd lost her pocket book to an opportunistic mope. 'You too, Adele. I want a full update.'

Adele began with a precise summary of our activities, both at the crime scene and on Broadway, in Bushwick. Sarney listened, nodding from time to time, until Adele began to explain why the blocks around Palmetto Street had to be re-canvassed.

'If the car wasn't within sight of Ellen Lodge's house,' he interrupted, 'then where was it?'

'On Fresh Pond Road or Myrtle Avenue where there's more traffic. Or maybe they just kept moving.' Adele played with the buttons of her red blazer for a moment, then looked up at Sarney. 'The important question here is how they knew Lodge was going to leave the house when he did.'

Sarney looked at me, but when I remained silent, he quickly assumed the role of devil's

48

advocate. 'Maybe,' he noted, 'the shooters made a few passes and got lucky. Maybe they kept circling the block until he came out.'

Adele settled herself against the seat. 'You want me to believe that two ghetto gangsters, out to avenge the death of their boss seven years ago, roamed through a white neighborhood like Ridgewood until they just happened on their target? Gimme a break.' She rushed on before Sarney could respond. 'But even if they did, it only brings up another question. How did they know he was staying with his wife? Was that also a lucky guess?'

Sarney was a smart boss, smart enough to endure the foibles of his children. That Adele Bentibi was fabulously opinionated was something he just had to live with. He grinned and raised his hands, palms out. *'No mas, no mas.'*

As for me, I was already bored with the debate. The widow had presented us with a motive and we would have to check it out. Though the re-canvas was obviously important, it was unlikely to turn up a suspect. Even if a dozen people re-called seeing two black men sitting in a car, it would be just another piece of the puzzle.

'Whatta ya say we go over this again,' Sarney continued. 'In case I have to do a press con-ference.'

This time Sarney took notes. I watched him carefully, looking for signs of my own fate. Under ordinary circumstances, nothing draws the bosses to a microphone like a celebrity homi-cide. But Lodge's celebrity was another matter. The official pronouncement at the time of his

49

sentencing was that he'd dishonored the job and was punished appropriately, a judgment clearly designed to put an end to the matter.

I let my eyes close for a moment, envisioning David Lodge jumping that fence. He must have known his fate because the little yard dead-ended against a brick wall. But he hadn't accepted it. Even at the very end, he'd turned his head away from the bullet. Was that last bit of resistance an act of defiance? *Fuck you, I'll never surrender?* Or no more than animal instinct, a worm wriggling at the end of a hook?

'Yo, Harry, you with us?'

I looked up at Sarney. 'Right here, lou.'

Sarney smiled. I, too, had my foibles, and daydreaming was one of them. 'Your partner and I were discussing where you want to go next. We thought it'd be nice to hear your opinion.'

'Well,' I told him, 'as soon as I get back to work, I'm going to call up the Legal Bureau, have them draw up a subpoena for Ellen Lodge's phone records. She says her husband got a phone call just before he walked out the door. Be nice to know where it came from.'

'That's admirable, Harry, but could you try to think a little more long-term?'

'How 'bout tomorrow?'

'That'd be fine.'

'David Lodge spent the last six and a half years in prison, right? So if we want to know what was on his mind yesterday, when they opened the gates, we have to go up to Attica, talk to the staff, talk to his old buddy from the Eight-Three, Peter Jarazelsky.'

50

'Attica,' Sarney reminded, 'is north of Buffalo. That's an eight-hour drive. Each way.'

'That's how come we have to fly. But don't fret, boss, we'll pick up Lodge's old case file and study it on the flight. We'd have to do that anyway.'

Sarney thought about it for a minute. He was going to have to get approval for the expense, an annoyance to be sure, but the trip couldn't be avoided.

'You really think Jarazelsky will talk to you?' Sarney finally asked.

'Lieutenant, I'd bet my life savings against a quarter that once you call up to Attica and make the request, Pete Jarazelsky's gonna welcome us with open arms.'

SIX

It was after ten by the time we finished up the last of the paperwork. The re-canvas had gone better – and slower – than we expected. Altogether, we'd spoken to nineteen honest citizens, each of whom had walked along Palmetto between eight-thirty and nine. None recalled seeing two or more individuals, black or otherwise, sitting inside a red Toyota.

By now, Sarney had obtained authorization for a trip to Attica. That was the good news. The bad news was that I was flying off to Buffalo alone.

51

David Lodge's autopsy was scheduled for nine o'clock the following morning and Sarney wanted Adele to be there. Myself, I was more than pleased with my end of the deal, but it was strictly Bill Sarney's call. He'd nominated Adele to witness the autopsy, then arranged for her to interview a sergeant named Merkovich who worked out of the Gang Unit at OCCB. Spott's crew, it seemed, was still in action, led by his brother, DuWayne.

I didn't quibble with Sarney's decision. By this time, David Lodge was the talk of the town and Sarney wasn't the type to leave himself uncovered. But the scheduling of the autopsy did catch my attention. Typically, homicides were autopsied several days after the event. Somebody down at One Police Plaza had given the ME's office a nudge. The question was why, if the big dogs were in such a hurry, they hadn't offered any help to the lowly squad detectives who'd caught the case – or taken the case away altogether.

The phone began to ring as I was buttoning my coat. I watched Adele answer, then signal me to pick up the extension.

'Would you repeat that, Sergeant Schniederman?' she asked.

'I said, "You're not gonna believe this, but we're temporarily unable to locate your file."'

'The Lodge file?'

'Yeah, that one.'

'Could it still be at the Eight-Three?'

'Nope, we swept out the Precinct's closed files two years ago.'

'How many files would that be?'

'I didn't count 'em, detective.'

Adele took a deep breath. 'What I'm trying to get at, sarge, is whether the Lodge file was the only file missing.'

'If you'll excuse me, detective, *missing* was not a word I used. *Unable to locate* was what I actually said.'

'Then are you unable to locate *all* of the Eighty-Third Precinct's files?'

'Not at this time.'

That was as far as we got. Efforts were being made to recover the requested file, but results could not be guaranteed. So sorry, and good night.

'Do you know how files get swept out?' I asked Adele once she'd hung up. 'You ever watch the process?' When she shook her head, I continued. 'Four guys arrive in a van during the late tour. They empty the filing cabinets into boxes, then transport the boxes to the archives.'

'And?'

'And nobody checks to be sure that every file is actually there. When the files are removed, the Property Clerk gets a list of the case files that are supposed to be in the drawers, a list compiled as each case is closed, not when the files are transported.' I shrugged into my coat, already cold. At the time, I was driving an eight-year-old Nissan with a pronounced intolerance for temperatures below ten degrees. The Sentra would take forever to warm up, assuming it started in the first place.

53

'How do you know this?' Adele asked.

'My second year on the job, I sprained my back so bad I had trouble sitting in a patrol car for more than an hour. The lieutenant was a merciful type. He let me work in the house for a couple of months, which was how I came to supervise one of these transfers. But the point is that Lodge's file could have been yanked while it was still at the Eight-Three.'

'Well, I don't see how that's a problem.'

I buttoned my coat, taking my time about it. 'It's not gonna be a problem, not for us, anyway. It's gonna be a problem for Sarney when we inform him tomorrow morning.'

'Don't be so hasty, Corbin.' Adele was still seated behind her desk. 'The prosecutors are also holding a copy of the case file. They would have gotten it when the case was being prepared for the grand jury. I have a friend in the DA's office, somebody I know from my group. What I'll do is call her tomorrow and ask her to speak to her supervisor. Maybe we can drop in, get a quick look-see off the record.'

'You wanna do this before you speak to Sarney?'

Adele rose from her chair and stretched before winding a silk scarf around her neck. The flaming-red scarf matched the red of her blazer almost exactly. 'Of course.'

'Sarney's worried, Adele. I can hear it in his voice.' I pulled on my gloves. 'That's why he asked us not to play any games.'

Adele folded her arms across her chest, her eyes narrowing as she gauged my resolve. For good detectives, bending the rules is a matter of instinct, and Adele's suggestion was no big deal – certainly, we had every right to the file. But procedure required that we make a formal request through the NYPD's Legal Bureau, then wait for the DA to comply, which might take days, or even weeks.

'Look, partner,' I finally said, 'the simple truth is that Bill Sarney's holding my marker. I owe the man.'

'For a promotion to detective, second grade, that has yet to come through?'

I shook my head, taking care to keep my language simple. 'I've been a guest in Sarney's home. I attended the wedding of his daughter and the christening of his son. That's why I can't think of him as just another boss. And that's why I'm going to honor my pledge to keep him informed.'

Adele didn't respond right away, probably because my position caught her by surprise. 'Alright,' she finally said as she slid into her coat, 'we'll do it your way, Corbin. But time isn't on our side here. If we don't move quickly, the case is going to get away from us. Ellen Lodge has an agenda, and we both know it.'

I took that thought with me to the Sparkle Inn. Sparkle's was more than the place where everybody knew my name. It was the place where everybody had, at one time or another, looked into that heart of darkness at the epicenter of a cop's life. Fraternity and brotherhood are the words traditionally used to describe the herding instinct of cops. But it was a new age and several female detectives greeted me when I came through the door. They included, among their number, Nydia Santiago. Nydia had once described my partner as 'Martha Stewart with a badge.'

The Sparkle's owner, Michael Blair, had a Dewar's and water awaiting me by the time I reached the bar. Blair was in his early fifties, a former detective from the Eight-Three who'd mortgaged his pension to buy the joint. He had pale blue eyes that darted suddenly to yours, as if he was trying to catch you in an unguarded moment. He hit me with one of those looks now.

'I heard,' he said as I found a stool, 'you stumbled into the Lodge case.'

Before replying, I raised the traditional toast to Sparkle, who stood behind the bar. Sparkle was a life-size manikin constructed from papier mâché. Long ago, before Blair purchased the bar, somebody had painted Sparkle's face and hair so that she slightly resembled Marilyn Monroe, then dressed her in a sequinned gown. Lit by a spotlight mounted just ahead of her toes, Sparkle did, indeed, sparkle.

'Bad news travels fast,' I finally said. 'Just as well.'

'Why's that?'

'Because I came here looking for a heads-up.'

This was an avenue closed to my partner. As I said, she'd never visited Sparkle's, or any other cop bar, which was probably for the best. That indifference to the opinions of her peers, which I admired, would have gotten a cold reception at

56

the Sparkle Inn.

But that wasn't true for me. I was the guy you could go to for a favor, even for a short-term loan, maybe enough to settle your bar bill. I was the guy you could talk to about the wife, the kids or the girlfriend. I was the guy who listened to your endless gripes and actually seemed to care. I was the guy who got along with everyone.

'I was in the Precinct when Lodge killed the perp,' Blair readily admitted, 'only I didn't catch the case. The man you need to talk to is seated at his usual table, but there's no guarantee he'll give you the time of day.'

I glanced over my shoulder at the broad back and wide shoulders of a notoriously anti-social detective named Linus Potter. Potter's neck was so much thicker than his small head that he appeared to be defectively manufactured. Perhaps that was why he usually parked himself in a corner and drank with his back to his peers.

When I carried my drink to his table and set it down, Potter didn't so much as glance in my direction. Nor did he budge when I took a seat. Only when I finally said, 'I caught the Lodge case and I'm looking for some guidance,' did he raise a pair of small blue eyes that looked right through me.

I responded by folding my arms across my chest. Despite the hostile glare, Potter was an easy read. Once he realized that he couldn't intimidate me, he'd either tell me the truth or tell me to go fuck myself. Indecision was not in Potter's DNA.

'It was a nothin' case,' he finally growled. 'We

57

got everything but a confession. And we woulda got that, too, except the hump was too drunk to remember what he did.'

Potter went on to describe the evidence against Lodge in enough detail to convince me that his own memory was accurate. And that evidence was impressive. Nevertheless, as the details accumulated, I realized there was a weak link in this perfect chain. Anthony Szarek, the man Potter called the Broom, had provided Russo with an alibi and put Lodge alone with the prisoner. But who vouched for Tony Szarek, a cop unfit for any duty beyond running out for doughnuts and sweeping the floor?

'This cop, Szarek, is he still on the job?' I asked.

'Retired three years ago.'

'You have any idea where to find him?'

'Matter of fact, I know exactly where to find the Broom.' Potter's smirk was positively gleeful. He'd been setting me up for this punch line all along.

'And where's that?'

'Mount Olivet Cemetery. He ate his gun two weeks ago.' Potter leaned forward to jab a thick finger into my shoulder. 'What I heard, the Good Life didn't agree with the Broom. You know the one I'm talkin' about? The one that goes from the rented room to the fucking bar to the rented room to the fucking bar. All the days of our fucking lives.'

I made one more stop, at a YMCA swimming pool on East Twenty-Third Street in Manhattan.

58

The pool was managed by Conrad Stehle, my former high school swimming coach, now retired. Along with a few others, Conrad had given me permission to use the pool at night, when you can swim laps without plowing your head into the bony rump of a frolicking senior citizen.

Not that I had anything against frolicking seniors. In fact, living long enough to become a senior citizen is definitely one of my aims. That's because, for most of my adolescence, I didn't expect to make twenty-one.

I have little sympathy for lawyers and sociologists who blame criminal behavior on early childhood experience: 'My client only shot that storekeeper in the face, leaving him to spend the rest of his life contemplating his scar tissue, because his mother was a junkie and he never had a chance.'

The way I see it, there's no point in looking back. If you blame your parents for your troubles, they can just turn around and blame their own parents, who will most likely blame their parents, who will most likely ... What you end up with, if you go too far down this road, is an amoeba blaming a virus.

'Yo, the mother-fucker messed with my genes. What could I do?'

Personal responsibility is the key to improving your life. That's my story and I generally stick to it. Still, there's no getting away from the fact that my life could have taken another direction; that except for a few lucky breaks, I might have been the one in the hump seat, making my own pathetic excuses.

My parents were cross-addicted to every intoxicating substance on the face of the planet, but they were educated and they were not poor. That was my first break.

At age thirteen, I was spending most of my life on the street, dodging the hustlers and the gang bangers as best I could. When I was beaten unconscious at age fourteen, I learned to cultivate an expression that revealed the extent of my determination not to repeat the experience, and to carry a knife. These were necessary adaptations for someone who never considered the possibility of going to his parents, or his teachers, or the cops.

I was halfway to feral by the time I reached high school. There was me and my few streetwise bro's, and there was everybody else. That you could never trust the everybody else was a simple given. Along with the fool's belief that doing well in school was for jerks. The way I had it, success was failure. Except in athletics.

Three months into my freshman year, a notice pinned to a cork board in the hallway caught my attention. The swimming team was having tryouts on the following afternoon. Like most of the neighborhood kids, I'd been spending a good part of my summers at the Asser Levi pool on Twenty-Third Street. I was the fastest swimmer among my friends and had even done well against older kids. So, why not?

Twenty-four hours later, carrying my bathing suit and the cleanest towel I could find, I walked into a locker room and met Conrad Stehle. That was my second break.

Conrad got me through high school, berating me, cajoling me, whatever it took. During those years, I ate more dinners at his and his wife's house than at my own. The funny part is that I never asked myself why he made the effort; I just assumed I was worthy. Even later on, when I realized just how stupid that was, I finally decided the question wasn't important enough to ask. Conrad Stehle had turned a punk kid with a bad attitude into a high school graduate, a punk kid who'll be forever grateful, and not only for the diploma. Conrad made me a swimmer, as well, long distance as it turned out. In my senior year, I was among the better high school swimmers in New York State. For a kid with few positive accomplishments, the cheap trophies I earned were shields that protected me from the street's many temptations.

But 'among the better' was not Olympic caliber, or even college scholarship material. When I emerged from high school with a diploma and a pair of empty pockets, I had to choose between work and the streets. My answer, guided by Conrad, was the United States Army.

The army was good for Harry Corbin, especially the camaraderie, and I eventually came to feel about my platoon as I had about the other members of my swimming team – the 'us' part of it at least as important as the trophies. Thus, by the time I was honorably discharged three years later, I was well prepared to join the 'cop family' Ellen Lodge had mentioned, the one that had walked away from her.

61

SEVEN

My third break was swimming itself. On a purely physical level, distance swimming demands
that you learn to calm your mind. This is literally
true. *Stroke/stroke/ breathe; stroke/stroke/
breathe; stroke/stroke/breathe; stroke/stroke/
breathe.* Every stroke is designed to pull you
through the water with maximum efficiency,
every breath to fill your lungs completely.

Take this to the bank. Mental agitation of any
kind interferes with these goals. When you're
angry, or even frustrated, your stroke becomes
ragged and you wobble from side to side in your
lane. Your lungs become tighter as well – a
definite no-no when you get less than a second
to breathe between strokes.

All of this is compounded by the conditions.
With your ear plugs in, you hear nothing beyond
the splashing of your arms and legs. With your
goggles on, you see clearly only when your face
is in the water. A red stripe on the bottom of the
pool, which you dutifully follow, becomes your
visual universe. In the end, your attention turns
inward simply because there's no other place for
it to go.

I remember learning this lesson the hard way.
Whenever my stroke was off, Coach Stehle

would have me swimming laps until I was ready to sink to the bottom. Then he'd have me do a few more.

Initially, I took the obvious course. I tried not to think about anything that might upset me. Fat chance. I was a confrontational child and I needed my enemies. But what I did learn to do, finally, was strip my thoughts of emotion. An image would come into my mind – of my parents, for example, huddled around a mirror striped with lines of cocaine while I foraged through the cupboards in search of dinner – and I'd observe it without any feelings at all. Or I'd imagine Ramon Arellano trying to intimidate me in the lunch room without further imagining myself driving a knife through the side of his throat.

By the time I finished my junior year, I was pretty much addicted to swimming. The pool was the place where I could look at myself without arousing emotions like fear, rage and self-contempt. Not that I liked the angry fool I saw. But at least I didn't hate him. Sure, he was a jerk who did everything he could to ruin his life. But he was my jerk and I could make of him what I would.

In my senior year, I began to redefine myself. I didn't want to be a jerk any more. I knew that going in. Putting a face to the new self I hoped to create was much more difficult. What did I hope to become? The question was never directly answered. Instead, as I swam my way through high school, then through a long tour in Berlin, I not only became less angry, I began to like my

63

life, as it was and as I hoped it would be. I wasn't asking for much. I had no grand ambitions. I just wanted an ordinary life, as free from the chaos of my childhood as possible.

And so I continued to believe as I walked out of the locker room and stood by the edge of an empty pool fourteen hours after the murder of David Lodge. The air around me, cool enough to produce goose bumps, was saturated with humidity and the odor of chlorine. Though it'd been years since I'd loosened up before a workout, I hesitated long enough to draw a few deep breaths, gradually expanding my lungs. Then I dove into the water and began to swim.

For the first few laps, as the muscles of my shoulders and back gradually stretched out, I didn't think about much of anything. The water flowed over my face and body, holding me in an embrace at once tender and distinctly sexual. The sensations were luxurious, as always, and I basked in them, knowing they came with no strings attached. This was purely for me, purely about me. This was mine.

Still, I knew where my thoughts were headed once I settled into a steady grind. In the army, I'd learned to smell trouble coming, to avoid it. No confrontations, especially with officers, that was the name of the game. And that meant no black-market bullshit, no cigarettes smuggled off the base, no drunken brawls, no pregnant *frauleins*.

When I became a cop, it was more of the same. Be where you're supposed to be and don't jam up the sergeant. Write your traffic tickets, twenty-five parkers and five movers, every month without fail. Make certain that your monthly activity reports are complete and current.

Bottom line: not being a pain in the ass to my superiors on the chain of command worked for me. I pretty much had the ordinary life I wanted. Maybe it was a bachelor's life, untrusting and sometimes lonely, but half the kids I hung with in my adolescence had been to prison, and not a few of them were dead. So if my glass was a few inches short of full, I wasn't complaining.

The red stripe beneath me never shifted when I got down to business. The pull of the right and left sides of my body remained in sync even as I admitted that a new element had entered my ordinary life. I needed to examine that element and I decided that I would. As soon as I figured out what it was.

But I was sure about one thing. Lodge's face had been plastered all over the evening news and wasn't likely to disappear anytime soon. The press would be watching the investigation; the bosses, too. When it comes to protecting the job, the big dogs at the Puzzle Palace are all white knights. And all willing to sacrifice a peasant or two, if that's what it takes.

I rechecked my position as I kicked out of a turn. By then, I was at the peak of my strength, in a swimmer's high, my body running on full automatic. When my hands cut the water, I felt as if I was about to yank the other side of the pool toward me. An illusion, naturally, like the powerful sense that I could go on forever. I'd get tired soon enough, at which point the far end of the pool would shift into full retreat, growing more distant with every turn.

Methodically, I reviewed the day's events, evoking a series of images beginning with the body of David Lodge sprawled on the frozen ground and finishing with Detective Linus Potter's nasty smile when he told me that Tony Szarek, the Broom, was dead. It was all so convenient: the ski masks, the river of brass, the carefully aimed *coup de grace*, the double-parked Toyota, the forbidding TEC-9, the widow's evasive answers. Every element led toward DuWayne Spott.

I'd come up against staged murder scenes a few times in the past. In each of those cases, the staging was an afterthought, a coda to a rage-motivated attack. The Lodge scene was a lot more elaborate. Clearly the scenario had been planned in advance. Just as clearly, it hadn't been planned by DuWayne Spott. The purpose of staging is to lead investigators *away* from the guilty party or parties, not toward them.

So what did all this mean to me? I was climbing out of the pool, a half-hour later, when I finally decided that I couldn't answer the question. I just didn't have enough information. Meanwhile, there were cold winds blowing out there. Sailing into them made no sense at all.

I went to my locker for a towel and found the light on in Conrad Stehle's small office. I wasn't surprised. Conrad had been subject to periods of insomnia ever since his wife, Helen, died two years before. Typically, he refused to toss and turn between the sheets, opting to stroll the few blocks from his house to his office at the Y. Sometimes he swam laps in an effort to wear himself out, but usually he settled for doing a little paperwork in the hope that one of his buddies would happen along. As I included myself in that group, I stuck my head in the door.

'Evening, Conrad.'

'Ah, I thought that was you I heard thrashing around in the pool.'

Conrad Stehle was closing in on seventy, a tall stocky man with the barrel chest of a true swimmer. He'd been a champion in high school, winning statewide tournaments six different times in three different categories. At one point, the now-defunct New York *Herald Tribune* had pronounced Conrad 'a future Olympian'. Those dreams had come crashing down when he returned from the Korean War with a purple heart and lungs too weak to support active competition.

I peeled off my goggles and cap, then fished out my ear plugs. 'I caught the David Lodge case. Did you hear about it?'

Conrad's green eyes widened slightly and he tilted his chin in the air. A bit of a cop buff, he liked nothing more than to discuss an investigation, and I sometimes used him as a sounding board. Lodge's celebrity, of course, only sweetened the mix.

'Just let me dry off,' I continued, 'and I'll be right back.'

Fifteen minutes later, when I returned, Conrad had a bottle of Cointreau sitting on his desk, along with two plastic cups. He poured an inch of the liquor into each cup, then passed one to me. 'To crime and punishment,' he said.

'Amen to that, brother.'

I clinked plastic, drained the cup, then drew an outline of the investigation thus far, including my numerous misgivings. Though I'd meant to be brief, I found myself explaining my reaction to Adele's maneuver with the Lodge file, my pending transfer to Homicide, and my equally pending promotion.

'The reassignment and the promotion, Conrad, they're both at the absolute discretion of the bosses.'

'And that's what you wish to protect?'

I shrugged. 'I don't care all that much about the promotion, although I could definitely use the money. But Homicide? Even as far back as the Academy, and we're talking fifteen years here, I wanted to be a homicide detective. Now I'm only a few months away.'

Ordinarily, Conrad had the listening skills of a psychiatrist, but my whiny complaints, on that night, evoked no more than a slight toss of the head as he removed a stubby cigar from his shirt pocket and ran it beneath his nose. He'd stopped smoking on the day Helen, a chain smoker since adolescence, died of lung cancer.

'I don't think you're worried about this file. I think you're worried that you can't control your partner.'

'Yeah, there's that, too. But I'm sure of one thing: if I play it by the numbers, I can't get hurt.'

'And those numbers include keeping Lieutenant Sarney informed?'

'At all times, Conrad. At all times.'

I left Conrad's office with a happy heart, and carried my good mood back to my apartment where I called Adele. It was a quarter to twelve and I knew she'd be watching the first half-hour of the Letterman show. Letterman was better, she'd told me, than a sleeping pill.

'Adele,' I said when she picked up the phone, 'the Broom is dead.'

'The broom?'

'Patrol Officer Anthony Szarek, retired.' I detailed my conversation with Linus Potter, laying heavy emphasis on the timing of Szarek's suicide, just two weeks before Lodge's scheduled release, and Szarek's devotion to alcohol.

'So what does this mean to us, Corbin?' Adele asked when I finished.

'According to Potter, Tony Szarek holds the case against Lodge together by putting Lodge alone with the victim. But who speaks for Tony Szarek?'

'Nobody,' Adele replied without hesitation, 'and now he can't speak for himself. But I'm still asking the same question. What does this mean to us?'

'Szarek was a drunk. He was the weak link.'

'I'm not disagreeing with you, Corbin, but it's getting late.'

'And you want me to come to the point?'

'Please.'

'The point is that the shit's hit the fan, and I

69

intend to maintain a low profile until I see if it's aimed in my direction.'

'This isn't like you, Corbin.'

'I don't care. Everything goes across the lieutenant's desk, every move we make. That way, the bosses can't protect themselves without protecting us. Remember, it's not just us. Sarney's also at risk here.'

'Yes,' Adele finally admitted, 'I could hear it in his voice.'

EIGHT

I know what I expected as I approached the Attica Correctional Facility in my rented Plymouth: soot-stained granite walls, ancient and forbidding, topped by coil upon coil of gleaming razor wire. But Attica's walls weren't soot-stained, or topped by wire, or made of granite. They were poured concrete and they appeared, from a distance on that day, as white as the fields of snow surrounding them. The effect was more Camelot than Tower of London, an illusion compounded by octagonal guard towers set into the walls like rooks at the corners of a chess board. Imposing in themselves, the towers were large enough to accommodate fully enclosed rooms behind their battlements, rooms to which the guards undoubtedly retreated on frigid winter days. These rooms were topped by funnel-shaped roofs covered with festive orange tiles.

From inside the Plymouth, with the heater running on high, it was a beautiful day. The sun at my back fired the edges of the undulating dunes with a wavering line of pure silver. The sky ahead was intensely blue and seemed to grow directly from the prison walls. Even the few sunlit clouds, though clearly in motion, could have been details in a painted backdrop.

But I wasn't going to be able to stay inside the car, enjoying the picture-postcard scenery, a fact of life that became painfully obvious when I finally turned into a parking lot surrounded by snow banks higher than my head. The temperature outside was minus six degrees, the sun no warmer than an uncooked egg yolk, the winds strong enough to stir up mini-tornados of snow. I was wearing a really nice wool coat, a coat suitable for a Broadway show or an uptown dinner. But when I stepped from the car – bravely, I thought – my coat afforded me all the protection of a terrycloth robe.

By then, thanks to a long delay while airport security cleared my weapon, I knew a lot more about David Lodge. The wait had left me plenty of time to read New York's three daily papers, each of which had uncovered a different piece of the investigation Adele and I were conducting.

A *Times* reporter named Gruber had somehow wangled an interview with Ellen Lodge. Her husband, she'd told Gruber, had claimed, on more than one occasion, to fear a revenge-motivated attack. According to Ellen, 'He was wired when he left the house. I could see that.'

71

Eva Hinckle made an appearance in the *Daily News* where she described Lodge's murderers as 'black males'. According to the reporter covering the story, Carl Gonzalez, Eva was certain because (as she only now remembered) the ski mask worn by one of Lodge's assailants had slipped as he got into the red car, exposing the back of his neck.

The *New York Post* hadn't gotten to any of the witnesses. Instead, a 'highly placed source within the NYPD' had told a reporter named Ted Loranzo about the location of the abandoned Toyota and the TEC-9's recovery. The main focus of Loranzo's story was the relationship between the TEC-9 (which Loranzo described as a 'machine pistol') and gangster rap. Profusely illustrated with photos culled from album covers depicting black men holding TEC-9s, the text made no effort at subtlety. The police, Loranzo told his readers, were concentrating their efforts on friends and associates of Clarence Spott.

So, the cat was out of the bag. All those blatant clues were never meant to fool the investigators unfortunate enough to catch the case. They were there because reporters need blatant clues in order to write slanted stories. Stories that somehow failed to mention Ellen Lodge's evasiveness, or Otto Hinckle's observations, or the convenient placement of the Toyota. Had Loranzo asked himself why Lodge's killers didn't park the car legally? If they had, the car might not have been discovered for weeks and would almost certainly have been stripped of anything as valuable as a TEC-9 by the time it was.

Accompanied by a corrections officer in a parka suitable for Antarctic exploration, I proceeded from the main gate to the administration building along a path bordered by snow banks even higher than the ones in the parking lot. The guard's name was Bardow and he hesitated when we finally reached the door.

'Are you here about the Lodge murder?' he asked.

With the sun in his face, Bardow's pale irises retreated into near invisibility. I focused on a spot where I thought they might be and said, in the most sincere voice at my command, 'Do you think we could talk about this inside?' By that time, even my balls were numb.

'Oh, right.'

With the door safely closed behind us, I admitted that I was, indeed, investigating the murder of David Lodge. Then I asked, 'Did you know him?'

'Sure. Lodge was an ex-cop. Up here, that makes him a celebrity.'

'What was he like?'

'Big – way over six feet. He lifted weights almost every day.'

'So, he wasn't somebody you'd mess with?'

'This is Attica. Anybody can be shanked. But Lodge wasn't a guy you'd go out of your way to antagonize, that's for sure. Not that he gave us any trouble. Mostly, he kept to himself.'

Though I would have liked to extend the conversation, we'd already reached the reception desk and I had time for just one more question.

73

'What about an inmate named Jarazelsky, another ex-cop?'

'Pete Jarazelsky was a horse of a different color. He took protective custody around six months ago.'

Deputy Warden Frank Beauchamp's business-like smile was firmly in place when I walked into his neat office. His grip, when he offered his hand, was equally businesslike. 'So, you're here to interview Pete Jarazelsky,' he said as he pointed me to a chair and resumed his own seat.

'Actually, I'm here to learn anything I can about David Lodge ... What do I call you? Dep? Deputy Warden?'

'Frank'll do.'

'OK, then I'm Harry.' I paused long enough to offer a manly nod which he returned. 'One thing strikes me as a bit strange, Frank, about Lodge. He was an ex-cop and I thought ex-cops went someplace where they could do easy time. Not places like Attica.'

Beauchamp wagged a finger in my direction. 'Well, you're partly right, Harry, and partly wrong. The system does maintain a minimum-security facility out on Long Island, a kind of honor farm. Celebrity prisoners, including cops and politicians, usually get sent there. But Lodge was never eligible because he was a violent felon.'

'And that's why he came to Attica?'

Beauchamp shook his head. 'Lodge started out at the Cayuga Correctional Facility, in Moravia. That's medium security. He went into their pro-

74

tective custody unit and stayed for almost two years.'

'I can understand why he went into protective custody, given that he was cop,' I said, 'but not why he came out.'

'Protective custody is nothing more than segregation. You stay in your cell twenty-three hours a day, you get an hour for exercise, you get two showers a week. After a while, even the yard looks better.' Beauchamp picked up a chunk of quartz crystal lying on top of a stack of papers and stared at it for a moment. 'When your lieutenant called me yesterday, I went through Lodge's file, lookin' for an answer to your question about how Lodge got to Attica. Turns out, he was transferred from Cayuga more than four years ago, but his file don't say why. So what I did was call over to Cayuga, ask a lieutenant I know, a huntin' buddy, for a heads-up.'

I leaned forward and laid my elbows on the desk. 'Now why,' I asked, 'do I think this is gonna be good?'

Beauchamp's brown eyes were sparkling and his smile was back. We were two cops exchanging stories now, which is exactly what I wanted.

'Seems like a month after Lodge came out of segregation, a man named Jimmy Fox, a white supremacist from Syracuse, was killed with a shank. A month after that, Lodge was on his way to Attica.'

'You're saying Lodge killed Fox?'

'The administration's snitches kept naming him, but he was never charged because there was no evidence.'

'Then why the transfer out of medium security?'

Beauchamp sneered. 'Let's just say, in the correctional system, we have ways to punish offenders without putting the state to the expense of a trial.' He returned the crystal to his desk and leaned back in his chair. 'Now I expect you're gonna ask me about the motive. Why would Lodge kill Fox?'

'It was right on the tip of my tongue.'

'Well, it goes like this. When you first come into the system, no matter who you are, somebody's gonna test you, see if maybe you wouldn't mind becoming a victim. That's just the way of it.'

'And David Lodge, he passed the test?'

'That's the word I got.'

We were interrupted at that moment by a uniformed officer who told us that Pete Jarazelsky was waiting in an interview room down the hall. Beauchamp waved him off, then asked, 'Anything else I can do for you, Harry?'

'Yeah, Jarazelsky. An officer told me he's in protective custody. Was somebody after him?'

Beauchamp laughed. 'Old Pete, he's a work of art. He snitched out so many inmates, the whole prison wanted a piece of his ass. Now I don't know who finally caught up with him, but he took a serious beating right before he went back into protective custody.'

I nodded. 'Seems like a good reason to spend twenty-three hours a day behind bars. But let me ask you this: Jarazelsky was sent up for burglary. How'd he end up in Attica with David Lodge?'

'No mystery there, Harry. It was the luck of the draw, simple as that. Pete asked for protective custody right out of the box, just like David Lodge, only instead of being assigned to Cayuga's unit, he was assigned to ours. The way the state sees it, if you're in protective custody it doesn't matter what prison you're sent to. If you're protected, you're safe.'

'Until you ask to come out.'

That brought another laugh, then an explanation. 'When Jarazelsky couldn't take being alone with himself all day, he asked to go into population. It was his bad luck that the population in question was the population of Attica.' Beauchamp rose from his chair and stepped around his desk. 'But there is one other person you need to see after you finish with Jarazelsky. Lodge was a trustee his last year with us. He did office work for our psychiatrist, Dr Nagy. From what Nagy told me, they got pretty close.'

When Beauchamp offered his hand, I knew my time was up. I had no complaints. Inspired no doubt by Lodge's celebrity, Beauchamp had definitely gone the extra mile. Still, I made one further request before I left his office. I asked if he'd assign one of his subordinates to compile a list of David Lodge's visitors over the past two years and fax it to me.

77

NINE

If it had been up to me, I would've interviewed Nagy first, leaving Pete Jarazelsky to simmer. But Jarazelsky had been brought to the administration building all the way from C Block as a courtesy when I might have had to interview him in the bowels of the prison. The least I could do was accommodate Beauchamp's schedule.

The starkly functional room Beauchamp had chosen for the interview had been designed for small conferences. A sound-dampening ceiling and two banks of fluorescent lights above, a long table surrounded by upholstered office chairs on wheels, a polished tile floor. Two flags, of the United States and the State of New York, stood against a cinder block wall.

When I came through the door, Jarazelsky's dark eyes jumped to mine. I returned his gaze, hoping for a peek into his heart before he composed himself. No such luck. His eyes immediately dropped to the table, leaving me to make the first move. He was wearing an orange jumpsuit and his wrists were cuffed to a leather belt at his waist. For a moment, I considered the grand gesture, asking the guard to unlock the cuffs, but decided against it. This wasn't an interrogation and I wasn't going to get hours and hours to wear him down.

I finally introduced myself as Detective Corbin, then took a seat across the table and stated my business. I was here to investigate the murder of David Lodge. I deeply appreciated his voluntary cooperation. I looked forward to any assistance he might offer.

'Hey,' Jarazelsky said when I ground to a halt, 'me and Davy, we were tight. I'm talkin' about on the street, back in the Eight-Three, and up here, too. So, any way I can help, I'm happy to do it.'

Jarazelsky was a short, unimposing man with jug ears and a drooping nose that fell to within an inch of his upper lip. His dark eyes were large and slightly bulging, his mouth slightly open as he watched me intently. He'd now made point number one, confirming Ellen Lodge's claim that Jarazelsky and her husband were prison allies.

'When was the last time you saw Lodge?' I asked.

'A couple months ago.'

'Months?'

'Well, see, I got into a beef with some niggers and hadda take segregation. It's only temporary, though.' He leaned across the table, his voice dropping in tone and volume. 'I know Davy woulda looked out for me, but I didn't have the heart to jam him up after he got his release date.'

'Right.' I rolled my chair back a few inches and crossed my legs, but made no further comment. I wanted to see what Jarazelsky would volunteer.

'Anyway,' he said after a moment, 'I knew Davy was goin' to his old lady's house. He told me he was gonna stay there while he looked for a job.'

'Do you know where he planned on looking for this job? Did he contact anyone before he left Attica, maybe some of his old buddies at the Eight-Three?'

Jarazelsky shrugged. 'I can't say for certain. He could've.'

I opened a notebook and wrote my own name three times, then looked back up. Between the bulging eyes and the jug ears, Jarazelsky's face had a bat-like quality, especially when he tilted his head down. Although his appearance also had a menacing aspect, I sensed the wariness of a small mammal caught in a trap. Whenever he shifted his weight, the chains that bound his wrists and ankles rattled softly.

'Tell me what David Lodge was like,' I said. 'What did he do with his time? Did he have any hobbies? Like to write letters? Play basketball? What'd he talk about when you were alone?'

'He lifted weights,' Jarazelsky said after a moment.

'That's it?'

'What can I say? Davy was pretty quiet. And he was never my cellie. We mostly got together in the yard. But you could take this to the bank: Davy was nervous about his release. The guy he clipped, Clarence Spott? Well, Spott's brother, DuWayne, took over the crew after his brother's passing. I was still at the Precinct when this happened, so I know what I'm sayin'. DuWayne put the word out that he wasn't gonna sit for his brother gettin' murdered by no honkey pig.'

This time, Jarazelsky's eyes gave him away. He was searching my face, gauging my reaction. Having confirmed (without prompting) the second element of the widow's statement, he wanted to know if I was buying his story.

'Are you telling me that Lodge was directly threatened by DuWayne Spott?'

'Like I said, Davy was real quiet. It wasn't always like that. Back at the Eight-Three, when he was still drinkin', he was pretty much out of control.'

Jarazelsky hadn't answered the question, but I let it go. I wasn't all that interested in his tale because it didn't address the point Adele had raised in Sarney's office. How would DuWayne Spott know that David Lodge was going to his wife's house upon release?

But I still had a choice to make. I could leave Jarazelsky's story unchallenged or I could send a message.

'Do you have a release date, Pete?'

Jarazelsky tried for a smile, but didn't quite make it. 'Six months.'

'You get out in six months?'

'Yeah.' He tried to bring his hand to his face, but the cuffs held him back. 'Ya know,' he told me, 'Davy was over at Cayuga for a couple of years.'

'And then got transferred to Attica?'

'Right.'

'How'd that happen?'

Again, Jarazelsky lowered his voice and leaned across the table. 'Davy told me that he ran into a problem with another con at Cayuga. He didn't name no names or nothin', so don't get ya hopes up, but he did say the beef came from outside the joint. Like, he was bein' set up.'

'So, what did he do about it?'

'He did what he *had* to do.'

For me, it was attack or retreat time. There was nothing to be gained by prolonging the interview, not unless I wanted to shake him up by pointing out that a black gangster from Brooklyn was highly unlikely to hire a white supremacist from Syracuse to pull off a hit.

Instead, I backed off. First, there was that fan thing I'd mentioned to my partner. As far as I could tell, it was still on high, still spewing excrement. And then there was the distinct possibility that Jarazelsky could be turned. In just six months, he was scheduled to leave Attica, to go from a place where his life was always in danger to a place of moment-to-moment safety. If I was somehow able to put his release date in jeopardy, he'd most likely roll over. He was, after all, a snitch by nature.

But I had no way to threaten Pete Jarazelsky, not then, and I wrapped up the interview a few minutes later. Jarazelsky continued to watch me, as he'd been watching me all along, with the look of a man immersed in a poker game. Would I call his bluff? Would I concede the pot? There was a lot at stake here for Pete Jarazelsky and he would have been wise to keep his anxiety to himself.

I fished a business card out of my wallet and

laid it on the table. Jarazelsky wasn't a large man and the jumpsuit made him appear even smaller. 'Any time you wanna call me, Pete,' I told him, 'I'm open for business. And I appreciate your talkin' to me when you didn't have to. I owe you one.'

Dr Vencel Nagy's interview room was neat as a pin. The tiled floor gleamed, the small wooden table and the chairs to either side had been polished to a frenzy; a bank of vertical filing cabinets against the far wall might have been resting on a showroom floor. The individual responsible stepped to one side when I entered the room, in deference to the uniformed guard escorting me. A small black man, he clutched a spray can of furniture polish and a soiled gray cloth to the breast of his orange jumpsuit as if fearing a robbery. But my escort never even glanced at the prisoner as he led me through a door to our right and into Nagy's windowless office.

The contrast between Nagy's office and his immaculate interview room could not have been greater. Not only did mismatched bookcases, crammed to capacity, stand against every wall, but the spaces between the bookcases were filled with dusty books stacked on top of each other. Towers of books sprouted from a threadbare Persian rug, as they did from Nagy's desk where he'd created a wall of books. If I sat down, I'd no longer be able to see him, which might have been all to the good. Dr Vencel Nagy's hands were jumping from his mouth to his ears to the fringe of snow-white hair along his scalp like cockroaches in search of a crevice. When he finally jammed them beneath his armpits, I was distinctly relieved.

'Please, sit down,' Nagy said after I introduced myself. In his sixties, his powder-white skin was criss-crossed by hundreds of fine wrinkles.

'Do you think I might remove some of these books first?' I shifted one of the stacks to the floor before he could answer, then stepped around another pile and dropped into a metal chair. I could see Nagy from this position, although it was like peering through a window.

'So, tell me what you are traveling all this way to find?' Nagy had a pronounced eastern-European accent. His vowels were thick, his consonants hard. His tone was that of a man used to having his questions answered.

'To find out who killed David Lodge,' I replied without hesitation.

Nagy turned to his left, his gaze drifting to the ceiling, and laughed, a heh-heh-heh devoid of amusement. 'With this I cannot help you,' he eventually admitted. 'David wasn't the sort of convict who made enemies. He was very quiet, very self-contained.' Suddenly, Nagy's hands were on the move again, bouncing over his chest and shoulders before settling at his waist. 'You don't know how much I miss David. This idiot they have sent me? You've seen him?'

'I have,' I admitted.

'David, for me, wrote up the charts, kept the files, answered the phones. This lunatic, he's all day with the vacuum cleaner and the rags and

84

the bucket. From a medication chart, he knows nothing. From filing, he can't tell A from Z.' Nagy paused long enough to slide his hands beneath his thighs. 'So, other than identify Lodge's killers, how can I help you?'

'How close were you to Lodge? Was he open with you?'

'We spoke together often. David was very smart, but somewhat obsessed.'

'Obsessed with what?'

'With his innocence.'

Bang, a wild card, face up on the table. I saw it hit the top of Nagy's desk, watched it quiver for a moment before settling down. 'Were you Lodge's therapist?' I asked.

Nagy's head made another left turn and he again laughed at the ceiling. 'Therapy is not what I do here, detective. Here I treat...' He shook his head. 'No, no, no. Treat is too grand. What I do is control a population of psychotics with various medications.' He smiled, his nearly lashless eyes narrowing slightly. 'Left to their own devices, you see, my patients tend to disrupt the prison routine.'

'And the warden wouldn't like that?'

'No, she wouldn't. But medications were not for David. He was under control.' Nagy's hands fluttered up to pat the sides of his face when he paused. 'Do you know about the blackout? David's blackout? Do I have to explain it?'

'Are you talking about his claim that he didn't remember killing Spott? I always figured that was so much propaganda.'

85

'There you are wrong, detective. David could not remember.' Nagy leaned forward. 'Think of how this would be for you. Not remembering the event that turned your life on its head. Are you guilty? Are you innocent? How can you know? And how can you accept your punishment when you are not knowing?'

I nodded, wanting nothing more, at this point, than for Nagy to continue. But the only things I encouraged were Nagy's hands which did a ten-second dance, graceful as an aerial ballet, before he shoved them into his pockets.

'For David,' he finally continued, 'the issue settled on the murder weapon, the blackjack. The blackjack belonged to him, true, but it had been sitting in his locker for months. Now, did he go to his locker that night, retrieve the weapon, then return to Spott's cell? This is the question David asks.'

'And what was his answer?'

'First, David considered motive. Why did he want to kill Spott? Because Spott hit him? If this is the case, then killing is motivated by rage. But this is also very strange because if David was enraged, he could have killed Spott much earlier. David was not only having his gun and his nightstick with him, he is big enough to kill with his bare hands.'

I smiled and leaned back. 'I see what you're getting at. Lodge murdering Spott in a moment of rage is inconsistent with his going to his locker for a specific weapon. Inconsistent, but not impossible.'

'And there you are seeing David's dilemma.

Logic can never bring certainty.'

'No, it can't. But tell me, doctor, did anybody else at the precinct know about the blackjack?'

Nagy's lower jaw was large enough to produce a pronounced underbite. He thrust that jaw at me and raised a remarkably still finger. 'This blackjack, it was a Kluugmann. It was collectible.'

'Say that again?'

'Kluugmann was a company that manufactured very high quality blackjacks and saps. They went out of business many decades ago and their products are collected. You can buy them at auction.'

'So, Lodge showed his Kluugmann to all his buddies, then stuck it in his locker and forgot he even had it.' Which was just what I would have done.

'Now you are getting the deal. Would he even have remembered the weapon's existence in the midst of a towering rage? A *killing* rage? This is what it boils down to with David.'

I shifted to Lodge's stay in Cayuga at that point, but the good doctor professed ignorance, again insisting that Lodge was generally reticent except when discussing the Spott murder. And Nagy merely shrugged when I told him that Lodge was a suspect in a prison homicide.

'This does not surprise me. In here, they are saying you must learn to walk the yard like a man. This is the first task, to walk through the yard without projecting fear. David was able to do this.'

'And that makes him a killer?'

'I am only saying, detective, that I am not

87

surprised by what you are telling me.'

Nagy didn't like being challenged, that was obvious. His head again turned to the left as his hands went into their little dance, touching, patting, pulling. By now it had become clear, even to me, that Nagy was suffering from an illness. Whether physical or psychological in nature was still up in the air.

'Tell me,' I finally said, 'about Lodge's thinking right before his release. Did he have specific plans? What was he looking forward to?'

'Sometime in the last few months of his incarceration, David finally recovered a memory of the night Spott was killed. That was when he became convinced of his innocence.'

'Did he say what it was that he remembered?'

'No, only that it was a fragment, a piece of the puzzle. But this I will tell you. If he had other concerns, he did not discuss them with me.'

'He never mentioned a man named DuWayne Spott?'

'Never.'

'What about a job, his wife, his old friends?'

Nagy's face twisted to the right, then the left, both motions so exaggerated it took me a moment to realize he was merely shaking his head. 'David was an obsessive type. You can see this in his body-building. Six days every week, never missing a day. It was how his mind worked.'

As I waited for Nagy to slow down, I played with the facts as I now understood them. A cold and sober David Lodge emerged, a Lodge obsessed with his innocence, a Lodge capable of

murder. Without doubt, if Lodge was truly innocent, he'd present a formidable challenge to
those who'd framed him. Killing Lodge was a
rational response to that challenge, despite the
risks.

Suddenly, Nagy jumped to his feet and pointed
a trembling finger at the door behind me. I was
startled enough to reach for my weapon (which
I'd surrendered in the reception area), but when
I turned it was only Nagy's assistant. He was
standing motionless in the doorway, still clutch-
ing his can of polish and his rag.

'I have told you twenty times already to stay
out my office,' Nagy shouted. 'Never you are to
come in here. Are you hearing me? Never.'
Nagy's donkey jaw had risen almost to his nose
and his glittery blue eyes were circles of indignation. 'If you were not my patient, I would hit
you with a chair.'

TEN

It was eight o'clock by the time I got back to
Queens and the One-Sixteen. Jack Petro, a squad
detective and a good friend, was standing fifteen
feet away when I entered. He nodded sympathetically as I walked over.

'This one a keeper, Harry?'

Jack was asking me if the case would be transferred to Homicide or a task force at Borough

Command. In the normal course of events, high-profile cases were routinely taken away from precinct detectives, a development I would have welcomed.

'If that's the plan, no one's told me about it.'

I looked over his shoulder and saw Adele seated at her desk thirty feet away. She was staring directly at me, her gaze sharp and contemptuous. She'd been awaiting my return for hours and now I was bullshitting with my buddy. How predictable.

'My partner's giving me the evil eye.'

Jack's smile dropped away and his expression became grave as he tossed me a snappy salute. 'Time to report, soldier.'

Like many of my peers, Jack professed not to know why I continued to partner with Adele Bentibi when I had more than enough seniority to demand a change. He knew that I'd once been on the verge of marching into Sarney's office to do just that, even though it was clear that Adele was my perfect complement. Her strengths were crime scenes and physical evidence, while mine were interviews and interrogations. But partnering is about more than solving crimes and there's no hell quite like spending all of your working hours with someone whose company you'd rather avoid, even if you're physically attracted to her.

Simply put, like everybody else, I found Adele insufferably opinionated, and the fact that her judgments were usually right meant next to nothing. Plus, I'd only agreed to work with her as a favor to Bill Sarney. Adele had come to the

116th Precinct with a reputation. 'Difficult to get along with,' that was how Sarney explained it, a little character flaw that I should overlook, at least temporarily.

I don't remember my attitude on the day I agreed to work with Adele. Perhaps I was resentful, the fair-haired boy imposed upon. Or maybe I took the assignment with good grace – I was definitely out to please at the time. But after three months, I was certain that I'd had enough. Adele was very abrupt, seeming to dismiss my opinions before I managed to state them. More to the point, she was blind to a number of deficiencies related to her poor communication skills. I could not convince her that an interview is not an assault, an interrogation not a cavalry charge.

Eight hours a day? Day after day? I didn't think so.

'Martha Stewart with a badge' was the way Nydia Santiago had described my partner, and I could see where Nydia was coming from. But she'd gotten it wrong. I found this out when Adele told me her story over dinner.

I remember that it was the perfect night for a confidence. Adele and I had spent the prior ten hours in pursuit of a rapist named Joey Garglia, running from friend to relative to friend, sometimes threatening, sometimes cajoling. Finally, at six-thirty, Joey's mother had called. Her son was sitting in her living room and he was ready to surrender.

By any standard, it'd been a very good day, a

day of hard work and real accomplishment which we were capping with a decent Italian meal and a couple of drinks. Though I wasn't expecting much, the alcohol made me bold enough to ask an impertinent question.

'So, tell me, Adele, what's your story? How'd you become a cop?'

My partner never did answer the second question, not directly, but her response to the first part was enough to change the way I understood her. Permanently.

Adele could trace her family of Sephardic Jews back to the twelfth century when they lived in an area of northwestern Africa called the Maghreb. For centuries, she explained, their lives were reasonably stable, as were their relations with their Christian neighbors and Muslim rulers. Then the Almohad Dynasty had emerged at the head of a puritanical movement that tore the region apart. The aim was to purify Islam, a deed accomplished by the forced conversion of Christians and Jews; by the sale of Christians and Jews into slavery; by the slaughter of whole villages. Adele's family had fled, ironically enough, to Spain, from which they were expelled by Queen Isabella in 1492, the year Columbus sailed his little fleet in search of India.

I was munching on a crispy slice of bruschetta, and well into my second drink, when I finally realized that Adele wasn't talking about a succession of parents and grandparents stretching back nine hundred years. Her ancestral legends were tribal. Still, I was completely absorbed. My concept of family was so far removed from

Adele's that we might have been different species.

From Spain, the 'family' went to Istanbul, on the shores of the Black Sea, then to Baku, on the Caspian, then to Baghdad, Tunis, Cairo and back to Istanbul. Restless as gypsies, they were always on the move, always calculating the dangers around them.

They were in Damascus in 1840 when things again came to a head. A Capuchin monk and his servant disappeared. A Jewish barber was tortured until he admitted the men were murdered because their blood was needed for Jewish rituals. More Jews were then arrested and tortured until the Ottomans, at the request of the British and French governments, ordered the surviving Jewish prisoners released.

But the Damascus Affair was only the first of many similar persecutions that finally drove the Bentibis (by then, Adele was speaking of her actual family) out of the Islamic world. They'd gone to Belgium first, in 1948, then come to New York, settling along the southern end of Main Street in the Queens neighborhood of Flushing. Adele was the youngest child of the youngest child to make that journey.

We were outside by the time I realized that Adele had answered my second question in her own way. Her voice hadn't betrayed a hint of self-pity when she told her tale. Nevertheless, I now understood that, for Adele Bentibi, the job was about justice.

And I understood something else, as well. I'd spoken to a number of cops, including Jack

93

Petro, about my intention to seek another partner and it had almost certainly gotten back to Adele. In the family-like atmosphere of a New York City precinct house, secrets are rarely kept for any length of time. So, why had Adele, ordinarily so closed, suddenly confided in me? What message was she sending? I played with both questions before I decided that revealing herself was Adele's way of asking me to continue the partnership. Partners, after all, tell each other everything.

It was hot on the street, especially in contrast to the heavily air-conditioned restaurant, and foggy as well. As I stood out on the sidewalk with my hands in my pockets, the fog settled around my face and throat, hot and slick, like the breath of an animal. Adele was standing in front of me, her face turned up, her dark and slanted eyes for once soft and vulnerable. I stared down into those eyes for a long moment, the urge to take her into my arms, to taste her mouth, nearly overwhelming. And I was almost certain she'd respond, that I wouldn't be rejected. Adele was leaning forward, her weight on the balls of her feet, as if about to sprint, and she continued to stare into my eyes until I finally chickened out.

'Goodnight, partner,' I said, making a feeble attempt to keep my tone casual. 'I'll see you in the morning.'

'Corbin,' Adele said as I approached her desk, 'look at these. Tell me if you see what I see.'

I watched Adele lay eight crime scene photos, in two rows of four, on my desk.

94

'Am I allowed to hang up my coat first?'

'Of course.'

The detective squad at the One-Sixteen covered most of the second floor of a three-story brick building on Catalpa Avenue. The layout was simple enough: a large room broken by the lieutenant's office, a door leading to a corridor, a corridor leading past three interview rooms. There were ten desks in the main room, set back-to-back. They were all in use when the squad was fully staffed, but times were tough and the NYPD, once 42,000 cops strong, was down to 35,000 and still shrinking. Our own little squad had been making do with eight detectives for almost a year.

When I came back to my desk, I settled down immediately. The photos were of Anthony Szarek as the Crime Scene Unit had found him two weeks before. The Broom was lying on his back, with his head propped up on pillows. A trail of spatter led from his left temple, across the bed and the floor, to a wall about eight feet away. The spatter caught my attention first, and I studied a series of photos depicting the blood trail closely, but found nothing out of place. I turned, then, to a close-up of the contact wound an inch from Szarek's right ear. The starburst pattern was similar to the one I'd observed on Lodge and perfectly consistent with suicide.

'Was he drunk?' I asked without raising my eyes.

'Very good. The Broom's blood-alcohol level was .32 when the trigger was pulled.'

'That's drunk enough to be unconscious.'

'Yes, it is.'

My gaze finally settled on the only photo I'd yet to consider. This one had been taken to illustrate the position of a .38 caliber revolver, a Smith & Wesson, relative to Szarek's hand and body. The weapon, a few inches from his fingers, was not out of place, and my eyes drifted eventually to his fingers, following them over his hand and wrist, then along his arm to the sleeve of his white T-shirt. It's what I didn't see that finally grabbed my attention.

When a bullet is fired into human flesh, small drops of blood and minute bits of tissue are propelled backward, in the direction from which the bullet came. If the Broom had been holding the gun to his head, there should have been blowback on his hand, his wrist, the T-shirt. But there wasn't, at least none I could see.

'Anybody test for blood?' I finally asked Adele. 'On Szarek's right hand and wrist?'

'The assistant medical examiner who performed the autopsy. It was negative.'

'What about gunpowder residue and nitrates?'

'Those tests were also negative.'

The information was designed to set off alarm bells. No blowback? OK, I could live with that. No residue? I could live with that as well, though my suspicions would be aroused. But the absence of any physical evidence demonstrating that Szarek held the gun to his own head was a red flag that could not be dismissed.

I gathered the photos and passed them to Adele. 'Two questions. First, how'd you get the photos? Second, did Lieutenant Bill Sarney authorize us to investigate Szarek's death?'

'I got the photos and the reports from a friend of a friend at the 94th Precinct. The lead detective on the case, by the way, was a lazy asshole named Mark Winnman. Mark was happy to go along when the medical examiner reported manner of death as probable suicide.'

'Did you bring up the lab findings with Detective Winnman?'

'I did, and guess what? By the time the reports came in two weeks later, the case was closed. Winnman, he didn't even read them.'

'Just stuck 'em in the file and forgot about 'em? That how it went?' When Adele responded with an amused smile, I continued. 'But you didn't answer the other question, partner. Did you tell Sarney you were gonna check out Szarek's death before you did it?'

She shook her head.

'How about afterwards?'

'Afterwards, yes. I brought the photos and the lab reports to his attention.'

'And how did he react?'

'Badly.'

I took a moment to get my temper under control, but I couldn't shake the feeling that partnering was a one-way street for Adele. 'So what's it gonna be?' I finally asked. 'Games all the way down the line? Because you're acting here as if I don't exist.' I silenced her reply with a wave of my hand. 'What you do reflects on me. I can't say it any plainer than that. Your consequences are my consequences.'

Adele looked at me for a moment, her eyes

97

progressively hardening, and I realized that her thirst for justice would always come before her loyalty to Harry Corbin. An instant later her words confirmed that insight.

'Feel free to disown me,' she declared, 'whenever you find it convenient. In the meantime, are you ready for dinner? Because I've been waiting for you since five o'clock.'

But I wasn't ready, not quite. I took three DD5s from my desk drawer, one each for Beauchamp, Jarazelsky and Dr Nagy, then wrote up meticulous summaries of each of their interviews. When I was finished, I carried them directly to Bill Sarney's office. Sarney and I had reached a point in our relationship where, at least in private, I called him by his first name.

I took a chair without asking permission, careful to keep my tone casual as I summarized the fives I tossed on his desk. If Sarney wanted to raise the issue of Szarek's case file, he'd have to do it himself.

He didn't wait long, only until I shut up a few minutes later. 'What's going on with you, Harry?' he asked. 'Why would you expand your investigation to include an ex-cop who committed suicide without telling me in advance? You couldn't have thought I'd be OK with that.'

Adele's consequences were mine, just as I'd predicted, but I might have tried to shed them by disowning her. *Hey, Bill, I'm not her father. What she does on her own time is her own business. I can't be with her twenty-four hours a day.* Instead, I made a promise I couldn't keep. I told

98

Sarney that it wouldn't happen again.

'I need some idea of where this is going, Bill. Otherwise, me and Adele, we have no choice. We have to follow wherever the trail leads. You can see that, right?'

Sarney grinned. 'A couple of hours from now, just in time for the eleven o'clock news, an Inspector named Rita Meyers will make two announcements at a press conference. First, she'll tell the reporters that the Ballistics Unit has matched the TEC-9 found in the Toyota with fourteen shell casings discovered at the Lodge crime scene. Then she'll announce that a man named DuWayne Spott, whereabouts unknown, has been named as a person of interest. You understand, Harry, this is the first time a boss has appeared in connection with the case.'

I'd asked Sarney for a heads-up and he'd complied. I had no beef here. 'So where does that leave me and my partner, Bill? Do we continue to investigate?'

'Harry, you can color to your heart's content, as long as you stay between the lines. Now, there's one more thing. I'm not stupid. I know you can't control your partner's urge to self-destruct. But what I'd like you to do is keep an eye on her. If she jumps the tracks again, I wanna be the first to know.'

'It's not that easy, Bill. You're asking me to spy on my partner.'

There was an edge to my voice, and I'm sure Sarney heard it. But he wasn't intimidated. He leaned forward in his chair and lowered his chin until he was looking at me through his eyebrows. 'Sometimes in life,' he explained, not unkindly, 'you gotta watch out for your own ass. If your partner understood that, we wouldn't be having this conversation.'

ELEVEN

It was almost nine before we finally sat down to a meal, this one in a diner several blocks from the precinct. By then, Adele and I were observing a somewhat uneasy truce. Nothing had been resolved, of course, but there was no way, between Dr Nagy and Tony Szarek, we could sit across from each other and not discuss the case. We were cops, after all.

So we began with something easy: trashing Detective Winnman's reputation. According to Adele, not only hadn't he read the lab reports, he'd failed to speak to Szarek's family and friends, or to conduct a routine canvas of the building. From Winnman, we moved to the Broom, eventually conceding that suicide could not be ruled out, not absolutely, by the ME's findings. Not that it mattered all that much. For the time being, our hands were tied. Sarney had already told Adele that if the Szarek case was reopened, she and I would not be the investigators.

Gregorio, our waiter, showed up at that moment with a pair of Heinekens, which he set on the table. Though Gregorio also brought two glasses, Adele and I quickly pushed them to the side. They were still warm from the dishwasher, one of the hazards of ordering beer in a diner.

'According to Sarney,' I began, 'there's gonna be a press conference tonight, at which a boss named Meyers will tell the world that DuWayne is a person of interest, and that some of the shell casings recovered at the Lodge scene were fired by the TEC-9 found in the Toyota.'

I watched Adele's cheeks flame. 'Ellen Lodge and Jarazelsky are both lying,' she declared, her tone bitter and contemptuous, 'and the job is buying into their lies. I went to OCCB this morning and spoke to Sgt Merkovich. DuWayne Spott isn't a ghetto don, not even close. He's a pimp and a low-level cocaine dealer. According to Merkovich's snitches, there are only four men in his entire crew, most of them relatives or kids he grew up with. He couldn't have known when Lodge was going to be released, much less where Lodge was headed. It's simply impossible.'

I broke a salted roll in half and buttered one end. 'What was Sarney's reaction when you told him about Lodge's file being ... How did that jerk from Archives put it?'

'Unable to locate at this time.'

'So, what'd Sarney have to say when you told him Lodge's file was temporarily unlocatable?'

'He said he'd make a formal request to the DA's office for their copy, plus he'd contact CSU and the crime lab to see what they had in their own files.'

'He offer a time-frame?'

'Nope. But there's good news, too. We'll have Ellen Lodge's phone records tomorrow morning.'

Our dinners arrived a few minutes later: meat, gravy, potatoes and a few broccoli spears that'd been stewing for the better part of the day. As I ate, I allowed myself to fall into the minds of the conspirators, a practice I commonly follow prior to interrogations. From their point of view, the news coming from Jarazelsky must have been devastating. Lodge's recovered memory would be meaningless in a court of law. The only way he could prove his innocence was by persuading somebody else to confess.

By this time I knew quite a bit about David Lodge, and not only from Nagy and Beauchamp. The newspaper stories had included extensive accounts of the events leading up to Lodge's guilty plea seven years earlier. One item in particular had caught my attention. According to the ME, Clarence Spott had been severely beaten prior to being struck with the blackjack. That beating had occurred outside the precinct and had been delivered by David Lodge, who'd already been the subject of a dozen civilian complaints alleging police brutality.

What would I do if I was one of the co-conspirators, say the man at the top of the pyramid, and I learned that Lodge was coming after me? What would I do to protect myself? What risks would I take? What level of fear would Lodge inspire, this large violent man who spent his days in Attica's weight yards?

The death of the Broom was one answer to those questions. Ellen Lodge and Pete Jarazelsky provided two more answers. Like Szarek, they were weak links, points at which a good detective places the splitting wedge before driving it home. Nobody would rely on them unless they were desperate.

'Eva Hinckle called this morning,' Adele said, 'to report her newly surfaced memory. She was very definite. The ski cap rode up and she saw the back of the driver's neck. He was black.'

'Which proves what? Even if she's right?'

'Don't you read the newspapers, Corbin? It proves that DuWayne Spott and his army of ghetto gangsters killed David Lodge.'

Lieutenant Bill Sarney was a compulsive organizer and the walls of his office were dominated by a series of cork boards. As Adele and I sat before his desk the following morning, I found myself caught up in the notes and departmental notices pinned to the boards. What struck me was that the paperwork was absolutely square to the frame and the colored pins holding them had been placed at uniform heights.

'Alright, guys,' Sarney declared once we were seated. 'What's up?'

'Nothing you don't already know, lou,' I replied. 'Our day's just gettin' started.'

Sarney's tone was supremely casual, and his face gave nothing away. 'Ah, but that's the point, Harry. I want to know what you're going to do with your day. That's why I asked you to stop in.'

Adele handed Sarney a printed document, Ellen Lodge's phone records, which Adele had taken off the computer a few minutes before Sarney called us into his office. Two days ago, she pointed out, at 9:01 a.m., an incoming call from a pay phone was taken by someone at the Lodge residence. That didn't surprise me; as a cop's wife, Ellen Lodge would expect us to check her records. But a second, outgoing call did catch me off-guard. It was made to a cell phone at 9:06 and lasted a mere nine seconds.

'My partner and I think,' Adele told Sarney, 'that we should begin with another visit to Ellen Lodge. We can ask her about the second call and return her husband's personal effects at the same time.'

'Fine,' Sarney replied without hesitation. 'What else?'

'Dante Russo. He was Lodge's partner on the night Spott was killed. We think he should be interviewed.'

'You know who Russo is?' When neither of us jumped to reply, Sarney nodded once, then continued. 'Russo is the PBA's Trustee for Brooklyn North. He knows everybody. So, please, unless you have enough evidence to secure an arrest warrant, don't get in his face.'

The Patrolman's Benevolent Association represents every uniformed cop in New York City below the rank of sergeant, some 27,000 in all. That they have clout – in city and state government – as well as with the job – goes without saying. Dante Russo was a Trustee, one of only twelve. This gave him clout within the PBA.

104

Under ordinary circumstances, I would've made a call to an old partner now working in the personnel bureau and asked him for a peek at Russo's service file. But that wasn't going to happen here. We were going to play by the rules and that was all she wrote.

TWELVE

It was snowing when Adele and I left the precinct to re-interview Ellen Lodge. The snow-flakes, large and virtually weightless, fell out of a pewter sky, drifting ever so slightly as they made their way to an already-covered sidewalk. The snow covered the streets and the radio cars parked at the curb as well. It softened the right angles of the shotgun tenements, gathering in the window frames, and rounded the knobby branches of Marino's Maple, planted three decades before to honor an officer slain in the line of duty.

When I finally took a step, the snow floated up, playful as baby powder, then settled back on the supple leather of my tasseled loafer where it proceeded to melt. 'How bad is this supposed to be?' I asked Adele.

'You didn't check the weather before you left home?'

'I barely had time to shave.'

'Well, don't worry, it's only a snow shower.

It'll be sunny by noon.'

Adele got busy on her cell phone while I drove the few blocks to Ellen Lodge's home. Like every PBA trustee, Dante Russo would no longer wear a uniform and have no assigned duties. His job was to move from precinct to precinct, conferring with delegates, handling union-related problems as they arose.

Adele's first call went to PBA headquarters where she was told that Russo still worked out of the Eight-Three and she should contact the desk lieutenant. From the desk lieutenant, she was shuttled to the precinct's executive officer, then to the community affairs officer, before Dante Russo finally came on the phone.

I half-expected Russo to make some excuse – if he wished, he could stall us for weeks – but after a brief conversation Adele hung up.

'So, that's that,' she said. 'Officer Russo will receive us at eleven.'

'Guess he's not afraid of us.'

'Must be the Jarazelsky interview.'

Adele was referring to a phone call Pete Jarazelsky had made from prison the night before. The call was to Christian Barrett, a talk-radio host who'd once declared that high rates of infant mortality among black and Latino Americans was God's way of cleansing the ghettos. Ever the good soldier, Jarazelsky told Barrett that fear of assassination by former associates of Clarence Spott, including his brother, DuWayne, had been uppermost in David Lodge's mind on the day he walked out of prison.

The story was too big to be contained, coming

106

as it did after Ellen Lodge's *New York Times* interview. Every station had run with it on the morning news, every newspaper as well.

'We're being out-flanked,' Adele observed as I pulled to the curb in front of Ellen Lodge's house. 'You know that.'

'I know it's worse than that. The final nail in DuWayne Spott's coffin is about to be hammered home.'

'And after that you're off the hook?'

'I was never on the hook, Adele, because I never took the bait. You want to do justice. I know that, partner. And I'm even willing to admit there's nothing more satisfying in life than closing a cell door behind a violent predator. But crime goes on. Like death and taxes.'

I managed to get my left foot out of the car before Adele spoke up. 'The detectives are small and the job is big. Know thy place.'

'That's right, Adele. In the real world, the cockroach never crushes the shoe.'

'The cockroach just crawls into its hole.'

Funny thing about partners. After a while, they get to know each other so well, they even know when to shut up. That I wasn't going to get in the last word was a foregone conclusion.

I expected to find Ellen Lodge frantically coping with her toddlers, but there were no children in the rooms through which she led us, only games and mats and tiny tables stacked against the walls as though awaiting collection. Which, in fact, they were.

'The parents pulled their kids,' she told us.

'After what happened, you can't fault 'em. I'm waitin' for Goodwill to come and pick up the junk.'

Though her tone was edged with defiance, Ellen Lodge's gray eyes seemed weary to me, weary and disappointed. I wondered if she'd expected her husband's death to lift a burden, only to find the weight on her shoulders increased many times. I wondered, too, if I might take advantage of her vulnerable state, if I might exploit her misery. Sarney had ordered us to go easy on Dante Russo. He hadn't said anything about Ellen Lodge. She was in play.

Ellen led us across the lower floor of the house, then up a staircase to a sitting room where she dropped into an armchair. The chair and a matching couch were upholstered in an elaborate pattern of intersecting vines and blossoms. The colors were vivid, especially the scarlet roses which matched the ruffled curtains on the bay window. I stood there for a moment, taking it in, before deciding that the room was far too bright for Ellen Lodge. It was a room that spoke to the woman she wished to be. Or, perhaps, to a woman she once was.

Adele and I took seats on opposite ends of the couch. I was going to conduct the interview and I didn't want my subject distracted. First, I took Ellen Lodge over old ground. Had any memories surfaced? Anything about her husband's immediate plans? Anything from his letters? How about his demeanor when he left the house?

The last question finally brought a response more complex than a simple shake of the head.

In her *Times* interview she'd described her husband as 'wired'.

'Well, I don't know exactly. I mean he, like, ran upstairs, grabbed his coat and tore outta here, so you gotta figure somethin' was botherin' him.'

I might have reminded her that her original description of David Lodge's movements didn't include running, grabbing or tearing, but I let it go. Instead, I asked about the phone call that inspired her husband's agitation. Again, she told me that she hadn't recognized the voice, that she was only sure it belonged to a man who didn't have a foreign accent.

'I was in such a rush. You know, with the kids. I wasn't payin' that much attention. In fact, for all I know, the guy coulda been black.'

Score one for Ellen Lodge.

'You told us the call to your husband came in around nine o'clock,' I continued. 'How close to nine would that be?'

'Within a few minutes either way.'

I opened my jacket, plucked Ellen's phone records from the inner pocket, then carried them over to her chair. When I knelt down, my face was within arm's length of hers. 'Would this be the call, this one at 9:01?'

'I'd say so.'

'Now what about this one at 9:06? It went to a cell phone and lasted only a few seconds. I was wondering what that call was about.'

Lying to somebody on the other side of the room is one thing; lying to somebody two feet away is another. Though Ellen managed to deliver her lines, she couldn't look me in the eye.

'I was callin' a girlfriend,' she declared, 'but I got a wrong number. I didn't have the time to re-dial.'

I returned to my seat on the couch, then took a moment to re-fold the document and slide it into my jacket pocket. I was stalling for time as I tried to decide whether or not to go in hard. When I looked up, Ellen Lodge was staring at me.

'So,' I said, 'the girlfriend you were trying to reach, her number must have been very similar to the number you called, right?'

I watched her stiffen and knew any direct assault on her story would result in a display of defiance; that I'd only strengthen her resolve. Thus, when she told me she couldn't recall her friend's number offhand, that she'd have to look it up, I simply changed the subject.

'You remember Tony Szarek, the cop they call-ed the Broom?' I asked. 'He was gonna testify that he left your husband alone with Clarence Spott.'

'Sure, how could I forget? What about him?'

'Szarek's dead. Two weeks ago. The medical examiner said "probable suicide", only there wasn't any note. But then again, Szarek's blood alcohol level was four times the legal limit, so maybe he was too drunk to hold a pencil. Or maybe he was passed out. Of course, if he was passed out it's hard to see how he could shoot himself, but you never know. The Broom, he put your husband alone with the prisoner. I tell ya, when I heard he was dead, I took it hard. He was

110

the first guy I wanted to talk with, Ellen. After you, of course.'

I glanced at Adele, then nodded. She took a manila envelope from her bag and passed it over. The envelope contained David Lodge's personal effects, but I didn't open it right away. Instead, I held it in my lap as I continued to address Ellen.

'You know what I keep thinking?'

'No, what?'

'I keep thinking that if your husband believed he was innocent, a conversation with Tony Szarek would have been prominent on his to-do list. Definitely.' I paused long enough to laugh and shake my head. 'Imagine a guy like David Lodge confronting a miserable drunk like Tony Szarek. How long before the Broom rolled over? An hour? A minute? A second?'

Ellen Lodge folded her arms across her chest. 'What's this have to do with me?'

'Probably nothing,' I admitted, 'but did you know your husband was friendly with the prison psychiatrist?'

Ellen ran the fingers of her right hand through her short hair, her eyes closing momentarily as she reviewed her options.

'No,' she finally said, 'I didn't.'

'Funny your husband never mentioned it in his letters, because David used to work in the shrink's office and they were pretty tight. Anyway, the shrink's name is Vencel Nagy and he claims that your husband left prison fully intending to prove his innocence. And not only didn't he fear revenge, he never even mentioned Du-Wayne Spott's name.'

111

I stood up and approached Ellen Lodge again, only this time I remained standing. At six-three, I towered over her.

'You put yourself out front when you lied to me and my partner,' I told her matter-of-factly. 'And when you lied to the *New York Times*. Now, maybe everything'll go smoothly; maybe the nightmare will just fade away. But if it does not, if there are a few potholes down the road, you gotta figure someone's gonna come lookin' for Ellen Lodge the way they came lookin' for the Broom.'

I took a business card from my shirt pocket and dropped it in her lap. 'My cell phone number's on the card.'

By this time Adele was standing in the doorway. I took a step toward her, then turned around.

'Oh, yes, I almost forgot. We just came by to return your husband's personal effects.' I reached into the manila envelope, took out David Lodge's wallet and placed it on a table to Ellen's left. 'One wallet.' Then I dipped into the envelope again. 'One Department of Correctional Services photo ID.' Then again. 'One appointment card with a parole officer named Paris Blake.' Then again. 'Twenty-two dollars in bills.' Then again. 'One treasured photograph.'

I placed the photograph in her hand, forcing her to look at herself, posed on a strip of sand in her blue bikini, her youthful sexuality as innocent and unaffected as her smile. That her husband had kept that photo with him throughout his prison years was as inescapable as the fact

112

that she was no longer the girl in the picture. She was smaller now, and frightened, a middle-aged woman who'd taken so many wrong turns she no longer believed there was a right one out there.

Ellen Lodge continued to stare down at herself and I continued to stand in front of her. Maybe she was waiting for me to go away. I can't be sure. But eventually, though she didn't speak, she looked up at me through gray eyes that seemed drained of emotion.

'Any hour of the day or night,' I reminded her. 'I'll be there for you. All you have to do is dial my number.'

THIRTEEN

'I'm sorry, Corbin,' Adele told me as the door to Ellen Lodge's house closed behind us and we descended to the street, 'for what I said about you wanting to be rid of the case.'

I didn't respond and Adele, apparently, decided that I was still angry. But I hadn't been angry in the first place. As I've already said, Adele had a sharp tongue and I'd learned to live with it. No, what had captured my complete and undivided attention was the ankle-deep snow beneath which my shoes had disappeared. I'd had these loafers for years, had polished and conditioned the leather until the shine appeared to come from within. More to the point, having long ago molded themselves to my feet and toes, they were far and away the most comfortable shoes in my closet.

I don't like to think of myself as a fuck-up, a label applied to me often enough in the past. But this was beyond fuck-up. This was actually subhuman.

'You were very good in there,' Adele continued. 'The widow didn't know whether she was coming or going.'

I responded by opening the trunk of the Caprice and searching through our evidence kit until I found a handful of sterile gauze pads. Then I tossed the keys to Adele.

'If I don't dry these shoes,' I explained, 'I'm gonna end up throwin' 'em away.'

Though it took her a moment to shift gears, Adele didn't argue. She slid behind the wheel, then unlocked the passenger's door. Inside, I wasted no time. I took off my shoes and began to work the gauze into the leather. For all my good intentions, I succeeded only in transferring brown polish from the leather to the gauze pads to my fingers. The shoes remained as damp as ever, as did my socks and feet.

I was still holding my shoes a few minutes later when the cell phone in my jacket pocket began to ring.

'Do you want me to get that?' Adele asked.

Ignoring my partner's sarcasm, I jammed my damp feet into my damp shoes and answered.

'Corbin here.'

They're gonna roll your boy tonight, Harry.

114

Unless you find him first.

The phone went dead while I was still fumbling for a response. I put it back in my pocket, then repeated the message to Adele, doing my best to imitate my anonymous informant's gravelly whisper.

'The plot thickens, partner,' she said. 'Must be all that excrement pouring off the fan blades.'

It was still snowing hard enough to dot the windshield between swings of the wipers. Ahead of us, the rear end of a mini-van swung out as the vehicle tried to negotiate a right turn on the hard-packed snow. We were headed for the adjoining precinct, little more than a mile away, which was fortunate. City-wide, traffic would be a nightmare.

Adele finally broke the silence. 'Can we assume,' she asked, 'that the "boy" we need to find is DuWayne Spott?'

I shoved my feet under the heater, consigning my loafers to their fate. Somehow, dry was looking better and better. 'Either that or some devious miscreant wants to throw us off the track. But here's a problem we need to deal with right now. Sarney told us to go ahead with the interview, but not to get in Russo's face. What exactly did he mean by that?'

'What do you think he meant?'

I replied without hesitation. 'You ask a question. You accept the answer that you're given.'

'Corbin, are you suggesting that I'm argumentative?'

'Perish the thought, partner.'

* * *

115

We met Dante Russo in the office assigned to the precinct's Community Affairs Officer. Russo was alone and sitting behind a desk near the center of the room when we arrived. He motioned us to a pair of small armchairs, explaining that the CAO, Justin Moore, was over at Bushwick High School, delivering an anti-drug lecture to the freshman class.

'Ya know what I'm sayin', right? This is your brain. This is your brain on drugs. Meanwhile, the little humps know more about dope than he'll ever know.'

As I sat down, I slid my chair toward the end of the desk, separating myself from Adele. The first thing I noticed, before Adele fired off a single question, was that Russo's warm and friendly voice didn't match his expression. He sat with his jaw thrust forward, staring down at us along the length of his long nose. The net effect was disdain, an impression reinforced by his full lips which were noticeably compressed.

'So,' he said, 'what can I do ya for?'

Adele crossed her legs, attracting his rapt attention. 'I don't know if you're aware of it,' she told him, 'but Clarence Spott's case file is missing.'

Russo took a second to answer. 'No, I wasn't.'

'Eventually, of course, we'll get a copy from the DA, but for right now, we're kind of dancing in the dark.'

'What can I do to help?'

'Well, why don't you run down the events leading to Spott's arrest?'

We got the official version, of that I was

116

certain, the one that held Dante Russo blameless. Clarence Spott was a known drug dealer whose photo had been on display in the muster room for weeks. Russo had recognized him, stopped his car, finally ordered him to get out. Then, in quick succession, Spott called Lodge a pig, Lodge slapped Spott, Spott punched Lodge, Lodge reacted predictably.

'I eventually managed to pull him off, but Dave's a big guy and—'

'Was,' Adele corrected.

'Was?'

'Dave *was* a big guy. Now he's dead.'

Russo's chin rose a millimeter even as his tone became more confidential. 'Dave was mostly OK when he was sober. But he couldn't lay off the bottle, not for more than a couple of days. I tried to convince him to check into rehab, but askin' for help wasn't his style.' When Russo paused, Adele simply nodded for him to continue. 'Anyway, after I got my partner under control, we transported Spott to the house. Lieutenant Whitlock – he was the desk officer – told us to dump him in a cell, which we did. I was out front, talkin' to Whitlock about whether we should get medical attention for the prisoner, when I found out he was dead. The last I saw of Dave, he was in the cell area with an officer named Szarek.'

'The Broom.'

'Yeah, the Broom.'

'He's dead, too.'

Russo shrugged. 'I heard he ate his gun.'

'Then you heard wrong.' Adele put her fore-

117

finger to her temple and mimed pulling a trigger. 'He put one in the side of his head.'

Adele was working herself up. That much was obvious. What was equally obvious was that she wasn't looking at the situation from her subject's point of view. Russo was holding his nose so high that he might have been sniffing for the carcass of a dead rat. But it was the disconnect between Russo's tone and his expression that interested me most. The differences were so pronounced that he might have been two people. Not that I felt he was the victim of some obscure personality disorder. Russo's mastery of the vocal part of his act was impressive – his voice remained honey-smooth and he would not be flustered – but he still needed work on the visual part. He was giving his hand away.

By then, I was sure that Russo was lying, and not without reason. The way he was telling the story, he'd immediately intervened on Spott's behalf. That wasn't true. Spott's extensive injuries had been inflicted in the course of a prolonged beating. More than likely, he and Lodge had carted Spott off to some quiet corner of the precinct where David Lodge had administered a serious tune-up while his partner watched out for the sergeant.

Russo, of course, was in no position to admit to any of the above. He'd escaped punishment because the story he offered the bosses suited their interests, the same story he now offered to Detectives Corbin and Bentibi.

'Ate his gun,' Russo told my partner, 'is just a figure of speech. Szarek and I were never friends.' Russo's lips expanded into a smile that didn't come within a shouting distance of his eyes. 'Anything else?'

'Just a couple of items. You told me that you pulled Spott to the curb around three-thirty in the morning.'

'That's right.'

'And he was the only one in the car?'

'Right again.'

'So, I was wondering what happened to the car? Did you search it?'

'Gimme a break. My partner was bleeding, the prisoner was bleeding. No way did I have time to worry about Spott's car.'

'But you notified the sergeant that you were transporting a prisoner to the house, right?'

Russo shook his head. 'What with all the blood, I thought my best move was to get inside and let the desk officer sweat the details.'

'Well, did someone go back later? Was the car towed into the precinct?'

Russo's chin finally came down. 'Look, the way our snitches are tellin' the story, David Lodge was blown away by DuWayne Spott who first swore to take revenge seven years ago. So you'll have to excuse me if I don't understand why you wanna know what happened to Clarence Spott's car.'

'It's just that...' Adele waved her hand, a circular gesture that might have meant anything. 'I mean, all this happened on Knickerbocker Avenue. That's the main drag in Bushwick, the shopping district, and there's a subway stop at Myrtle Avenue, too.'

'At three-thirty, everything's closed up. And the subway – if it should happen to be on time, which mostly it isn't – runs every twenty-five minutes.'

Adele smiled brightly. 'What about CSU? Didn't they process the Knickerbocker scene? Why didn't they tow the car to their evidence yard?'

Russo's chin resumed its customary jut and his smile vanished. 'Detective, I have no idea what happened to Spott's car. As you can imagine, the house was swarmin' with bosses at the time. Internal Affairs was there too, and they had lots of questions.'

He should have let it drop at that point. The first rule of resistance, in a police interrogation room or on a witness stand, is never volunteer anything. But Russo needed to impress the two pissant detectives who'd come to question him. He couldn't help himself.

'They were gonna try to take me down with Lodge,' he finally added, 'but I lawyered up right away.'

'How about your partner? Did Lodge get a lawyer?'

'Hey, I was the PBA delegate. Helpin' cops out is what I did. No way I'd let the cop-haters from IAB get their hands on Davy.'

FOURTEEN

When we left the precinct house at Knickerbocker and Myrtle a few minutes before noon, the snow had stopped. Although the sun wasn't shining (as Adele had predicted), there were breaks in the lower cloud banks that revealed thinner and much brighter clouds high above. The temperature and the humidity were rising as well. Within a few hours, the snow, driven by liberal applications of rock salt, would turn into an icy, leather-destroying slush.

'Anything to say?' Adele asked as I started the Caprice.

'You fucked up.'

'Seriously?'

'Definitely.'

'How so?'

I finally turned to look directly at her. 'You fucked up when you said Spott was originally pulled over on Knickerbocker Avenue. We didn't get that from Linus Potter and it wasn't in the papers. That means you saw the case file. I don't think you wanted me to know that.' I put the car in gear and pulled away from the curb. We'd only have time for a quick lunch and I headed for the Taco Bell a quarter-mile away.

'So, what's the harm? Who's going to know?'

'The harm is that you're not going to stop. You're like a junkie. The harm is that you led me to believe that you were gonna let Sarney get Lodge's file. When you had it all the time.'

'Are you very pissed off?'

'No, not really. It's too predictable.' I might have added that once this case was disposed of, I intended finally to seek another partner, that I was drawing a line of my own. But there was no point to that, either. 'Anything else in that file I should hear about?'

'Nobody gave a statement, not Szarek, Russo or Lodge, for two weeks, so the investigators didn't know where the original contact with Spott took place. By the time they found out, Spott's car was long gone. It was never recovered.'

Adele had my complete attention now and I motioned her to continue.

'Russo, he drew a pass for three reasons. He had no prior brutality complaints on his record, he was willing to testify, and he didn't have blood on his uniform, not his partner's or Clarence Spott's. That supported his claim that he took no part in the original beating.'

'It also means he didn't kill Spott in that cell.'

'You're wrong there, Corbin.'

'How so?'

'A single blow from a blunt object rarely produces spatter. It's the follow-ups that spread the blood.'

'Explain that.'

Though my tone was anything but challenging, Adele frowned. 'Slap your right fist into your

122

left palm,' she ordered. 'Now do it again and imagine that your palm bled between the first and second impacts. You see? When Spott was struck, he naturally started to bleed. A second blow would have impacted this blood and scattered it. In the process, Lodge's killer would have gotten blood on him.'

'But there wasn't a second blow?'

'According to the ME, Spott was killed by a single blow that crushed the back of his skull. Russo – or anyone else – could have delivered it and come away clean.'

I slid to the curb in front of the Taco Bell, dropped my ON OFFICIAL POLICE BUSINESS placard onto the dash board and shut off the car. Though I hadn't begun to complete the puzzle, I could now see a few of the pieces.

'Something else,' Adele said as we got out of the car. 'The bosses scapegoated the desk lieutenant, Justin Whitlock. The theory was that Spott should have been transported to an emergency room, not dumped in a cell. Whitlock was run out of the job after a departmental hearing and a series of appeals. The way it reads in the file, he was lucky to keep his pension.'

I got on the horn to Bill Sarney after we finished eating, summarizing our interviews with Ellen Lodge and Dante Russo, then repeating the anonymous tip I'd received on my cell phone. If Sarney was unhappy with Russo's treatment, he didn't say so. He jumped right on the tip.

'You think he was talking about DuWayne Spott?'

'That would be my guess, lou, but it would've been a lot more helpful if he'd told us where to look. Adele got the names of a few relatives from the gang unit yesterday, but if DuWayne isn't willing to make himself available, we're not likely to find him. Not in the short term, anyway.'

When Sarney told me that we'd have to look anyway, I didn't argue. Instead, I changed the subject.

'I want to jam Pete Jarazelsky's parole,' I told him. 'Jarazelsky's a rat in his heart. He'd roll over on the Pope if he thought it was in his best interest.'

'Keep goin'.'

'First, Jarazelsky took protective custody after a bad beating, so he's doing hard time. Second, he's scheduled for release six months down the line. What I was thinking...' I stopped suddenly as an idea caught my attention, a sequence of events which I filed away for later. 'I was thinking it might be possible to contact Jarazelsky's parole board, tell 'em we have strong reason to believe that Pete obstructed a homicide investigation and maybe they should reconsider their decision to release him.'

After a moment, Sarney told me that he'd 'look into it', then went on to other matters. The NYPD lab, he explained, had done a preliminary analysis of the blood evidence. All of the samples they'd examined contained Type A blood, matching Lodge's blood type. DNA results would follow in forty-eight hours. The Toyota had also been examined. While no fingerprints had been found, blood, fiber and hair evidence were recovered. The blood was all Type A. The fibers were black wool and might have come from the masks worn by the shooters. The hairs, two of which were dyed, had been deposited by four different Caucasians.

I wasn't overly concerned with any of this physical evidence. A comparison of two human hairs, unless they contain some obscure deformity, can never be said to match, not the way fingerprints match. The best that can be said is that a comparison doesn't exclude the defendant. Fibers are better evidence, but unless very rare, just marginally.

Nevertheless, after hanging up, I dutifully relayed the information to Adele before describing the sequence of events that had caught my attention a few minutes before.

'According to Nagy,' I told her, 'Lodge became certain of his innocence about six months before his release. Around the same time, Jarazelsky caught a bad beating and asked for segregation. Why can't these two events be directly related?'

'You mean Lodge beat the information out of Jarazelsky?'

'Exactly.'

'That presumes Jarazelsky knew the truth about Clarence Spott.'

'Or some piece of it that convinced David Lodge that he was innocent.' I smiled and shrugged my shoulders. 'It's only a theory, Adele, but it's a theory that makes sense. Pete Jarazelsky takes protective custody after Lodge kicks his

125

ass, then contacts one of his pals in the city. He explains the situation and measures are taken to eliminate the threat.'

'Any idea who that pal would be?'

'Dante Russo's obviously a possibility, or Ellen Lodge, but it could be someone unknown to us. What we need to do is take a closer look at Jarazelsky himself, but what we're actually going to do is waste our time searching for Du-Wayne Spott.'

FIFTEEN

We spun our wheels for the next seven hours, running from relative to acquaintance to relative, never even close to finding DuWayne Spott. We did pick up little tidbits, however, teasers that confirmed the information Adele had gotten from the gang unit at OCCB.

Our first stop was at the apartment of Du-Wayne's aunt, Mrs Ivy Whittington, in the Bushwick Houses. Ivy sat us down in her living room, insisted we take tea, then patiently answered our questions.

DuWayne, it turned out, had lived most of his life in the shadow of his brother's violence, a mama's boy until he reached adolescence.

'Clarence was a handful,' Ivy explained. 'You could whip that boy from morning till night, didn't do no good. No, sir. Clarence jus' take that whippin' and do what he gonna do.'

'And DuWayne?'

'Now DuWayne, he near about worshipped his big brother. Wanted to be just like the boy. Onliest thing, he was a sweet child. No kinda way did he have the heart for that life. Tore me up when the streets got him.'

Ivy's prim living and dining rooms were smothered with lace doilies – the couch where Adele and I sat, the chairs facing us, the end tables, the polished tops of a dining-room table and a long sideboard. The doilies echoed the oversized lace trim on the collar and sleeves of Ivy's tan dress, which she'd buttoned to the throat. A widow in her mid-seventies, her eyes swam behind thick-lensed glasses with amber frames large enough to hide her forehead.

I'd run across Ivy Whittingtons in the past, black women who'd seen everything there was to see, who'd suffered every kind of sorrow life has to offer. Always polite, they maintained their dignity with an iron will and their eyes gave nothing away.

'See, what happened, after that cop murdered Clarence, the city offered Reba – that's Clarence and DuWayne's mama – a two hundred thousand dollar settlement. Reba's lawyer, he says, "You hold out, Reba, you'll get a lot more." But Reba was always flighty. She took the deal and went off to Trinidad with Quentin.'

'Quentin?'

'Her new husband. Quentin's from the Islands, a musician.'

127

'And what about DuWayne? Did she cut him in?'

'She gave the boy a little somethin', but he just turned around and stuck it in his arm. See, the way it was, DuWayne couldn't keep up with his brother. That's why he started usin' the drugs. So he wouldn't have to face himself.'

At that point, I made my pitch. 'I won't insult you,' I told her, 'by saying that half the cops in New York are looking for your nephew. You've read the papers, watched the news. You know. But what I am gonna say is that if DuWayne surrenders, he's gonna be a hundred times better off. I'm not asking you to tell us where he is, even if you know. Just talk to him, Mrs Whittington, put the facts out there. Does he really want to be in some apartment when a SWAT team breaks through the door?'

Ivy stopped me with a wave of her hand. 'Is there a warrant out on the boy?' she asked.

When I admitted there wasn't, she smiled, exposing teeth so pearly-white they could not have been her own. 'Now why,' she asked, 'would a damn SWAT team be lookin' for somebody who ain't wanted for nothin'?'

Though I didn't have a ready answer, I persisted, explaining once again the benefits of voluntary surrender, finally offering my business card. Ivy held the card up to the light, as if examining it for flaws. 'DuWayne and me don't stay in touch,' she finally said. 'You wanna speak to DuWayne's cousin, Kamia. She and DuWayne, they run with the same crowd.'

'Does Kamia have an address?'

128

'She does now. The Fire Department carried her over to the hospital, Wyckoff Heights, day before last. Matter of fact, I'm fixin' to go over and visit. Kamia's my first daughter's girl.'

In the course of the afternoon, we interviewed Kamia (who'd overdosed on heroin), along with another five individuals, including one of Spott's hookers. They insisted that David Lodge was not on DuWayne's agenda. Sure, DuWayne might have made some kind of threat seven years ago when Lodge was sentenced, but that was just DuWayne shooting off his big mouth.

'See, DuWayne, he keep his bitches in line,' we were told at one point, 'but he don't wanna get it on with dudes. Hear what Ah'm sayin'? The nigga's a punk.'

By seven o'clock, when the lieutenant summoned us back to the house, Adele and I were both ready to call it a day. Most of what we'd been told merely confirmed what we already knew. No one, for instance, remembered DuWayne even mentioning Lodge's name in the last few months. DuWayne had all he could handle trying to maintain his perilous hold on the hustler's life. What with all the dope he was shooting, he couldn't take care of his women properly and his stable was on the verge of disintegration.

What had struck me, as the interviews piled up, was how eager people were to speak to us, even the street-wise who ordinarily wouldn't give us the time of day. I judged their enthusiasm

129

to be an indication of truthfulness. They were outraged by the media's treatment of DuWayne Spott and they wanted to correct the record. As if DuWayne not killing Lodge somehow made him an innocent bystander.

But they couldn't tell us the only thing we needed to know at that moment: Spott's where-abouts. One acquaintance had seen DuWayne on Sunday, in the early afternoon, but nobody had run across him since then. Disappearing wasn't like him, they insisted. DuWayne mostly kept a close eye on his women because they were all he had left.

'Once on a time,' Kamia explained from her bed, 'DuWayne used to do deals. But like, for the last year, he jus' into his dope. That's what he livin' for.'

I'd accepted Kamia's statement with a nod, then asked if any other cops, maybe someone from the Eight-Three, had been to see her.

'Uh-uh,' she replied, 'you the first.'

I'd asked the same question at each interview, and received the same response. If any effort was being made to locate DuWayne, aside from our own, they knew nothing of it.

When I brought this up to Adele on the way to the house, she merely shrugged. 'I'm disappoint-ed,' she told me.

'Because we're the only ones looking for Du-Wayne?'

'DuWayne's already dead.'

'That's one possibility, but it doesn't answer my question.'

'I'm disappointed with you, Corbin. What's

130

happening here isn't right.'

But I already knew that, and when my cell phone began to ring, closing off the discussion, I was grateful. I answered quickly, turning my face away from Adele who was still glaring at me. I was expecting to hear Bill Sarney on the other end, but it was my informant with his death-rattle whisper.

You're too late, Harry. Four-Eight-Three Ingraham Street. In the back.

We drove in silence, down Wyckoff Avenue and across Flushing Avenue, the traditional dividing line between the workers and their workplaces, and into the industrial section of Bushwick. It was past seven, the sun long ago set, and most of the low-rise warehouses had shut down for the night. Though vibrant during the day, the short blocks were very quiet now, the single exception being a waste management plant busy dispatching a column of green refuse trucks on their nightly run to collect Manhattan's commercial waste. Surrounded by a rusting chain-link fence, the intensely lighted yard seemed as garish as a Las Vegas hotel.

By contrast, the four hundred block of Ingraham Street was absolutely deserted. Pale orange light fanned outward from the only functioning street lamp, collecting in the mist and the slushy puddles at the curb. That it failed to reach the warehouses on either side of the street goes without saying, but Adele and I had no trouble locating 483 Ingraham. Almost dead center on the south side of the block, a single abandoned

131

tenement rose two stories above its industrial neighbors. The tenement's brick had been painted white decades ago, and its paint had now cracked into thousands of tiny shards. The shards cast leaf-like shadows that danced in the flashlight beams Adele and I played over the tenement's facade. From where we stood on the sidewalk, the building was in compliance with city code. The windows had been replaced with sheets of plywood and the door sealed with cinder blocks upon which some helpful city worker had painted the number 483 in red letters.

Followed by Adele, I walked to the eastern corner of the building, to a narrow alley. Though the alley was no more than five feet wide, the walls on either side were covered with graffiti, mostly tags, but with a few figures as well. A purple dragon holding a bleeding woman in its mouth; a pit bull with a goofy expression and the physique of a superhero, and a black Jesus hanging from the cross.

Adele unbuttoned her coat, removed her automatic and laid it across her body with the barrel pointing at the wall. She took a step, but I reached out to stop her. 'We're going to have a look around,' I said, 'but we are not going to remove *any* item of evidence. Under no circumstances, no matter what. We leave the scene the way we found it.'

Adele's smile widened and her eyes narrowed slightly, as a cat's eyes narrow with pleasure when its back is stroked. Driven by warming temperatures, the mist had thickened, beading on

132

Adele's hair and on her shoulders and her dark lashes.

I took out my own weapon, let it drop to my side. Adele was already in the alley.

SIXTEEN

We emerged, finally, into a back yard of packed earth dominated by an alianthus tree that rose to the tenement's roof line. Moisture dripped steadily from the tree's branches onto mounds of trash that virtually filled the yard. The trash appeared to be mostly industrial – bits of old machinery, crushed shipping pallets and card-board boxes. Adele and I worked our way through puddles of filthy slush, toward the rear of the yard, until we could see the whole of the tenement's back wall. In the center of the building, a narrow door had been closed off with cinder blocks, like the door in front, but some enterprising mutt had punched a hole in the cinder blocks large enough to slip through.

I went inside first, holding the flashlight well away from my body, shouting, 'Police,' as loud as I could. Abandoned tenements are haunted by the street's ultimate bottom feeders, the terminally addicted and the truly insane, either of whom might pose a serious threat to life and limb. Especially if surprised.

But DuWayne Spott was one bottom feeder

133

who would never again pose a serious threat to anyone. He was lying on his back, on a mattress, his coat beside him, the right sleeve of a Los Angeles Lakers sweatshirt pushed up almost to his shoulder. A thin belt, a tourniquet, circled his arm just above his elbow, while a disposable syringe rose from his forearm like an upraised finger. Though open, his unblinking eyes were fixed and dull, his chest neither rising nor falling.

Adele ran her flashlight over the stretch of concrete floor between herself and Spott, illuminating a dozen well-formed shoe impressions. Carefully avoiding them, she approached the mattress and squatted to verify the obvious. First, she placed her fingers to Spott's throat, then laid her ear on his chest, finally nodded once. Then she began to manipulate Spott's joints and muscles in an effort to measure rigor mortis. Typically patient and thorough, she worked his fingers, elbows and shoulders, his knees, hips and neck, his eyelids, mouth and jaw.

I remained on my feet. We were in a small room, no more than ten by twelve, with a door on the far wall that led to a corridor. While I managed to keep one eye on Adele, I never lost track of that door.

'How long?' I asked.

Adele lifted Spott's arm to examine the flesh along the underside. Spott was relatively dark-skinned which made post-mortem lividity harder to identify, but after a moment she lowered his arm to the mattress. 'Lividity is fairly well advanced, but there's no sign of rigor yet. I'd put

134

time of death somewhere between two and three hours ago.'

I crossed to the door and shined my flashlight into the corridor. Through a second door to my right, I saw another mattress and a pile of blankets. A portable electric heater, resting next to the blankets, was plugged into an extension cord which ran beneath the window and into the back yard. I walked up to the heater and switched it on. It cranked up without hesitation, emitting a loud hum as the coils began to glow.

When Adele joined me a moment later, I said, 'You think it'd throw enough heat to keep Spott alive for a few days? It's been cold as hell all week.'

Adele let the beam of her flashlight play across the floor until it met the red eyes of a large rat. One paw resting on an open can of Vienna sausages, the rat had raised itself up and was sniffing the air, its head swiveling from side to side. Unfazed, Adele continued, systematically exploring the room until she came upon a series of semi-liquid puddles that had the unmistakable shape, color and texture of human vomit. 'Look there, Corbin,' she said. 'That tells the whole story.'

The sequence I imagined at that moment – of DuWayne carried to this building, of DuWayne's cold-turkey withdrawal, of DuWayne begging for dope, of DuWayne vomiting in the corner – seemed flawless to me. When his captors finally offered him a taste, he hadn't hesitated, not for a split second.

I walked back toward the body, letting my eyes take in the little touches, the open glassine en-

135

velope, the guttered candle, the disposable red lighter, the tiny ball of cotton lying in the bowl of a blackened tablespoon. As I approached, I tried to summon up a trace of pity for DuWayne Spott but came away empty. He was a player who got played. It happens all the time.

'I'm gonna call in the troops,' I finally said.

'Better come in here and take a look first.'

When I complied, Adele, ever the impresario, yanked up a corner of the mattress to reveal the point of the charade, a TEC-9 semi-automatic handgun with an extended magazine that had to be a foot long.

Two uniforms by the Eight-Three's arrived first, followed by the Eight-Five's patrol sergeant, two detectives, a squad lieutenant named Burke and the Crime Scene Unit. This was all routine and I let Adele conduct the relevant briefings, only nodding agreement when absolutely necessary. But then Bill Sarney turned up in the company of the precinct commander, followed shortly by an inspector from borough command and a deputy chief from One PP. Sarney's attitude as he approached the deputy chief was so deferential he might have been a house servant on a southern plantation.

I remember watching the network vans rolling up, a pair of cops refusing to let them turn onto Ingraham Street, frantic reporters behind a web of crime-scene tape, the unblinking eyes of a dozen video cameras. I kept thinking that maybe Adele was right, maybe the bad guys had played their last card, but that card was a beauty. The

136

bosses were about to bet the house on DuWayne Spott. Never mind the fact that neither Mr Spott, nor any of his associates, could possibly have acquired the number of my cell phone. And never mind the faint ligature marks encircling Spott's wrists, either. Those were details that could easily be put to the side. The important thing was that whatever doubt the voting public might have had about DuWayne Spott's guilt would be wiped away by the recovery of the TEC-9. The job could now bury David Lodge, once and for all, simply by going along with the script.

It ended very nicely. A deputy inspector whose name I've long forgotten approached Adele and me, offering his hand for a quick, firm shake. He told us that we'd done a great job, but the case was going over to a special unit in the Chief of Detectives Office. We should return to our squad, write whatever fives were necessary to cover the day's events, then copy the entire Lodge file and place the copy on Sarney's desk. Forthwith.

Sarney was waiting for us when we arrived and he was smiling. I told him about the second tip, the one that had carried us to Spott's resting place. He listened carefully before also congratulating us.

'You guys have a few days coming,' he told us, 'and I want you to take them. I don't expect to see either one of you before Monday. *Capisch*?'

When I began to write up my fives a few hours later, the interviews of Ellen Lodge and Dante

137

Russo seemed part of some ancient history I'd discarded long before. I can't say I hadn't expected this sort of an ending, or that I didn't feel relieved to have concluded the business without having to inform on my partner. But there was a bitterness as well and I couldn't get the taste of it out of my mouth.

Mike Blair had a drink waiting for me before I reached the bar. When I chugged it down, he refilled my glass without me having to ask. 'It's goin' bad, right?' he said. 'The Lodge thing?'

'I'm done with it,' I explained. 'The case's gonna be run from the Puzzle Palace. What I think they'll do – if they haven't already done it – is put the murder on DuWayne Spott, then hunt for a second shooter among his associates.'

'That's good you're getting clear of it. Because I've been hearing things.' Blair's eyes jumped to mine, a quick penetrating glance designed to catch me off-guard.

'Like what?'

He leaned out over the bar. 'Nobody's talkin' against *you*, Harry. Everybody knows you're a cop's cop. But your partner? The word out there is that she has a hard-on for the job.'

I might have debated the logic of the charge, given Adele's gender, or I might have defended her, but I didn't do either. Instead, halfway through a third scotch, I carried my drink to Linus Potter's table and sat down without being invited.

With Potter, you had to get past the gargantuan shoulders and the tiny head and the buzz cut

138

before you could see what he really looked like. Far from raging, his blue eyes were slanted at the corners and a little sad, while his mouth, beneath a thick brown mustache, was free of tension. The impression I got was of a man who knew his life might have gone in a different direction if not for circumstances beyond his control.

'Tell me about Lieutenant Justin Whitlock,' I asked. 'What happened to him?'

Potter laughed, then let his eyes drop to the table. I think he was waiting for me to go away, but I simply held my ground, as I had at our first discussion. Gradually, his eyes came up. This time, they appeared amused.

'Whitlock, one day he calls Dave into his office. He tells Dave that complaints are comin' from all over the house and nobody wants to ride with him. So Dave, what he does is throw a tantrum, figuring he can intimidate Whitlock. He tosses his chair, kicks the waste basket, slams his hand on Whitlock's desk.' Potter laughed again, a deep chuckle that rumbled in his chest. 'And it works. Would ya believe that? Instead of puttin' the asshole on suspension, Whitlock teams Dave up with Dante Russo, one bad deed leading to another, if you take my meaning.'

I pushed my chair back, started to get to my feet, then sat back down. 'Lemme ask you somethin' serious, Potter, if you don't mind?'

He looked at me for a moment, then nodded.

'I got two things on my mind. First, my shoes are ruined from the snow and my feet are freezing. Second, the Broom, he didn't commit suicide. And what I can't figure out is which one

139

is bothering me the most.'

Potter was still laughing when I walked out of Sparkle's a moment later.

SEVENTEEN

The highlight of my weekend was a pair of stories in Sunday's *New York Times*. I lived in a middle-income housing development on the east side of Manhattan called Rensselaer Village. My two-bedroom apartment, for which I paid $950 per month, was an inadvertent legacy from my parents who'd resided in the complex for the better part of four decades. In line with New York's complicated rent laws, after my father and mother split for a retirement community on Long Island, I simply inherited the 800 square feet, along with the extremely low rent. Nearly identical apartments in my building now went for three grand a month.

When my parents announced that they were off to the burbs, I was living in Sheepshead Bay, Brooklyn, and considering the possibility of relocating to Maplewood, New Jersey. Instead, I went to live in the heart of the great financial engine that drove Sheepshead Bay, Maplewood and everything else within a radius of fifty miles. I was pleased, to be sure, but still cautious. Before moving in, I had every stick of furniture removed, including the curtains on the

140

windows, the artwork on the walls and the cabinets in the bathroom. Then I had the rooms painted, the windows washed and the floors refinished with two coats of clear polyurethane specially formulated for basketball courts.

If I'd known a priest, I'd have had an exorcism performed as well.

The two stories appeared in the Metro section. The first, and by far the larger, revealed the latest developments as related by Deputy Chief Simon Kramer in the course of a press conference. Kramer had begun the conference by announcing that the gun found by Detectives Bentibi and Corbin near the body of DuWayne Spott had been positively linked to the murder of David Lodge by the Ballistics Unit. Moreover, two prints left by Spott's right index finger were found on the automatic's receiver. Then he went on to confirm a pair of facts already leaked to the media: Spott died of an accidental heroin overdose and he was alone when his body was discovered.

A twist of the knife, our names appearing in the paper. The integrity of the crime scene was now guaranteed by my and Adele's personal integrity. It was no longer possible to suggest the gun had been planted without suggesting that Adele and I had planted it.

But if the first story had the feel of a nail driven into a coffin, the second managed to at least crack the lid. It's author, Albert Gruber, had somehow wangled a phone interview with Dr Vencel Nagy.

David Lodge, Nagy told Gruber (as he'd told me) had not been fearful as his release date approached, nor had he spoken about the possibility of assassination. Instead, though Lodge still had no clear memory of his whereabouts when Spott was murdered, he was convinced of his innocence.

The Gruber story had almost certainly been planted. At the very least, the reporter had been fed enough information about Nagy to inspire a phone call. My first thought was of Adele. They were already talking about her in the One-Sixteen. If she was blamed for the leak, the buzz would grow louder. Of course, there was also the possibility that Adele was guilty as charged. I'd left the precinct right after finishing the paperwork, my goal to avoid another lecture. Of Adele's plans for the weekend, I knew nothing.

Mike Blair's voice sounded in my ear at that moment. *Nobody's talkin' about you, Harry. Everybody knows you're a cop's cop.*

At six o'clock, too restless to stay inside, I headed over to the Y. There were people in the pool, swimming laps, and I had to share a lane with a teenage kid who kept sprinting forward as if trying to reach the end of a punishment. He splashed water in my face every time I went by.

After a choppy half-hour, the kid took off, leaving me alone with thoughts I was unable to arrange in a sequence that reached any good end. Maybe the rumors would die away. Maybe Adele would back off. Maybe we'd resume our regular duties. But the bitterness would remain, of that I was certain. David Lodge would become the part of my career I avoided thinking about.

And I knew I could take his killers down. I had no doubt whatever. The bad guys' blitzkrieg strategy was driven by necessity. They needed DuWayne Spott in the ground and the Lodge murder closed before the various discrepancies Adele and I had uncovered were closely scrutinized. And the emergence of the wild card, Vencel Nagy, had compounded the pressure. If it wasn't done quickly, they must have known, it wouldn't be done at all.

I stayed at it for another forty-five minutes, but I couldn't settle into my stroke. For once, I was unable to separate the events from the emotions they aroused. And I didn't even know who I was angrier with, Adele or Sarney. Because they were both right. Letting David Lodge's killers off the hook went against every instinct. On one level, I was as outraged as Adele. But that didn't make Sarney wrong. There were definitely times when you had to watch your own ass, when you had to acknowledge your place in the greater scheme of things. Otherwise, you paid the price.

I carried that last thought through a shower and the short walk to Rensselaer Village, where I picked up the phone and called Adele. When she answered after several rings, I told her about Mike Blair's warning, repeating it almost word for word. Her reaction was predictable.

'What,' she asked, her tone amused, 'must I do to make amends?'

'How about telling me that you didn't plant

143

that story in the *Times*.'

The question was meant to surprise her and she didn't respond immediately. Determined not to speak first, I listened to her breathe into the phone as she weighed her answer. Of one thing I was fairly certain: she wouldn't lie to me.

'Everybody loves you, Corbin,' she finally said, 'but you have the instincts of a shark.'

'That's not an answer.'

'Look, what I do on my own time is my own business. I don't have to account to you. After all, you're a "cop's cop".'

'Forget it, Adele. I'm not buying into the guilt trip. I didn't start that rumor and I'm not spreading it around.'

'Thank you.'

'You're welcome. Now, let me back up a little. You do know the story I'm talking about, right? Gruber's story in the *New York Times*?'

'I read it.'

'Did you plant it?'

'I don't have to answer to you, Corbin. I've already said that.'

'I'm your partner, Adele. You don't hide something like this from your partner.'

But Adele wasn't buying into any guilt trips, either. 'I won't be in next week,' she announced. 'I've got eight vacation days coming and I've decided to take them right away.'

'And what if Sarney doesn't allow you to take them?'

'Corbin, sometimes you're very naive. Sarney can't wait to be rid of me.'

144

EIGHTEEN

I was sitting behind my desk at nine-thirty the following morning when Jack Petro entered the squad room carrying a box of donuts from Acme Cake, a commercial bakery located in the Eight-Three. Jack set the donuts on a filing cabinet, opened the box and shouted, 'Breakfast is served.' Within seconds, he'd drawn a crowd.

I paused long enough to fill a mug with coffee so thick it might have been used to caulk a boat, then joined Petro, Bill Sarney and two other detectives, Esteban Arroyo and Carl Stein. After a few minutes, Arroyo and Stein drifted off. Jack followed a moment later.

'You guys wanna try teamin' up?' Sarney asked, his tone sincere as far as I could tell. 'You and Jack?'

'And after Adele's vacation?'

Sarney looked at me for a moment, his gaze speculative, as though I'd caught him by surprise. Then he leaned forward and dropped his voice. 'Bentibi's on her way to a desk job at Borough Command. In fact, the only reason I let her take her vacation days was because I wanted to be rid of her as soon as possible.'

'Ya know somethin', lou,' I said. 'It's just not right, punishing someone for doing the job they were trained to do.'

Again, Sarney's look became quizzical. 'What is it with you and this broad?' he asked. 'Because if you're worried about leavin' her to swing in the breeze, you should remember that she put the noose around her own neck.' When I didn't answer, he smiled and reached out to tap my shoulder. 'Alright, she's your partner, Harry, and I'm sorry I asked you to keep an eye on her. But Adele is history, and so is David Lodge. The way I count 'em up, those are blessings.'

Jack Petro waved me over to his desk as the door closed behind our commander's retreating back. 'You see the paper today?'

'I haven't.'

Petro took a copy of the *Times* from his briefcase. The story he wanted me to read was in the Metro section and by the same Albert Gruber who'd interviewed Vencel Nagy. This time Gruber had gotten to Ivy Whittington and Kamia Thompson, Spott's aunt and cousin. Gruber used their words to create a portrait of a born loser, then asked the same question Adele and I had asked. How could a junkie-pimp like DuWayne Spott know when David Lodge was due for release or where he was going?

Gruber was an investigative reporter and could easily have found Ivy and Kamia on his own. But he could not have described the DuWayne Spott crime scene, as he proceeded to do, right down to the heater, the stolen electricity and the vomit, without help from someone who'd been there.

'Being as I'm an experienced detective,' Jack

146

said when I looked up, 'I can tell from your pained expression that you're an innocent man. Can I also assume that you've heard the talk? About your partner?'

'Yeah.'

'Then what ya gotta figure is the further away you get, the better it's gonna come out. This woman, she don't know when to lay off. I'm tellin' you this as a friend.'

He was right, of course. Adele had never understood the job, had never tried to understand. Somehow, she'd come to believe she could use the job to further her own ends. I was troubled by no such delusion, but Adele had one advantage, nevertheless. She could walk away and suffer only economic consequences. For me, the job was as close to family as I'd managed to get in my life. The thought of giving it up was not, at that moment, something I was willing to entertain.

Jack took off at that point, back to his own desk, leaving me to my thoughts. I sat there for a moment, annoyed with myself and with the situation, until my eye was attracted to a fax sitting on Adele's desk. The fax was from Deputy Warden Beauchamp, the great white hunter, and listed David Lodge's visitors during the four years of his incarceration at the Attica Correctional Facility. There were only two names on the list: Ellen Lodge and Linus Potter.

Prison, a felon with long experience once told me, is a lonely place. As time goes on, the letters and the visitors stop coming and you get the feeling nobody even remembers your name. But

147

Linus Potter had been faithful, showing up in early December and again in late May or early June every year. Ellen Lodge was another matter. She'd visited her husband exactly once, five months before his release.

We had a good time that week, Jack and I, putting away a homicide on Tuesday and an armed robber a few days later. Both were gifts. The murderer was kind enough to slay his victim, a rival for his wife's affections, in full view of three witnesses who knew him well. He surrendered peacefully when we knocked on his door an hour later. The stick-up man's mistake was his target. The discount linen store he robbed was protected by three video cameras, each of which got a clear shot of his face.

An hour after viewing the tapes, Jack and I put a name to that face: Paul Rakowitz, a junkie-thief who'd been tearing up the Bushwick and Ridgewood precincts for several years. A day later, we ran him down in a shooting gallery on Troutman Street. He, too, surrendered peacefully.

The murderer, Paolo Baez, admitted his guilt without hesitation, pride in his macho deed so evident his confession sounded more like bragging. 'Yo, and put this in,' he demanded, 'the *maricon* begged like a woman.'

Paul Rakowitz had a different take on his situation. He was a horse trader, give some to get some. 'I don't see any reason,' he told us, 'why we can't do business here.'

'Keep talkin', hump.' Jack could afford an

148

attitude because Rakowitz was dead meat. In addition to the video, three witnesses had picked him out of a line-up.

'OK, what I'm sayin' is this. I'm, like, connected.' After a brief pause, he added, 'In Bushwick.'

Jack patted his belly. 'Best get to the point,' he declared, 'because we're fast approachin' dinner and my tummy's startin' to rumble.'

'Like, I help out sometimes. You know, the cops.' Rakowitz was cadaver-thin, the pupils of his blue eyes mere pin heads. He had huge hands, though, which he opened and closed as though trying to raise a collapsed vein. 'You should talk to a Sergeant named Molinari. First thing out of his mouth, he'll tell ya Paulie's a straight-up guy.'

At that point, Jack left the room to call Molinari, leaving me to mind the prisoner. Rakowitz had committed a violent felony in our precinct and there was no disputing that he belonged to us. But an accommodation might still be made if he was crucial to some larger investigation in the adjoining Brooklyn precinct. At the very least, Molinari was entitled to a heads-up.

The interrogation room we occupied was small and nearly featureless. At one time, the walls might have been a pale beige – at least that would've been my guess – but neither walls nor ceiling had been painted in so long, they really didn't have a color. Above our heads, a single fluorescent tube buzzed in an industrial fixture. The top of the rusting fixture was piled with layers of gray dust that rose and fell like sand

149

dunes.

This was home to me, a setting so comfortable I looked forward to being here for hours at a time. As a matter of principle, I never gave up on an interrogation. As long as a suspect would talk to me, I'd keep going until I got a confession or my superior ordered me to relent.

Jack returned after only a few minutes. As he glanced in my direction, he tugged on his shirt cuff, telling me the story he would present was basically true.

'Bad news,' he declared as he sat down. 'Molinari says you're a piece-of-shit junkie and justice would best be served if I kicked your ass before turning the key in your cell door.'

Rakowitz was all indignation. 'I'm not dis-respectin' you,' he announced, 'but this I find hard to believe. I helped those guys out just last month with a burglary on Flushing Avenue. Speed King Auto Parts. Ask him.'

'Hey, listen to my words. Molinari's not gonna protect you. You understand?' When Rakowitz merely nodded, Jack shook his head. 'I want you to say it out loud. Say, "Sergeant Molinari will not protect me, so Detectives Petro and Corbin are the only friends I have in the world."'

Jack waited until Rakowitz copped to his utter dependence, then said, 'So tell me what you wanna trade, Paulie. What you got to give and what you hope to get.'

'OK,' Rakowitz said, leaning out over the table again, his voice dropping in pitch and volume. 'You ever heard of Paco Luna? They call him Demente.'

150

Paco 'Demente' Luna was Bushwick's resident drug lord, a man with a reputation so vicious he'd become well-known to law enforcement in the surrounding communities. That a miserable street junkie like Paulie Rakowitz could not deliver Paco Luna was a simple given.

'Talk's cheap,' Jack replied. 'You need to be a bit more concrete here.'

'Well, did ya ever wonder how come he's got no competition? Luna's Puerto Rican, but there's lots of Mexicans and Dominicans livin' in Bushwick. Usually, you go into a mixed neighborhood, you get to choose your product.'

'And that's not the way it is?'

'Fuck no. You don't deal with Luna's people, you don't get high in Bushwick. Now I'm not sayin' nobody else tried to set up. I'm sayin' they don't last long.'

'Paulie,' Jack said, 'you gotta look at the facts here. We got you for a violent felony. You can't buy your way out by givin' up some street dealer.'

'That ain't the point. It ain't about Luna.'

'Then what's it about?'

'It's about how he's, like...' When Rakowitz ran his hand across his forehead, it came away slick with sweat. 'Luna's protected, OK? He's got cops watchin' his back.' Another pause while his eyes scanned the tiny room as though searching for hidden witnesses. 'Hey, think about it. Luna's been runnin' the show in Bushwick for the last fifteen years. Nobody lasts that long unless they got connections. I mean, it's like obvious, right?'

151

NINETEEN

Rakowitz kept us going for another fifteen minutes, although it was clear from the beginning – when Jack demanded that he name these cops, when he failed to do so – that we were being treated to a street rumor so common it had risen to the level of myth. The cops, so the story went, were always bent, the man at the top always protected. I'd heard the same tale from Dominicans in Washington Heights and Rastafarians on Eastern Parkway, usually as I was closing a pair of handcuffs around their wrists. Why, they wanted to know, did we snatch the little guys who were only dealing to stay high when the big dogs went their way unmolested?

As I remember it, my usual response was a slap on the head and a demand that the offender 'Shut the fuck up.'

Still, Rakowitz was impressive. He told his tale forcefully, saving the best for last. 'OK, you know that Luna has a house on Decatur Street near Central Avenue, right?'

In fact, we didn't. Decatur and Central intersected in Bushwick, not our jurisdiction.

'Yeah, fine,' Jack said. 'So what?'

'So, I'm acquainted with a dude who was on a roof gettin' off when he seen cops go into that

152

building. They marched in like they owned the fuckin' place.' Rakowitz gave it a couple of beats before delivering the punch line. 'And this guy, he says he seen these cops before.'

'Your acquaintance, he got a name?'

'Bucky.'

'Bucky?'

'Yeah, on account of his teeth.'

'So, where can we find Bucky?'

'I don't know. I ain't seen him in a while. But everybody knows him. He grew up in the neighborhood.'

'Where?'

'I ain't sure.'

'How 'bout his real name? You know that?'

When Rakowitz leaned forward, beads of sweat dripped from his hair to splatter on the table top. 'I don't,' he admitted, 'but I could find him.'

At that point, Jack approached the prisoner, drew him to his feet and quick-marched him into a cage. 'The only thing you need to find,' he explained as he turned the key in the door, 'is a boyfriend. Before you become public property.'

By the time I walked into Sparkle's at nine-thirty, the joint was jumping. I took a moment to absorb the noise and the commingled odors of beer, tobacco and bodies huddled together after a long day's work, then crossed to the bar where Mike had a Dewar's waiting. Home sweet home.

I lifted my glass to Sparkle, as always. For some reason, she was looking especially vivid tonight. Her red, Cupid's-bow mouth was pursed

153

invitingly and her blue eyes were naughty and knowing.

'You do something to Sparkle?' I asked Mike, who was filling a pitcher with Guinness.

'I had her cleaned yesterday.'

'You don't clean her yourself?'

'Harry, you gotta be kiddin'. The woman I use, her day job's at the Metropolitan Opera!'

I was still mulling this over when Nydia Santiago called to me. She'd taken over the table usually reserved for Linus Potter, who was standing at the other end of the bar. 'Harry, c'mere a minute.'

Nydia was sitting with her two main girlfriends, Rose Fulger and Mary Contreras (known universally as Mary Contrary), and an Eight-Three detective named Chris Tucker.

'What's up?' I asked as I sat down beside Nydia.

'What's up with your partner?' she countered.

'What's wrong with her?'

'Why don't you tell me?'

'She's a cop hater,' Chris Tucker jumped in, his tone distinctly belligerent.

'Is that what she's accused of, Chris? Hating cops?'

'In the Eight-Three, they're sayin' she's an IAB rat. They're sayin' she was recruited while she was still in the Academy. You know that's what the headhunters do. They find the freaks, the ones that shoulda been social workers, and turn 'em into snitches.'

I'd stayed away from Sparkle's all week, avoiding a choice I knew I'd eventually have to

154

make. Nydia had just invited me to sever all connection with Adele, to close her case and get on with my career. It was Nydia's way of covering my back and I was certain she expected me to accept the offer.

Some ultimately rational part of me insisted that I seize the opportunity. Adele was going down. I couldn't save her, but I could save myself. And I wouldn't have to join the chorus of her accusers. If I simply announced that Adele and I hadn't spoken during the last week, it would be enough.

As always on crowded Friday nights, despite an ordinance that prohibits the use of tobacco in bars, the atmosphere at Sparkle's was clouded by cigarette smoke. I watched the smoke drift across the intense beam of light trained on Sparkle's rhinestone dress, watched it rise and fall in slow waves, now white, now gray, now black. I was hoping that some answer would come floating out of that mist, a once-and-for-all decision that I could live with. Instead, I became more and more angry, with Sarney, with Adele, with the job, and with half-drunk Chris Tucker who just happened to be close enough to bear the consequences.

'Chris,' I finally declared, 'I don't care what you say about my partner as long as you don't say it to my face. Ever again. You understand where I'm goin' with this, right?'

My amiable reputation was so at odds with the look on my face, it took my companions a moment to grasp the essentials. Nydia was the first to react. She put her hand on my arm, but

155

I shook it off. Chris Tucker's normally pale cheeks were flaming; his blue eyes seemed about to explode. Street cops are taught to confront any challenge to their authority. You back off once, so the lesson goes, you'll be retreating until the day you put in your papers.

'That was over the top, Harry,' Nydia said. 'That was uncalled for.'

I stood up, my eyes pinned on Tucker's. When he remained in his chair, I smiled before repeating my position. 'That goes for you, too, Nydia. I don't care what bullshit rumors you tell each other, just keep them away from me.'

Though my act was convincing – probably because I meant what I said – I lost my courage at that point. I should have gone on to say that my partner was an honorable cop who'd been around long enough to separate the good guys from the bad guys. If she was pointing fingers, she was pointing them in the right direction. Instead, I carried my empty glass over to Jack Petro, who was standing at the bar.

'What's up with Chris?' Petro asked. 'He's red as a beet.'

'Chris said something about Adele that I didn't want to hear. I had to ask him not to repeat those words in my presence.'

Like Nydia, Jack was solicitous. 'Harry, c'mon,' he said, 'don't get worked up. Whatever Adele's doing, she's doing on her own. Nobody's blaming you.'

Another should-have moment. I should have told my old friend that DuWayne Spott didn't kill David Lodge and that I was certain I could nail Lodge's true killers, but I settled for a shrug and a smile. 'Tucker's saying Adele's an IAB snitch. You believe that?'

'Harry, listen to me. It's not like Bentibi's gonna be shot at sunrise. She's just gettin' transferred.'

I turned away at that point, to ask Mike Blair for a refill. The larger truth, that Adele was still out there, digging her own grave, would only render her more culpable.

A few minutes later, too restless for the small talk around me, I carried my drink over to Linus Potter, edging in between his massive body and the wall. Potter was staring down into a mug of dark beer.

'What's new, Linus?' I asked.

'I'm havin' an anxiety attack,' he announced.

'About what?'

'You ever been smacked by pigeon shit? While you were just walkin' down the street?'

'Yeah, I have.'

'Not me. I never got smacked and I been around pigeons all my life.'

'That makes you overdue.'

'Which is exactly what concerns me. Forty-four years without gettin' smacked? My time is comin' soon. It could even be a multiple occurrence.'

Potter reached into the pocket of his overcoat and drew out a black Kangol cap which he placed on his tiny head. Amazingly, the cap was too small.

'Forewarned is forearmed, right? I went and

157

got me a little protection. Whatta ya think?'

'It's you, Linus. The real you, the one who never stopped visiting David Lodge.'

Potter's lips came apart in what I took for a smile. His eyes, though, didn't waver by so much as a millimeter. What he was about to tell me had been carefully thought out.

'Davy and me were partners for about six months, right before I got promoted. We did OK together.'

'Was he drinking then?'

'Yeah.'

'How'd you handle it?'

'I told him if he showed up drunk or drank on the job, I'd shove his head so far up his bony ass, he'd be lookin' out between his teeth.'

My turn to smile as I imagined David Lodge, knucklehead extraordinaire, cowed by Linus Potter. Potter's back was broad enough to support a grand piano.

'You told me you investigated the Clarence Spott murder. That must have been tough, being as Lodge was once your partner.'

'I exaggerated.'

'Exaggerated what?'

'It's four o'clock in the morning when I get a call from the lieutenant. He tells me there's been a homicide inside the Eight-Three, a citizen. An hour later, when I arrive at the house, IAB is already working the case. So what I do, more or less, is observe the proceedings. I wasn't even called to testify before the grand jury.'

Potter stopped long enough to drain his mug, then signal Mike for another. 'But what I told

158

you was true. Every piece of evidence pointed at Davy. And the consensus, at the time, was that his blackout was so much bullshit.'

'At the time?'

'Davy was a good cop who destroyed himself with booze. Clarence Spott was a piece of shit who deserved worse than he got.' Potter stuck out his hand to intercept a frosted mug sliding along the length of the bar. As he grabbed the mug, beer spilled over the rim and onto his hand. He licked the beer off his fingers, then resumed. 'I felt sorry for Lodge, so I went up to see him a couple of times a year. He really didn't remember what happened. That much was obvious. But he also thought he was innocent, at least at the end, which wasn't obvious. Something happened to him, though, after the last time I visited, something he remembered that made him sure.'

'How do you know that?'

'He wrote me a letter.' Potter withdrew a folded piece of paper from his jacket pocket. 'I been carryin' it around all week, figurin' you'd show up sooner or later.'

That little voice, the rational one, spoke again, demanding that I leave well enough alone. *Next thing*, it insisted, *you'll be calling Adele.*

I took the letter anyway, and read it through twice. It contained nothing I didn't already know. A memory had surfaced, a fragment, and Lodge had become sure of his innocence. The nature of that memory was not described, nor was Pete Jarazelsky's name mentioned.

'Old news,' I said as I returned the letter.

Potter refolded the page and stuck it back in

159

his pocket. 'Letters get screened goin' in and out of prison. Phone calls get monitored. Even face-to-face visits, the guards can listen in. So what I figure is that Davy was playin' his cards close to the vest. One thing I can say for sure: after seven years in the joint, he'd become a patient man. Took care of his body, too. Last time I was up to see him, he told me he was benchin' three hundred pounds.'

TWENTY

I got up the next morning and fixed myself a breakfast of fried eggs and toast which I washed down with two mugs of coffee. Then I spent the next three hours cleaning my apartment. A hated job, to be sure, but one at which I've become more efficient over the years. As I worked, I considered a pair of options: hiring a housekeeper or living in filth. But the reality was that I couldn't afford professional help, not while my credit card remained in deficit. And I couldn't live with the dirt, either. Not only did I fear the chaos, but nothing diminishes the female libido like food-stained upholstery, underwear on the floor and greasy pillowcases.

I put the vacuum cleaner away around noon and went to my computer. This was another chore I didn't look forward to. I hadn't checked my email for a week and I knew my inbox would be choked with spam. I found thirty-five pieces of mail awaiting me. The few from individuals whose names I recognized were opened first. They'd been sent by cop friends who'd moved on to greener pastures and I archived them, intending to reply at some later date. Then I went to work on the garbage.

Instant credit. Normalize blood pressure. Obtain a university diploma. Trace anybody anywhere. Enlarge your penis. Enlarge your breasts. The kicker was the domain address of a gay porn site: weaponsofassdestruction.com.

For the most part, I was able to delete the junk without opening it, but there were a number sent by individuals whose names I didn't recognize. It was possible (just barely) that I'd discover somebody trying to reach me on legitimate business among these.

Though each bore the name of a different sender, the first three were for a brand of septic tank cleaner. The fourth was from a gentleman who identified himself as B-Arnold. Initially, I judged the name to be a clumsy ploy designed to trick me into opening the message, but then my gaze drifted to the subject line: It Ain't Over Till It's Over.

For the next thirty seconds, I watched a white envelope turn round and round, like a dog chasing its tail. My primitive dial-up system was loading a photo. I can't say I knew what was coming, but I was impatient enough to wish I'd coughed up the extra twenty bucks a month and switched to broadband. Then an image appeared on the monitor, a head-shot of Dante Russo in uniform, facing front. The full-color photo had been shot against a white background, virtually guaranteeing that it had come from Russo's personnel file.

A few years before, on impulse, I'd purchased a digital camera, intending to pursue photography as a serious amateur. It hadn't taken all that long, a couple of months at most, before I admitted that I was virtually without talent. By then, however, I'd grown fascinated with the processing of images and was spending most of my time at the computer, working in Photoshop.

I had two problems with Russo's photograph, which showed him in full uniform, including a billed cap. First, I feared that citizens, shown the photo, would be drawn to the uniform and not the man. Second, as a PBA Trustee, Russo had no assigned policing duties and never wore a uniform. His job was to roam from precinct to precinct within Brooklyn North's territory, conferring with PBA delegates, troubleshooting problems the delegates were unable to handle.

What I might have done, if I was a true artist, was remove the cap and create a hairline from scratch. But that task was beyond my abilities. The best I could do was search through my archived photos until I found an individual with a hairline similar to Russo's, cut that hairline out, then paste it over Russo's cap before smoothing the rough edges. Though far from perfect, the final version I printed was serviceable, a 4x6 likeness that caught Russo with his chin up, his lips compressed, his dark eyes suspicious and superior at the same time.

I sat back in the chair and allowed my thoughts to drift. Not surprisingly, they quickly settled on Adele. I was sure Russo's photograph hadn't come from her. Adele's inability to manipulate was her biggest flaw. If she wanted me to look at Russo's picture, she'd have knocked on my door and shoved it in my face.

Last night, in Sparkle's, I'd briefly considered phoning Adele. Now I was thinking a little harder, thinking that maybe I should give her a warning, let her know the attack was intensifying. The charge made by Chris Tucker was not without foundation. Internal Affairs did, in fact, recruit cops while they were still at the Academy. These recruits were called field associates and their job, simply put, was to spy on their peers.

I didn't believe that Adele was a field associate. She was too independent, too unpredictable, a born rule-breaker who could never be trusted. But the truth didn't matter here. If Adele's peers decided she was an IAB rat, they'd be as likely to leave her hanging as come to her defense when she needed back-up. Especially those who had something to hide.

After a brief journey into the kitchen, where I opened and closed the refrigerator door for no good reason, I decided that I couldn't decide. The only thing Adele would want to hear from me, assuming she wanted to hear anything at all, was that I was ready to join her crusade. And I wasn't.

* * *

Twenty minutes later, I was sitting in the office of my high school mentor, Conrad Stehle, at the Y on Twenty-Third Street. It was Saturday afternoon, the pool full and Conrad busy. Nevertheless, when I knocked on his door and told him, 'I'm fucked, Conrad,' he waved me to a chair, then listened carefully while I reviewed the events following our last meeting. When I got to the punch line, the part about Adele's open rebellion, he nodded and smiled.

'For me,' I concluded, 'the whole business is about bad choices. It's like the deal they used to give murderers in Utah: the gas chamber, the rope, or a firing squad.'

Conrad took his little cigar from his pocket and tapped it on the cover of *Swimmer's World* magazine. His eyes closed for a moment, then opened again as he smiled. 'This business about losing no matter what you do, I have a hard time with it.'

'I'm sorry to hear that, Conrad. But if there's a clear win here, it's somehow eluded me.'

'What about David Lodge's killers? Putting them in prison, which we both know is where they belong.'

'The job's going to punish Adele, no matter how this turns out. If I do anything to help her, I'll be punished, too.'

'That doesn't answer the question.'

'Conrad, removing bad people from the general populace is an activity that satisfies my deepest needs. That's why I do it. But there's a price to pay here and...' I hesitated for a moment, sorting through the various conflicts, reducing

164

them in scope until I finally got my thoughts around an idea that didn't squirm out of reach. 'I don't want to be an asshole, a jerk,' I explained. 'Adele, she's got delusions of grandeur. Her goal is to right every wrong. Me, I try not to confuse myself with cartoon superheroes. That's because I know that when you leap off a roof, you don't fly up into the clouds, you go splat on the concrete. Besides, I didn't bury evidence, or look past witnesses, or try to dump the case in somebody else's lap. I conducted an honorable investigation, committing every scrap of information to paper, until the day I was relieved. What happens next is not my business.'

Conrad looked at me for a moment, his eyes bright, his smile amused, then got up and walked over to where a small coffee maker rested on a filing cabinet. He slid a filter into the basket, added coffee, then filled the tank with water. A moment later, the coffee maker emitted a wet belch, shortly followed by a hiss, then the patter of coffee dropping into a carafe.

I sat through the process, giving Conrad plenty of time to challenge my argument. I knew we'd eventually come back to the business at hand, as I knew the timing was strictly at Conrad's discretion. Sure enough, after serving the coffee and taking a quick sniff at the cigar in his pocket, he finally spoke.

'Now tell me what calamity will befall Harry Corbin if he just walks away from this case. If he does nothing at all.'

'You mean, if I desert my partner on the field of battle?' I returned his smile. 'That's not too good for the old self-image.'

'Could you live with it?'

'You not gettin' this, Conrad? The prize behind door number two is the same as the prize behind door number one. Yeah, I could walk away from Adele, and I wouldn't fall apart, either. But I'd have to grow a beard.'

'A beard? Why a beard?'

'Because that way I won't recognize myself when I look in the mirror.'

'I understand,' Conrad conceded after a moment, 'how that might not work out.' He filled the two mugs with coffee, then carried them over to his desk. Taken black, Conrad's coffee was as bitter as boiled espresso.

'The half-and-half?' I pointed to an open container sitting next to the little computer on his desk. 'You wouldn't remember when you bought it, would you?'

'Yesterday.'

I watched him lace his own coffee with two packets of sugar and a large dollop of half-and-half. When the half-and-half didn't curdle, I took the plunge, filling my own mug to the brim. 'There's something else,' I said, 'another factor working against Adele. You spoke about punishing Lodge's killers, about hauling the bad guys up to the bar of justice. Well, there's no guarantee that Adele and I can close this case, not working on our own. Obvious moves, like obtaining phone records and financial documents, will be closed to us, along with access to ballistics and the crime lab. And Pete Jarazelsky, that ultimate soft target? If the job doesn't back

166

us, we have no way to put pressure on him, even if he'd agree to an interview.'

'So, there's the possibility of risking everything for nothing?'

'I couldn't have said it better myself. All the pain, none of the pleasure. The ultimate lose-lose situation.' I leaned forward and cocked my head to the left. 'In my personal experience, people who launch themselves into lose-lose situations fall into three categories. They're either born losers, or psychotics, or both.'

'Tell me,' he demanded without turning around. 'Into which category does Adele Bentibi fall? Is she the loser? Or is she the psychotic? Or is she the psychotic loser?'

TWENTY-ONE

Like any other athlete, even a pseudo-athlete, I sometimes pause to check myself out in the mirror. I'm not obsessed, not like body builders where narcissism is the whole point. Just occasionally, late at night coming from the pool, I pause before a full-length mirror in the locker room to make a quick evaluation. And why not? No one can say I haven't worked for my body, that I haven't put in the hours.

A single glance is usually enough to assure me that I'm holding it together as I enter my forty-first year on the planet. Only occasionally am I dissatisfied; only occasionally do I suspect that my body has tipped over the edge, that the inevitable diminishing has begun.

My features undergo a similar shift at such times, rugged somehow becoming goofy. I have the good hair, as I've already said, but my eyes, always narrow, have been narrowed further by fanning crows' feet and a slight puffiness that no amount of sleep can erase. They are at different heights, as well, with the right a bit lower than the left, producing a cock-eyed look made worse by a mouth with a pronounced bias to the right and a noticeably off-center chin.

Not even in my most charitable moments would I call the face in the mirror handsome. My features are too unbalanced for that. But rugged is a tradable commodity for a middle-aged bachelor in New York, whereas goofy doesn't work at all. I knew because that crooked smile I flashed across a crowded room sometimes produced a quick frown, shortly followed by an exaggerated rolling of the eyes. *God, why do I keep attracting the losers?*

I relate to my apartment – which I finally re-entered some two hours later – much as I do to my body. Mostly, I feel comfortable when I lock the door behind me. I feel at home. But there are definitely times when the place seems more like a bad joke. From the roughly finished dining table and the captain's chairs, to the wall-to-wall Berber carpeting, to the green sectional couch and the bookcases framing the television, to the posters on the walls. Artificial is the first word that comes to mind, followed shortly by phony, then pathetic.

When I flicked on the lights that afternoon, I felt as if I'd been the unwitting victim of an apprentice decorator at a failing discount department store. Case in point, the posters on the living room walls were of extremely obscure, extremely bad movies, the kind that played rural Mississippi drive-ins in the 1950s. *Captive Wild Woman* (starring Acquanetta as the Gorilla Girl); *Juke Joint* (The Joint is Jumpin! The Jive is Jivin! The Jam is Jammin!); *Girl With An Itch* (Have Negligee, Will Travel!). I'd thought them clever enough when I'd accumulated them over a period of nine months, but now they seemed as superficial as the movies they were created to publicize.

Compounding the felony, I'd paid way too much for the posters, as a recent visit to a series of websites offering the same ones attested. But then I'd sunk more than I could afford into my furniture as well. My bedroom set had come from Stickley, the couch and bookcases from Ethan Allen, the oak dining table from a cabinet maker in Williamsburg who saw customers by appointment only. Which is not to suggest that my furnishings were top of the line by New York standards. Not even close. But they were definitely beyond the legitimate aspirations of a cop living on a single paycheck. Most cops I knew shopped at department stores on sale days.

I hung my coat in the closet, then went from room to room, turning on lights. When I got to my bedroom, I spent a few moments staring at a pair of low bookcases against the far wall. The

169

bookcases were made of walnut and too expensive, but that wasn't what caught my attention. There were more than a hundred books on the shelves, mixed fiction and non-fiction, all hard covers. With very few exceptions, these books were about New York.

Why did I have them? To show them off? To show myself off? Most of the women I dated were far better educated than I was and had far more prestigious jobs. Slipping an obscure fact into the conversation, or so I believed, made me appear sophisticated enough to be safe. Maybe I was a cop with a high school diploma, but I most likely wouldn't bite.

I continued to move through the apartment. Wherever I looked, I found not just the pitiful efforts of a dull mind, but evidence of pure desperation. Everything would *be* alright as long as I kept pretending that everything *was* alright. My apartment would be the home I'd never had. The job would be the family I'd never known. Even the women in my life had a place in the facade, a burden to endure. Their job was to stick around just long enough to convince me that I had the capacity to love. If only I found the right lover.

When the apartment was fully lit, I retreated to my tiny kitchen, to the wall phone next to the refrigerator. I stared at the phone for a moment, Adele's number a series of mad little beeps that repeated themselves as if somebody had pressed my REDIAL button. Then I dialed her number and put the phone to my ear. My reward was Adele's answering machine, where I left a

170

simple request that she call me back.

That done, that line crossed, I made a second call, to a Chinese restaurant on First Avenue called Mee. My dinner ordered, I began to set the table. I felt pretty good about things, comforted as I was by a battlefield maxim declaring that any decision, even a bad decision, is better than no decision. Then my phone began to ring and I walked back into the kitchen, expecting to hear Adele's voice.

'Hey, Harry, how's it going?' Bill Sarney asked.

'It's goin' alright, Bill. How's by you?'

'Me, I got a headache.'

'And its name is Adele Bentibi.'

'How'd you guess?'

Sarney was using that hearty, cheerleader voice he generally deployed before asking a favor. It was a voice I'd responded to in the past, as I'd responded to the occasional dinner we shared, or being invited to his home. We were friends and allies, Bill Sarney and Harry Corbin, and I had no reason to doubt his sincerity at that moment. But sincerity was no longer a relevant concept, for either one of us. Sarney had long ago decided that his interests and the interests of the job would never be at odds. That was his line, his personal line, and I'd stepped across it when I phoned Adele. I had no choice now, except to play him. Nailing Lodge's killers would be hard enough without telegraphing my intentions.

'So what's that bad girl done now?' I asked.

'We know she's the one leaking to the *Times*.'

171

'Know?'

'Yeah, we're sure.'

It was my turn to chuckle manfully. 'I could ask if you maybe tapped her phones, Bill, or somehow got your hands on her phone records, but I think I'm just gonna leave that dog lie. In the meantime, I haven't spoken to Adele in a week.'

That was at least technically true. Though I'd called her only a few minutes before, we hadn't actually conversed.

'Harry, look, we think it would be a good idea if you contacted her.' Sarney's tone dropped a half-octave as he shifted to that gossipy tone he used when he was passing on insider secrets. 'Let me level with you here. The bosses think those stories in the *Times* are not gonna be a problem. They're worried about what your partner—'

'Former partner,' I corrected. 'With the emphasis on the former.'

'Yeah, your former partner. The bosses wanna know what she's gonna do next. Like, specifically, if she's gonna go public. You can't blame them, Harry. They're scared because she doesn't give a shit about her badge or her reputation. They got nothin' to hold over her head.'

TWENTY-TWO

Initially, I refused Bill Sarney outright. If I remember correctly, I was pretty indignant. He was talking about my partner, after all. Turning my back on her was one thing. Loyalty didn't require me to go down with the ship, not when the captain had drilled a hole in the hull. But cops didn't spy on their partners, not in the cop world I inhabited, not in any cop world I could imagine. If word got out, I explained to my boss, I'd be branded a fink. And I'd deserve it, too.

But in the end, I allowed myself to be persuaded. Sarney's argument was succinct. He told me that what had happened to me was nothing more than bad luck. Most cops, even those who rise to the top, never have to make the kind of choice that was being shoved down my throat. Nevertheless, I was forced to decide, as he'd been forced to present the options. If I didn't go along, not only would I not be promoted, my and Adele's fate would be one and the same.

'So what you're saying,' I finally asked, 'is that I'll be branded a snitch unless I actually become a snitch?'

'Yeah, that's pretty much the way of it. The bosses have a job that needs doing and nobody except you to do it.'

After finishing dinner, I took out a yellow pad and settled down on the living-room couch. My goal was simply to list the various assumptions Adele and I had made in the course of the Lodge investigation, to subject each to a second evaluation. But I was still unable to concentrate and I found myself parked in front of the television thirty minutes later, watching the Knicks stumble through a dreary first half.

Down by eleven, the Knicks were heading into the locker room when my phone began to ring. I muted the TV and picked up the receiver, expecting to hear Adele's voice. I got her husband, Mel, instead.

Mel Bentibi was the most even-tempered man I'd ever known. He simply could not be drawn to any extreme emotion, a trait that drove Adele crazy. 'He plays the Zen monk,' she once told me, to cover up the fact that he has the inner life of an eggplant.

'Say, Harry, I've got a serious problem.' Mel cleared his throat. 'It's Adele. She's been injured.'

'Yeah, how so?' I smiled at that moment – a crooked smile, to be sure – while my heart tightened into a fist.

'She was mugged.'

'Where?'

'Coming into the apartment in Bayside.' Another hesitation. 'The thing about it is that I'm in Dallas. You know, on business. I'm not gonna be able to get away before Tuesday morning.'

'Can I assume that means your wife isn't

174

critical or dead?'

'Please, Harry, don't talk like that. Adele's in North Shore Hospital, in Manhasset. Her doctors tell me she'll be fine. They just want to hold her overnight for observation.'

'Does she have her cell phone with her?'

'No, they took it, along with her gun.'

'They?'

'Harry, I don't know the details. The doctors told me that she's under sedation.'

I'd double-dated with Adele and her husband several times in the past. Though I'd found Mel to be terminally bland, I'd generally been able to deal with him. But at that moment, I lacked the patience to beg the jerk for a set of facts as likely as not to be wrong, and I simply hung up.

It was eight-fifteen and North Shore Hospital was forty-five minutes away, even assuming light traffic on the dreaded Long Island Expressway. I threw on my coat and went out to my car, which was parked in front of the building. Once again, the Official Police parking permit on the dash had worked its magic and there was no ticket beneath the wiper blade. That was predictable, as was the Nissan's failure to start. It was bitter cold and the car had been sitting for two days.

I opened the trunk, removed a set of jumper cables, then attached one end of the cables to my battery. When an empty cab drove by a few minutes later, I raised both hands. In the left, I held the unattached end of the jumpers, in the right, a five-dollar bill. Within two minutes, the Nissan was up and running.

175

* * *

As I crested the Williamsburg Bridge, I got on my cell phone, punching the O, then waiting for an operator to respond. A few minutes later, I was speaking to the desk lieutenant at the 111th Precinct in Bayside, Queens. Her name was Fujimori and she clucked sympathetically when I identified myself as Adele's partner.

'They hit her in the face,' she told me, 'with some kind of club, maybe a baseball bat.'

'Once?'

'Apparently. Are you familiar with the lay-out?'

'I've been there.'

'Alright, Bentibi was attacked after parking her car in the lot behind her apartment building. She got lucky when a porter came through the back door as the attack started and her assailant ran away with her handbag. Also, Bentibi has a defensive wound on her forearm, a large contusion. We're assuming she managed to absorb some of the force of the blow.'

I took a second to visualize the scene. The Bentibis owned a condo in a hi-rise building a few hundred yards from Little Neck Bay. The surrounding blocks were all residential, mostly single-family homes, and very quiet. Beyond that, Bayside had been an upper-middle-class enclave for a century, with the nearest subway five miles distant – not the happy hunting ground for street muggers who depend on mass transit for a quick getaway.

'You get a lot of muggings in that part of town, lou?' I finally asked.

176

'I can't remember the last one.'

'How'd they escape?'

'They had a car.'

'You get a make, a plate number?'

'Negative. Bentibi was too disoriented and the porter ran over to help her. He only glimpsed the vehicle.'

'What about an ID? Either of them get a look?'

'Your partner doesn't remember what happened, but according to the porter, the bad guy had his face covered with a stocking mask. The most the porter's willing to say is that Bentibi's attacker was white.'

We went back and forth for a few minutes, until I was about to thank her and hang up. Then she added, 'They didn't get Bentibi's badge. She had it in her pocket. They got her weapon, but not her badge.'

I think the statement was meant to console. If so, the kind lieutenant had wasted her breath. Though the emotions running through my little brain were decidedly mixed, sorrow was decidedly absent.

The middle of Adele's face was swathed in bandages, her mouth below the bandages and her eyes above, swollen and discolored. But she was awake and oriented. When I came through the door, her head swiveled a few inches and the sliver of eye visible between her purple lids came to rest on my face. My greatest concern, on the way over, was that I would find her afraid. But Adele's gaze was steady and I had the distinct feeling that we were both explorers mapping an uncertain terrain.

A few moments before, I'd cornered a resident at the nurses' station. Neurology, she'd told me without looking up, had run a battery of tests and Adele's brain was not damaged, at least not as far as they could tell. On the other hand, the injuries to bone and soft tissue were extensive. Adele's nose had been virtually smashed and she would probably need further surgery, even though a plastic surgeon had 'popped it into place.'

I sat on the edge of an empty bed a few feet from Adele's. 'Next time you go for a nose job,' I told her, 'it'd probably be good if you picked a better surgeon. You're gonna have to have that one done over.'

Although Adele's lips were as thick as hot dogs, they parted in a semblance of a smile. Encouraged, I stumbled on.

'I know you're already thinking that I came out here to offer my assistance because I pity you, or because I'm suffering from some kind of Sir Galahad complex. But when you get home, you're gonna discover a phone message left by Harry Corbin before he found out what happened.' Leaning forward, I tapped Adele's knee, an unheard-of liberty. 'The fact is that I was already on a righteous path when Mel called from Dallas. You have no claim to the moral high-ground just because you got your ass kicked.'

Adele continued to stare into my eyes, until I straightened up and asked, 'Are you stoned?'

That brought a true smile and the merest of

178

nods. They'd given her some sort of pain killer, undoubtedly an opiate, which was doing its work quite nicely. Never-Never Land, here we come.

But Adele surprised me. In a series of excruciatingly slow movements, she worked her way to the edge of the bed and opened the drawer of a little nightstand, extracting a key ring which she handed over. As she would have needed her keys to get through the back door of her building and into her apartment, she'd probably been holding them when she was attacked.

I slid the keys into my pocket, then looked into Adele's eyes. Her lids were no more than a few millimeters apart, but her eyes glowed nonetheless, whether from the dope or the pleasure of seeing me, I couldn't know. After a moment, her lips began to move, her mouth to open as she attempted to speak.

She took a long time about it, working her swollen tongue behind her teeth as she struggled with the mechanics. When her words finally broke free, they were thick and rounded, the hard consonants slurred. Nevertheless, I understood her well enough.

'Why did you come back?'

'Why do you need to know?'

Always respond to a question with a question, a rule of thumb familiar to police interrogators and mental therapists alike. But it wasn't going to work here. Adele continued to stare at me, a bug-eyed lizard fixed on a crawling insect. I could answer, or I could be eaten. It was strictly up to me.

179

'You're my partner,' I finally said, 'and I have to defend you to the death or suffer eternal damnation. Call it cop culture, the mythology of the job, whatever. You don't leave your partner's back undefended, no exceptions.' I shifted my weight on the bed, but maintained eye contact until I was sure Adele wasn't going to be the first to speak. 'Only there's much more to it, which you already know.'

'Like what?'

'Like bodies in winter, like David Lodge's body on a lawn in the middle of January. That brown grass, it looks nice and soft, but when you kneel down, it's all frozen little knobs that get up between the bones of your knees. And then there's the blood. Blood that fresh isn't supposed to be hard, just like the sun isn't supposed to be cold. You remember the sun that day, Adele, how bright it was, how cold it was? I felt like I was sucking that icy wind down into my bones.'

That was it for me, as far as I wanted to go, and I lapsed into silence. A few minutes later, Adele pushed a red button attached to the sheet, releasing a jolt of whatever pain killer she was taking, then drifted off to sleep. I remained where I was for a short time longer, listening to the pulse of her IV pump as it forced a mix of antibiotics and saline into her veins. I knew there was work to be done, that the night would be long, that the faster I moved the better off I'd be. But I kept imagining the pain, not only from the blunt object that had crashed into Adele's face, but from the surgeries to come. I'd seen injuries like hers many times and I knew she'd never look the

180

same. Without doubt, she knew it as well.

I finally took my weapon from its holster, slid it into the pocket of my coat and left. A nurse pushing a medication cart looked up as I came down the hallway, a pretty woman in a starched uniform. I returned her smile without hesitation. The way I saw it, I had only one problem. When my Nissan fired right up a few minutes later, I had none.

I found three sets of files and a notebook, all neatly arranged on Adele's dining-room table. Though I might have hung around long enough to study them at my leisure, I packed them into a briefcase and went out through the rear of the building, avoiding the doorman. It was now approaching eleven o'clock and I wanted to settle down with a pot of coffee in my own apartment as soon as possible. Still, I made a stop on the way, driving to Woodward Avenue where it passes behind Linden Hill Cemetery, to the edge of the ridge that gives Ridgewood its name. The cemetery was by far the largest green space in the neighborhood.

I pulled the car to a stop along the curb, shut off the headlights and threw the transmission into PARK. Initially, I made no effort to organize my thoughts, content to stare out over a pair of auto Graveyards at a sliver of the Manhattan skyline nine miles away. The Chrysler Building was clearly visible, and the Met Life Building, somehow squat for all its two and a half million square feet. There were a dozen others, as well, that I didn't recognize, a four- or five-block swathe advancing from west to east.

Little by little, my thoughts slowed down, until I was left with the game I'd chosen to play, and with the stakes on the table. Adele had been viciously attacked and the most obvious suspects were Lodge's killers. But it didn't have to be that way. Chris Tucker's outrage, when I confronted him in Sparkle's, had been hot enough to singe the hairs in my nostrils. That he, or someone very much like him, had decided to teach Adele a lesson was entirely possible. And then there were the bosses. Sarney's call had come only a couple of hours after the attack on Adele. Had Sarney known about Adele when he called me? Had there been a hidden message in what he'd said?

I watched a police cruiser slowly climb the hill. It pulled to a stop alongside my car and the officer behind the wheel shone his six-battery flashlight into my face.

'Hey, Harry, what're you doing here? It's Paul Aveda.' Aveda turned the flashlight on himself, as if his word alone wasn't good enough.

'Sittin' and thinkin',' I responded.

'You don't need a lift home, do ya?'

'Paul, if I've ever had a more sober moment in my life, I can't remember it.'

'Ten-four, detective.'

Aveda's tail lights were still visible in the rearview mirror when my cell phone began to ring. My first thought was of Adele, but that was wishful thinking. The vaguely female voice on the other end of the line had been generated by a computer. That was evident in the odd cadence and the staccato delivery.

Sza-rek. Russ-o. Jara. Zel. Sky. Put their pieces to-ge-ther. It won't be that hard, if you have the balls.

The phone went dead at that point and I returned it to my pocket. Up ahead, framed by trees on either side of the road, the view was sliced by a set of telephone wires that crossed Woodward Avenue a hundred yards from where I sat. Adele and I often came here when the weather was good, to sit with the windows open, to eat a take-out lunch, to stare at Manhattan as if it was a fable passed down from one generation to the next. This was especially true on summer days when the towers shimmered in the distance like the after-image of a receding dream.

But on that Saturday night, with the temperature in the mid-twenties and the wind crisp enough to blow New York's soot into the Atlantic, it was more like staring through a jeweler's window. The triangular lights on the Chrysler Building seemed ready to leap beyond its spire and the windows in the glass towers, lit only by the moon, were sharp enough to count.

TWENTY-THREE

The Brooklyn neighborhood of Greenpoint is similar to the neighborhoods of Ridgewood and Bushwick in many ways. Established in the middle of the nineteenth century, Greenpoint, too, was created to serve the needs of manufacturers fleeing overcrowded Manhattan. The Civil War ironclad, Monitor, was built in Greenpoint, at the Continental Iron Works, and one of the first kerosene refineries in New York, Astral Oil, opened for business in 1867.

Both Continental Iron Works and Astral Oil were long gone by the time I drove into Greenpoint on that Sunday morning, replaced, along with most of the community's manufacturing base, by warehouses offering service-sector jobs at appropriately lower wages. But Greenpoint was still vibrant, having undergone several major population shifts in the past fifty years. The first had begun after WWII, when a half-million Puerto Ricans poured into Manhattan's two great *barrios*, East Harlem and the Lower East Side. By the early Sixties, the *barrios* were full and the Puerto Ricans began to move to neighborhoods in the outer boroughs. One of those neighborhoods was Greenpoint, where they came to dominate a section on the community's northeastern edge.

The second change came forty years later, after the fall of the Soviet Union. Free to emigrate for the first time in fifty years, Poles flooded Greenpoint's already sizable Polish-American community. So many, in fact, that a good number of the Latinos, now a mix of Puerto Ricans, Dominicans and Mexicans, had been forced out by rising rents.

I hadn't come to Greenpoint, however, in search of pierogies or stuffed cabbage, or even the peppered vodka. The material I took from Adele's apartment had included the case files of David Lodge and Tony Szarek, as well as Dante Russo's personnel file and Adele's notebook. I'd read the notebook first, but the only salient fact I uncovered was that Pete Jarazelsky had resided in Greenpoint until his conviction for burglary. As Adele had circled the address several times, it naturally caught my attention.

Tying Jarazelsky to the Broom involved no great detecting skills either: Tony Szarek was living in Greenpoint at the time of his death. But the last connection eluded me for several hours.

Because there was no entry in Adele's notebook to guide me, I got to Dante Russo's personnel file last. Russo was a sixteen-year NYPD veteran. His file included all of his evaluations, along with records of the tours he'd worked, the overtime he'd piled up, and his PBA Trustee status. If there'd been any civilian complaints against Russo, they would also have been included, as would commendations or departmental disciplines. But there were none.

185

I found Russo's evaluations to be universally bland. *Dante Russo is an experienced officer who continues to exhibit good judgment in the field.* This was true even in the year Clarence Spott was murdered. Russo's eager cooperation (along, no doubt, with his PBA connections) had apparently resulted in a complete whitewash. His yearly evaluation made no mention of either Clarence Spott or David Lodge.

It was all very interesting, this portrait of a careful, calculating cop, a cop who took as few risks as possible, a cop who should have gone out of his way to avoid partnering with a rummy like David Lodge. But it was also useless, and I was finally left with a PA-15, Russo's original application for employment with the NYPD.

Sitting there, I vividly recalled working on my own application. The PA15 required you to list every job you'd ever held, every school you'd attended, any contact with the police, the names and addresses of your parents and siblings, the names and addresses of third parties willing to recommend you, the address of every house or apartment in which you'd lived.

I'd fretted over my application for weeks, running from place to place, making sure I had each date and address exactly right. At the time, I was afraid that I'd be rejected if I messed up on a single detail. Russo, apparently, had approached his own application with equal care. His PA15 was typed and there were no white-outs.

Curious, I shifted to Russo's personal recommendations. There were six in all, half from PBA board members – Russo had obviously

186

been pointed toward a career with the union from the very beginning – and half from neighbors who claimed to have known Russo from his infancy. The neighbors were uniform in their praise of Dante's virtues, his honesty and reliability, his love of God and country. They could make this claim because they'd once lived within two blocks of him in the Brooklyn neighborhood of Greenpoint.

I got my first surprise of the day when I pulled over to the curb on Milton Street off Manhattan Avenue. For the most part, the housing in Greenpoint reflects the neighborhood's working-class character, a necessity because Greenpoint was developed before the mass transit era. Factory employees had to live within walking distances of the factories they manned – not just the workers on the floor, but the professionals as well, the engineers, the accountants, the corporate executives. I'd seen the same phenomenon operating in Bushwick and Ridgewood, upper-middle-class enclaves shoehorned into working-class communities.

Milton Street, from where I sat, was a prime example. Both sides of the block were lined with sturdy brick town houses fronted by trees whose branches swept over the road. Without doubt, the town houses had been constructed in the second half of the nineteenth century, their cost well above the lifetime salaries of ordinary factory workers.

The town house to my right, the one in which Anthony Szarek had been living at the time of his death, was in perfect condition, its yellow brick free of soot, every sill in place and level. On the second floor, despite the cold, a lace curtain fluttered behind a tall window. Somebody was home.

I got out of the car and buttoned my coat, grateful for the windless day, and for a gossamer-thin layer of gathering cloud. The weather was going to change and the way I figured, it could only get warmer. We were already at absolute zero and had been for more days than I cared to count.

I rang the bell and waited patiently before a set of oak double doors. My informant had invited me to connect Szarek, Russo and Jarazelsky, a task Adele had already performed. But connection isn't conspiracy, and my aim was simply to draw the ties that bind a little tighter.

The man who opened the doors was tall and barrel-chested, wearing a dark suit and a red tie over a snow-white shirt. I flashed my shield and ID, then asked him to identify himself.

He hesitated, his lips compressing slightly as he folded his arms across his chest. Finally, he said, 'Mike Szarek.'

Mike Szarek was Tony Szarek's brother. He'd been interviewed by Detective Mark Winnman. Winnman had found Mike's name in the deceased's address book, then killed two birds with one stone by notifying the family and conducting his one and only interview at the same time.

'You're Anthony Szarek's brother?'

'Yeah.'

'Can we go inside?'

188

'I'm on my way to church, me and the whole family. You should come back later.'

I put my hand out to prevent his closing the door. 'This'll only take a few minutes. We could do it right here if you want.' When he didn't respond, I told him that the circumstances surrounding his brother's death were being re-examined, then asked him to describe his brother's state of mind in the days leading up to his death.

No human head is truly round, but Mike Szarek's came close, an effect enhanced by a short, thick neck made even shorter when he hunched his shoulders. 'The cops have already been here. Some detective whose name I don't remember.'

'Winnman.'

'Yeah, Winnman.'

I slid my hand in my pockets and smiled the most ingratiating smile in my repertoire. 'Like I said, we're taking another look at your brother's death, going back over the details.'

'You think it wasn't suicide?'

'We're taking another look,' I stubbornly repeated. 'Nobody's drawing any conclusions.'

After a moment, Szarek's shoulders relaxed and he again met my gaze, an indication that he'd decided to tell the truth, at least as he saw it. 'What could I say? Like I told the other detective, me and Tony wasn't all that tight. Not that we were enemies or anything. It's just that I'm very active in the church. Tony, he never went to church, didn't believe in it.'

Szarek paused long enough to gesture at a

189

Roman Catholic church on the far side of Manhattan Avenue, then continued. 'And when Tony killed himself, he rejected God altogether. Now Tony coulda gone to Father Willenski, who's also a psychologist, instead of committing suicide. That's a mortal sin, suicide, and there's no way to tell the Lord that you're sorry once you pull the trigger.'

'Mr Szarek, believe me, I didn't come here to stir up bad memories. I just need to know if there were any specific events that led you to believe your brother was suicidal. Was he generally unhappy? Did he talk of killing himself? Did he make a suicide attempt in the past?'

'Like I said, me and him, we weren't so close.'

'Who could help me then? Who knew him well enough to answer those questions?'

Szarek frowned as it suddenly dawned on him that he'd walked into a trap. I needed the name of somebody close to the Broom. Mike would now have to furnish that name or be seen to deliberately obstruct my investigation. Myself, I didn't figure the man had the heart to confront me. He was a good citizen at bottom. Going one-on-one with cops was not on his agenda.

'You could talk to my sister, Trina Zito. Her and Tony got together once in a while.' Mike Szarek smiled for the first time. 'What could I say?' he asked. 'Trina's the family disgrace. She married a wop.'

I clapped him on the shoulder, one kidder to another. 'It might've been a lot worse, Mike. You gotta look on the bright side. She could've married a Jew.' I gave it a couple of beats, en-

190

during Szarek's quick frown. 'Say, do you by any chance know a cop named Pete Jarazelsky?'

Szarek's head jerked back as though he'd been poked in the eye. He was pissed now, and probably freezing cold, even standing back in the doorway. 'Jarazelsky's in jail.'

'I know that, Mr Szarek. I spoke to him recently. What I'm asking is if you knew him.'

'Pete grew up in the neighborhood, like all of us, but he was a lot younger than me so I can't say we were actually friends. But if we saw each other on the street, we'd nod hello.'

'What about your brother? Did your brother know Jarazelsky well?'

'They were both cops in the same precinct, so I guess they had to know each other.'

TWENTY-FOUR

'Yeah,' Trina Zito told me twenty minutes later, 'Tony drank pretty much all day, every day. But he wasn't unhappy and he went to work in the morning, so who am I to judge?'

'Your brother sees it differently,' I suggested.

Trina's husband, Fred, took that moment to put in his two cents. We were in the front room, seated on matching love seats. Though no more than a half-mile from Tony Szarek's town house, the Zitos' apartment was far more humble, five rooms in a frame tenement sided with textured yellow vinyl.

'You don't wanna pay too much attention to Mike,' Zito told me. 'He's worried about his inheritance. The guy was on the balls of his ass when Tony died. Him, his wife and his three kids. If we hadn't agreed to let 'em stay in Tony's house until it's sold, they'd be on the street.'

'Tony died without a will,' Trina explained. 'Mike and me, we're his closest relatives.'

'Is the estate in probate court?'

'Yeah,' Fred declared, 'and it's taking forever as it is. If Tony was murdered, we'll most likely never see a dime.'

'You've discussed this possibility?'

Trina Zito cleared her throat. 'When the cops said it was suicide, I figured they must know. I mean, there was an autopsy and everything. But I'm not surprised that you turned up, either. See, my brother had his pension, plus he made a lotta money in business and he was pretty healthy, so he had no reason to kill himself.'

'How big is his estate?'

To her credit, Trina answered the question without hesitation. 'What with the equity on the house and the bank accounts, we're probably lookin' at six hundred thousand.'

'You said Tony was in business?'

'Right, he was a partner in Greenpoint Carton Supply, on India Street.'

I leaned back and crossed my legs. Trina's tone was becoming more conversational and I wanted to put her at ease. 'One thing I don't get. If your brother drank from morning till night, how'd he

192

run a business?'

'That I couldn't tell you, detective. We used to have Tony over to dinner every couple of months and he occasionally took us out to a restaurant, but he never talked about his work. I don't even know the names of his partners.'

'Do you know for certain that he actually had partners?'

'He must've, because we don't inherit his shares in the business. They revert to the corporation. That wouldn't make a lot of sense if he didn't have partners.'

I nodded thoughtfully, then took Dante Russo's photo from my shirt pocket. 'You ever see this guy with Tony?'

Even as she shook her head, Trina Szarek echoed her brother, Mike. 'Me and Tony,' she declared, 'we weren't that close.'

'What about a man named Pete Jarazelsky?'

Fred Zito popped to attention, running his fingertips back and forth over the dense stubble on his chin. 'Don't talk to me about Jarazelsky,' he declared. 'I own an auto parts store in Williamsburg and I once hired Pete to work for me on Saturdays. The scumbag robbed me blind. Every time my back was turned, something else went out the door. And the guy was a cop, for Christ's sake.'

I nodded agreement, then asked the same question I'd put to Mike Szarek. 'If you and Tony weren't close, who should I speak with? He must have been close to someone.'

Fred and Trina looked at each other for a moment, then shrugged in unison. 'Yeah,' Trina admitted, 'there's someone alright.'

'And who might that be?'

'Ewa Gierek, his live-in lover. Ewa's suing for half the estate.'

'You know where she lives?'

'In Flushing, with her brother.'

Ewa Gierek was the whitest white woman I'd ever seen. Her porcelain skin was nearly translucent, her blue eyes pale and prominent, her hair so light that her lashes and brows were virtually invisible. A wintry landscape, to be sure, broken only by the scarlet lipstick on her small, Cupid's-bow mouth and the blush worked into her cheeks.

The image of Tony Szarek I'd been carrying up till then, of the pitiful Broom mopping his way through the last years of a stumble-bum career, vanished forever. Szarek was a few months short of his fifty-eighth birthday when he died. Ewa Gierek was no more than forty and might have been a good deal younger.

'If I could just come in for a moment,' I said. 'I want to talk to you about Tony Szarek.'

She nodded once and led me to a living room choked with oversized furniture: a leather sofa with rolled arms, two matching recliners, a pair of leather hassocks, a glass coffee table, a projection TV jammed into a corner. The wall opposite the sofa held four rows of glass shelves on which baseball memorabilia, mostly playing cards in lucite holders, had been arranged.

'My brother, Ryszard,' Ewa explained when I glanced at the display, 'he is dealer of these

194

baseball things.' Her accent was heavy and she spoke slowly, pronouncing the words with care. 'Even in Warsaw he is following Yankees. Crazy, yes? But he has made living from baseballs. This is good.'

'Is your brother home?'

'He is at convention in Chicago.'

I was about to launch into my usual pitch, the one about reopening the case, taking another look at the facts, but decided against it. Instead, I took out Dante Russo's photo and tossed it on the coffee table between us. 'Do you know this man?'

One thing about pale white skin, it's a definite impediment to successful lying. Even as Ewa shook her head, her cheeks flared as though someone had lit a candle inside her mouth. Under other circumstances, where time wasn't a factor, I might have let her falsehood stand. As it was, I pounced on her.

'Listen, Ewa, and listen closely. I'm here because I think person or persons unknown, motivated by money, put a gun to Anthony Szarek's temple and pulled the trigger. Can you hear me now? You're suing for half of an estate worth six hundred thousand dollars. As the Feds like to say, that makes you a person of interest. Of course, there are other persons of interest, who also stand to benefit from Tony's death, but they didn't start out by lying. See, I already know that you and this gentleman are acquainted, so maybe you wanna take a closer look before I leave with the wrong impression.'

By the time I finished, my voice had risen in

195

volume and my tone was self-righteous, despite the little fabrication at the end. The display was meant to be intimidating, but Ewa's eyes never left mine as she worked things out.

'I know him,' she finally admitted.

'Why didn't you tell me that right away?'

'Tony has always said to not talk about his business.'

'Tony's dead and buried, Ewa. It's time to save yourself, and just maybe your inheritance, too. Now tell me his name, the man in the photograph.'

'Dante ... Dante something.'

'And how well were Tony and Dante acquainted?'

Once she got into the flow, Ewa was forthcoming, at least as far as I could tell. Although she was routinely ordered to make herself scarce whenever Russo visited the Milton Street house, she believed Russo and Szarek to be partners in Greenpoint Carton. She'd seen them at the warehouse, conferring with the man who handled the company's day-to-day affairs. That man's name was Justin Whitlock.

I have an excellent memory, as do most good detectives, but it took me a minute to locate the name. Lieutenant Justin Whitlock had been the desk officer at the precinct on the night Clarence Spott was killed. Just as the Broom had placed David Lodge alone with the victim, Whitlock had provided Dante Russo with an alibi. Predictably, the job had made a scapegoat of Whitlock, forcing him into retirement.

'Justin Whitlock,' I asked, 'is he a partner?'

196

Ewa shrugged. 'I know only that when I am calling Tony at job, Justin is usually one to pick up telephone. When I am at job, Justin gives orders to workers.'

'Alright, I believe you. Tell me, did Tony ever mention a man named David Lodge?'

'I don't remember this name.'

'Did he seem worried about anything, say in the three months before he died?'

'Tony was party animal. Always out with friends. He worried about nothing.' She stared at me for a moment, her head cocked to one side, her Cupid's-bow lips so pursed they might have been found on the face of a doll. 'Why you are not asking about the loving brother?'

'Mike Szarek?'

'Yes.'

'I've already spoken to him.'

I stood at that point, intending to express my gratitude for her cooperation and be on my way to the hospital. But Ewa had other ideas. She placed herself between me and the door, backing up until the knob was pressing into her back. All the while, she attacked Mike Szarek's reputation. According to Ewa, he was a brute who'd been arrested twice for spousal battery. Moreover, he was a hypocrite of a Christian who hated and envied his successful, happy-go-lucky brother, even while receiving holy communion.

'Every Sunday I am seeing his face at ten o'clock mass at St. Anthony's. Never he is even looking in my direction. Always he walks out with nose in the air.'

I endured the diatribe for several minutes,

hoping some unrevealed tidbit would slip out, but it was just more of the same.

'Ms. Gierek, I have to leave,' I finally told her. 'But don't worry, I'll be talking to Mike Szarek again.'

Ewa turned far enough to unlock the door, then swung back to me. As I suspected, she had her exit lines ready.

'You Americans,' she said, pulling the door open, 'you are narrow peoples, all the time lying flat, like a ruler. Only one sin do you see, sin of sex. There are seven deadly sins but you only think about lust. How many times do I see big fat man on television screen telling world about sin of sodomy? What about sin of gluttony? What about sin of greed? Of envy? Of hatred? To these, you Americans are blind.'

I flashed a smile at that point as I slid by her into the hallway, thinking, *Lady, when you're right, you're right.*

TWENTY-FIVE

It began to sleet as I pulled out of North Shore Hospital's parking garage, intermittent sprays of frozen rain that chittered across the hood and roof, filling a heavy silence. I turned right coming out of the parking lot, toward Northern Boulevard with its many traffic lights, instead of the much quicker Long Island Expressway. After passing thousands of hours behind the wheel of a patrol car, I'd come to accept the fact that some New York drivers view adverse weather conditions as opportunities to indulge already suicidal impulses. Better to be traveling as slowly as possible, just in case some moron lost control on a curve.

Adele had been sitting in the lobby when I arrived at a quarter past four, a smallish figure in a bloodstained ski jacket. She rose on seeing me, but made no comment on my tardiness. When I asked her if she wanted to wait until I retrieved the car, which I'd parked in the garage, she merely shook her head.

As we drove toward Queens, I found myself wanting to tell her everything I'd done that day, all in a rush, like a child, and I wanted to listen to her adventures as well. I had my partner back and my emotions were running high. Till then, I hadn't realized how much I'd missed her grouchy attitude and condescending tone. One more reason to be walking down this road.

But the signals from Adele were a deal more somber. She sat alongside me as we drove through the town of Manhasset, staring out through the windshield at curtains of sleet that drifted back and forth across the headlight beams like schooling fish. I watched her tighten a seat belt already tight enough to constrict her breathing, then raise her chin. For a moment, I was certain she'd speak. Instead, she brought her right arm across her chest, sling and all, then settled against the seat.

I finally broke the silence as we approached

the Queens-Nassau border. There was work to be done, after all, decisions to be made. I told Adele about Sarney's call, the threats, the demand that I spy on her, the claim that the bosses were certain she was leaking to the *Times*.

'If we can't trust the phones – and we can't – it'd be better if you stayed with me in Manhattan,' I told her. 'If we were in the same place.'

Adele took a deep breath, holding the air down inside for a moment, finally releasing it with an audible hiss. Despite the swollen mouth, when she spoke, I understood her perfectly.

'I thought he would come,' she said.

Adele was talking about her husband, Mel, who was currently in Dallas, and whose failure to alter his plans didn't surprise me. I wondered what foolish dreams Adele had been nurturing. Had she hoped Mel would suddenly develop an emotional life, that she would find herself at the center of that life? If so, she'd been victimized by unrealistic expectations. Somewhere along the line, Mel had cut a deal with himself. So that he would never be hurt, he would never feel anything at all.

'Maybe,' I finally said, 'you should stash Mel in a corner for now, get back to him later.' I leaned forward to pull down the windshield's visor on her side of the car, revealing a mirror on the underside. 'After all, if we don't survive, Mel's not gonna matter a whole lot.'

Much to my relief, Adele abruptly shifted gears. She'd been humiliated twice in the last forty-eight hours, by the man who attacked her and by

200

the man who should have been there to comfort her. Right now, she was feeling helpless and helpless was definitely not her thing. It was time to fight back.

Though her lips were as swollen as ever, her skin purple above and below her bandages, Adele's speech was fairly confident, the new mechanics more familiar now as she described her activities during the week we'd been apart. There was very little I hadn't already guessed. Adele belonged to a number of associations open to women struggling with New York's various male-dominated law enforcement agencies, including the Department of Corrections and the District Attorney's office. Besides offering emotional support, the associations also functioned as mutual aid networks and Adele had exploited these connections to secure the various files. The single surprise was that she'd gotten a peek at the IAB file created when Pete Jarazelsky was arrested for burglary. Closely held, IAB files are difficult to secure under the best of circumstances.

'Jarazelsky,' she finally told me, 'was caught inside the warehouse, so he had no defense. He was alone at the time, but IAB suspected that he was part of an organized ring.'

'Did he roll over?' One thing about crooked cops, they usually start naming names before the cuffs go on. That would be especially true of a rat like Jarazelsky.

'No, he lawyered up right away.'

'You think Jarazelsky made the same mistake as David Lodge? You think he spoke to the PBA delegate, Officer Dante Russo, before he asked for that lawyer?'

'Pete Jarazelsky and David Lodge had the same lawyer, Corbin. A man named Theodore Savio.'

Adele was rolling the words in her mouth, stumbling over the syllables in a way that reminded me of Ewa Gierek, whose existence I revealed a short time later. My description of Ewa's milk-white skin, her invisible brows and tender years, was amusing enough to draw a genuine smile, which pleased me. By that time we were in Adele's apartment and she was filling a suitcase with clothing, doing it one-handed. She didn't ask for my help and I didn't offer it.

The phone began to ring downstairs as Adele closed the latches on the suitcase. If she heard it, I couldn't tell. She opened the drawer on her night table, took out a box and flipped off the cover, revealing a small automatic pistol. The weapon was designed to be carried in a pocket or beneath a waistband. There were no front or rear sights to snag on fabric and the shrouded hammer was buried in the gun's frame.

Adele had shown the automatic to me when she'd first purchased it as a back-up weapon. Though it didn't look like much, the AMT held five .40 caliber rounds. And like all semi-automatic handguns, it could be fired as fast as you could pull the trigger.

The phone stopped in mid-ring and Adele smiled before handing the weapon to me. 'Corbin, please, jacking a round into the chamber is beyond me at the moment.'

I took it a step further, ejecting the magazine to make sure it was full. When I handed the gun back to Adele, she tucked it into the sling covering her right arm. The weight caused her to wince slightly, the only concession to pain she'd made so far.

The sleet had turned to snow by the time we started out for Rensselaer Village and I stayed with Northern Boulevard, though I might have jumped on the Cross Island Parkway. I was in no hurry. It was Sunday night, the streets nearly empty, the snow outside thick enough to reduce the neon tubes defining the commercial landscape to smears of color that rippled across the windshield with each stroke of the wipers. A block away, the headlights of an orange sanitation truck cut across the intersection and I lifted my foot from the gas. The truck turned in front of us, exposing a rotary machine on its tail-end that spit circles of rock salt onto the asphalt. Though I kept as far from the truck as possible, pellets of salt cracked into Adele's side of the car as we inched by.

'Those files, they're useful,' I said after another long silence. 'But maybe not in the way you think. Remember, you can't admit you have them. Nor can we access financial records or obtain warrants of any kind.'

My remarks produced no more than a shrug. This was ground Adele had already been over and she simply changed the subject. 'Irony,' she observed, the word coming out: eye-own-eee. 'Tony Szarek's murder. If it has nothing to do with David Lodge.'

By this time, Adele knew the particulars of my day, knew that the Broom had a destitute brother who hated him and a young mistress who was suing for half of his estate. It was at least possible that one or the other (or even the good sister, Trina) had killed him. The ME's failure to discover traces of gunpowder residue on Szarek's hand had troubled me from the beginning. If his killer had simply touched the gun to Szarek's palm and the inside of his fingers after it was fired, the tests would have come back positive. Cops would know that.

But even if we'd made false assumptions, if we'd been drawn to the Broom by mere coincidence, examining his life had enabled us to connect Russo, Jarazelsky, Szarek and Justin Whitlock. The Broom's actual killer was now irrelevant.

'They had no time to worry about the Broom,' Adele continued. 'David Lodge was coming out of jail bent on revenge. He had to be taken down, no matter what the risks.' Adele reached out to lay the fingers of her left hand on my arm. Despite the bandages and raccoon eyes, her gaze was too intense for me to mistake her intentions. 'The panic is still out there. All you have to do is stir the pot.'

'Then what?'

'Then somebody will come after you, Corbin, just like they came after David Lodge, just like they came after me.'

We were up on the 59th Street Bridge by then, the Island of Manhattan before us completely

204

obscured by the snow. I watched Adele's hand drop to her lap and her gaze return to the accumulating snow on the roadbed. 'Corbin,' she said.

'What.'

'Thank you.'

'For what?'

That brought a little smile and a change of subject. 'How much are we supposed to get?' Adele asked, pointing through the windshield. 'How much snow?'

'Three or four inches, nothing to worry about. We should be looking at temperatures in the upper forties tomorrow.'

I thought back to the day I'd ruined my loafers, the day we found DuWayne Spott. At the time, I'd been the one without a clue. Now my feet were encased in a pair of waterproof Timberland boots and Adele was wearing flat-heeled pumps. It was a neat reversal of our customary roles, and not at all unpleasant.

Adele and I began to discuss tactics and overall strategy as we drove south along Second Avenue, a discussion that continued as I carried her bags into my apartment, as I made up the bed in the spare room, as I prepared a dinner of soft-boiled eggs and buttered bread that Adele managed to get past her swollen lips. We stayed at it until nearly ten o'clock when Adele finally plucked a vial of pain killers, Percocets, from her handbag. The Percocets had been prescribed and filled at North Shore Hospital, a kindness negated by a thoughtless pharmacist who'd topped the vial with a child-resistant cap. Though it couldn't be opened with one hand, Adele kept trying until I took the vial from her fingers.

'You know, Adele,' I said as I twisted the cap and shook out a round white tablet. 'It's OK to ask for help. Remember, no woman is an island.'

I watched Adele rise to her feet and carry the tablet into the kitchen. By this time we'd pretty much settled on our strategy and my thoughts had taken a more playful turn. Adele's body, when in motion, had always contradicted her customary air of self-control. Far from willowy, her shoulders were relatively broad, her confident stride an unconscious echo of the fearlessness so obvious in her gaze. I followed that body into the kitchen where I almost got up the nerve to make the move I'd been dreaming about for many months. That I settled for a glimpse of the nape of her neck as she bent over the sink had nothing to do with Mel, or with a justifiable fear of the shape her rejection might take. No, the reason I didn't press my lips to Adele's neck sprang from a fear of acceptance. This wasn't about a weekend rendezvous, two days of give and take before everybody goes home, the party's over. In many ways, Adele had remained a mystery to me throughout our partnership, but there was no mistaking this piece of the puzzle. Adele Bentibi was commitment prone.

A half-hour later, Adele retreated to her room, already a little woozy, and I was off to the Y for a swim. Though I'd hoped to relax into an easy rhythm, I never did find my stroke and spent forty-five minutes thrashing around. I didn't think about Dante Russo as I thrashed, or any of the other actors, or even about Adele. Instead, my thoughts drifted to the day Roderigo Carrabal slashed my chest on the basketball court behind the Jacob Riis Houses. At the time, we were disputing an out-of-bounds call.

Carrabal was trying for my face, which I managed to jerk out of the way. As it was, the gash ran from one shoulder to the other, passing just beneath my collar bone, and required stitches on the inside as well as the outside.

The stitches were sewn into my flesh at Cabrini Hospital on 19th Street by a sour-tempered resident who greeted every flinch with a disapproving scowl. Still, the resident was a deal kinder than the two detectives who interviewed me later on. They smelled an easy collar and when I insisted that I couldn't identify my assailant, they finally smacked me in the head, one after the other, before they took off.

I began to stalk Roderigo Carrabal long before my wound healed. He was never out of my mind, not for a waking moment. I felt that I'd been put to a test. If I didn't pass, I'd be engulfed by the fear still crouched somewhere in my subconscious, held at bay only by the promise of revenge.

Roderigo wasn't much of a fighter as it turned out. When I finally caught him alone, he looked at the length of pipe in my right hand and began to beg in a mix of Spanish and English that left no doubt as to his sincerity. It didn't help him, though.

TWENTY-SIX

I got on the phone at seven-thirty the following morning, to the NYPD's sick desk in Lefrak City where I explained that I was fighting a bad cold and would be out, probably for the next few days. The desk officer took my information without comment, then hung up. Ten minutes later, my phone rang. It was Bill Sarney.

'What's up, Harry?' he asked. 'I just got a call from the sick desk.'

I let my voice drop to a near whisper. 'I gotta keep it down,' I said. 'Adele's in the shower.' In fact, she'd come into my office and was standing ten feet away.

'She's staying with you?'

'Yup, I talked her into it. I didn't see any other way to keep track of what she was doing.'

'And that's why you called in sick?'

'Now you're gettin' it.'

After a brief pause, Sarney declared, 'I like it, Harry, but I do have one question.'

'And what's that?'

'You nailin' the bitch?'

'Nailing Adele? Shit, I'd rather get in bed with a crocodile. This is a woman who bites.'

When I glanced at Adele and found her smiling, my mood lightened for the first time in weeks. The sense was as much physical as psychological, a slight rising on the balls of my feet, a sharpening of my attention. No more conflict. Now I could focus.

'Yeah, well speaking of biting, you have any idea what she's up to?'

'Healing, Bill, is about all she can manage right now.'

'Yeah, I heard she got mugged.' Sarney delivered the party line smoothly, just to make certain that we were all in agreement. When I didn't argue the point, he continued. 'But I didn't think it was that bad. The lieutenant at the One-Eleven told me she only had a slight—'

'Wait a second.' I put my hand over the mouthpiece and counted slowly to five. 'Adele just turned off the water in the shower. We better make this quick. Look, all I know for sure is that she got her hands on the David Lodge file and she's been feeding bits of it to Gruber at the *Times*.'

'This is not news, Harry.'

'OK, the other thing is that she wants to go public with her injuries. You know, claiming that she was set up by other cops.' I paused again, this time only for a second, then said, 'I gotta go, Bill. She's comin' out.'

Adele was still smiling when I followed her into the office where she took a seat before my computer. I remember that her pajamas, blue and silky, were airing on the carefully made single bed, and that a vaguely floral scent hung in the air. I breathed that scent eagerly as I squatted behind her chair and peered at the monitor on the desk. Generally, my apartment smelled faintly of the chlorine I brought home from the pool.

Prior to Sarney's call, Adele had been checking out the source of the email I'd received on the prior morning, the one that included Russo's photograph. In my ignorance, I'd hoped the return address would be of value in identifying the sender. No such luck.

'A public library,' Adele told me, 'in Brooklyn.' After a moment, she added, 'Library computers are designed to serve people who can't afford their own computers, to give them open access to the internet.'

'Which means?'

'That anybody with a library card might have sent that email.'

I took the mouse from Adele and quickly accessed my new messages, hoping to hear from B.Arnold@midwood/BPL.lib. But I struck out there as well and shut down the computer.

'Time to get moving.'

Adele stood and followed me into the living room. She was wearing a pair of neatly creased white slacks over a loose turtleneck sweater. I imagined her slowly drawing her right arm through the sweater's sleeve, inch by inch, noting that her bra had defeated her altogether. Helping Adele dress was her husband's job, of course, one of those in-sickness-and-in-health obligations you take on when you pronounce your wedding vows. Another humiliation for Adele, for whom going bra-less had never been a possibility.

210

I walked to the closet nearest the front door and lifted a Kevlar vest from a hanger. Like most detectives, I rarely wore body armor on the street, my job not being all that dangerous. But things were different now, and I needed to acknowledge the changed circumstances. Removing my shirt and sliding into the vest did just that. There's nothing like the weight of Grade II body armor to concentrate the mind.

I made one stop before heading off to Greenpoint, at a tiny store on 14th Street where I contracted for a pair of pre-paid cell phones, putting 300 minutes on each one. Then I returned to my apartment where I gave one to Adele. She took the phone from my hand, then rose on tiptoes to kiss me on the cheek. Though the kiss was very gentle, she winced before settling on her heels.

'Take care,' she said.

A half-hour later, I was parked on India Street a hundred yards away from Greenpoint Carton Supply, munching on a fried egg sandwich and swilling coffee from a container large enough to hold a milk shake. The entire block was industrial, lined on both sides with sprawling two- and three-story brick buildings pocked with filthy windows. This was a world from which all pretense had been relentlessly scrubbed, a world devoid of corporate parks and instantly recognized logos. This was where you came to work, if you were a worker, or to make a profit if you were a boss; a place where you started early and you finished late and you never pretended, not

211

for a minute, that there was anything glamorous about your day.

New York City is, in many ways, as dependent on Greenpoint and similar neighborhoods in every borough as on the multinational giants in Manhattan. In fact, if you stripped Rockefeller Center of every item supplied by warehouses like Greenpoint Carton, you'd have a bunch of executives in two-thousand dollar suits crouched on bare floors, staring at bare walls.

My purpose, at that moment, however, had nothing to do with New York's complex ecology. I needed to know whether Greenpoint Carton was a functioning business. That question was answered at nine-thirty when five box trucks, solid twenty-footers with beefed-up rear axles, pulled from a small yard on the northern side of the building. Headed out on delivery runs, each bore a stylized GCS logo on its front doors.

I'd been hoping that Greenpoint Carton would fail the test, that it would come up a pure front operation. Though I'd still be unable to conduct a financial investigation, the knowledge could be useful. But that wasn't the case and there was nothing to do but get off my lazy ass and go to work.

My initial impression, when I entered Greenpoint Carton Supply, was of an impenetrable maze. Brown cartons of every size, stacked on wooden pallets, rose to the second-floor windows in a seemingly random pattern. The cardboard smelled like fresh sawdust and reminded me of Sparkle's in the early evening.

All around me, workers zipped by on forklifts powered by cylinders of propane. I expected one of them to slow down long enough to ask me what I wanted. They didn't, though I was favored with a number of curious glances, and I finally wandered across the face of the building until I found a set of stairs leading up. Again, though I was in plain sight, nobody challenged me as I climbed to a second-floor balcony fronting a small office.

For a moment, before going inside, I watched the activity below me. There were four active fork-lifts moving through the stacks, lifting pallets, carrying them to the rear of the building, where two workers in heavy jackets and woolen caps cut the straps binding the cartons. They were putting together orders for delivery on the following day. When the trucks returned in the late afternoon, they'd be loaded before the workers punched out.

I finally turned to an open door leading into a deserted office. The office was as starkly functional as the rest of the warehouse: three battered wooden desks topped by gray blotters, dusty computers and telephones so grimy I couldn't name their color. Along the back wall, a row of three-drawer filing cabinets caught my attention and I walked over to them, trying the first drawer I could reach. It was locked.

'Whatta ya think you're doin'?'

Though startled, I straightened up slowly before turning to face the man who'd addressed me.

'I'm looking for Justin Whitlock.'

213

'Well, you found him. And my question still stands. What the fuck you think you're doing in my file cabinets?'

Whitlock had that ex-cop look about him. In his mid-fifties, he was thirty pounds overweight, with a crepey neck that hung in soft folds and a red nose coarsened by one too many visits to the bottom of a bottle.

'You gonna play the outraged citizen, lieutenant?' I pushed a stack of invoices to one side, flashed my shield and sat on the edge of the desk. Though I was on Whitlock's turf, I was determined to dominate the space.

'I want you out of here.'

'Without even knowing why I came?'

Whitlock folded his arms across his chest and shifted his weight from one foot to another before cocking his head to the side. As this was a posture commonly assumed by superior officers annoyed by their subordinates, I failed to react appropriately.

'Of course,' I told him, 'if you already know what I'm doing in your office at nine-thirty in the morning, your demand is entirely reasonable.'

'Cut the bullshit, detective. You got no right to come in here without my permission.'

'If you wanna call the cops, Justin, I got the phone number of a good one. His name is Dante Russo and he works out of the Eight-Three. What I hear, he's got serious juice with the PBA.'

Again, Whitlock shifted his weight back and forth as he attempted to deal with the situation. I

214

had a badge and a gun and I wasn't leaving. What, if anything, could he do about it?

'I'm gonna call my lawyer,' he finally said.

'That wouldn't be Ted Savio, would it?' The question produced an unmistakable flinch. I'd tossed the dart blindfolded and hit the bull's-eye. For a moment, as his narrow eyes bulged and his ears turned bright red, I thought Whitlock was going to attack me. But then he calmed enough to ask the question he should have asked in the beginning.

'What do you want?'

'I want to know who got the Broom's piece.'

'What?'

'Tony Szarek's shares in Greenpoint Carton reverted to the company when he died. That has to be good news for somebody.'

'Well, it's not good news for me. All I do is work here. I'm a manager, not an owner.'

I covered my surprise with another question. 'And who manages you, Justin? Now that Tony Szarek's dead.'

Whitlock's face tightened down. 'You're fishing,' he declared, 'but I'm through biting.'

'You won't tell me who your bosses are? Why not, Justin? What have you got to hide?'

When he failed to reply, I decided to get moving. There was a lot to do and not much time to get it done. I straightened abruptly, then sauntered through the door onto the balcony before turning for a goodbye salute.

'Oh, yeah, before I forget. Pete Jarazelsky told me to make sure I gave you his regards.'

TWENTY-SEVEN

I'd tossed in the last bit for two reasons: to sow confusion and to protect Ewa Gierek. Jarazelsky was another of those wild cards, his prison also his protection. Was he being a good boy, keeping his mouth shut? Or was he cooperating? Lodge's murderers couldn't answer either question with certainty. Maybe Pete had taken the heat for the warehouse burglary, but he was a rat in his heart, a rat who knew far too much.

The sequence, as I read it, went like this: Lodge recovers a memory implicating Jarazelsky and persuades Jarazelsky to confess, after which Jarazelsky warns his co-conspirators. As this takes place months before Lodge's release, there's plenty of time to prepare a welcome-home party for good old Davy.

So much the better, then, if those party-givers now suspected that the untouchable Pete Jarazelsky provided the details that led me to Greenpoint Carton Supply. As for Ewa Gierek, the boys would have to be wondering what sort of alcohol-driven pillow talk might have transpired between her and Tony. My fear was that they'd decide to limit their exposure as I drew near. What is it they say about killing? That it gets easier as you go along? First there was Clarence

Spott, then Tony Szarek, then David Lodge, then DuWayne Spott. If the state managed to accumulate evidence of a conspiracy, Dante Russo and his pals would be looking at a first-degree murder indictment and a potential sentence of life without the possibility of parole.

I passed the afternoon working my various informants, finishing up at the apartment of Mejorana Delgado who supplemented her welfare and food stamps by snitching on her neighbors. Like my other informants, Mejorana repeated the crooked cop mantra. Everyone knew, or so she said, that Bushwick's most notorious drug dealer, Paco Luna, was being protected by crooked cops who routinely closed down every independent operation. Though I listened patiently, I didn't place all that much store in the information. Like Paul Rakowitz, Mejorana named no names. The important thing was that she knew the man called Bucky, whose real name was Maximo Chavez. Bucky was married to a woman named Nina Francisco who lived only a few blocks away.

'But if you talk to her, you gotta be careful, detective. Nina, she got a temper that could scare off a pit bull.'

TWENTY-EIGHT

The sun had broken through the clouds and the snow was gone by the time I stepped onto the sidewalk fronting Mejorana's Woodward Avenue apartment. I stood where I was for a moment, my eyes adjusting to the glare as I considered my next move. Mejorana had not only confirmed the existence of Bucky Chavez, she'd supplied his address. All to the good and I was encouraged. But Paul Rakowitz had insisted that Bucky could identify a cop he'd observed walking into Paco Luna's headquarters. Mejorana, who knew him well, hadn't mentioned anything of the kind.

My choices were simple. I had a second informant in Ridgewood, an Italian kid named Greg Ianuzzi. I could look him up or I could pay a visit to Bucky's wife, Nina Francisco. The problem with Ianuzzi, a small-time marijuana dealer, was that he could be difficult to locate. His only known address was the home of his parents, the place I'd be least likely to find him. Nina Francisco, on the other hand, had a fixed address and three children to hold her down. Plus, if Bucky had blabbed to Rakowitz, he would certainly have blabbed to his pillow mate. But there was a definite problem. Nina Francisco had a belligerent attitude and no reason to cooperate, while Ianuzzi was a professional snitch who sold information as readily as sidewalk vendors sell pretzels.

I went back and forth in my head as I walked the fifty feet to where I'd parked my car, as I unlocked, then opened the door. For all the care I took, I might have been in my own apartment. That changed in a hurry when a rat flew from the Nissan's interior, its naked tail whipping across my legs as it dropped to the pavement and skittered up the block.

My heart stopped in my chest at that moment, skipping several beats before reawakening with a thud against my rib cage hard enough to produce a groan. My knees wobbled and I reached out to the Nissan's roof for support while I watched the rat disappear into a storm drain fifty feet away.

My first real thought – when I'd recovered enough to actually have a thought – was that I'd have to set the now-defiled Nissan afire and hoof it to the nearest subway. I didn't see any way I could be in that car, with all the doors closed, and not hear the scrabble of rats' feet every time one of the tires rolled over a pebble. In fact, how could I be sure there wasn't a second animal inside right this minute?

'Yo, detective, you OK?'

I turned to find Mejorana leaning out the window of her ground-floor apartment. 'Yeah, I'm fine.'

'I'm glad to be hearin' that, 'cause you was always pretty white, even for a *blanco*. Now you're pale as a fuckin' ghost.'

Inspired, I finally dredged up the courage to stick my head inside the Nissan, to bang on the roof liner, then listen for the scrabble of tiny claws. I heard nothing, but still wasn't satisfied until I'd opened all four doors, checked under the seat and popped the door on the glove compartment.

The Nissan started on the first twist of the key, as though relieved to have escaped immolation, and I pulled away from the curb, my eyes still roaming the urban landscape. Inevitably, I turned to the questions of who and how, a pure waste of time. Any street cop – inspired, perhaps, by word of my encounter with Chris Tucker – might have gotten into the un-alarmed Nissan. As for the rat, the industrial neighborhood on the far side of Flushing Avenue was rat heaven. On the way over, I'd passed a cruiser from my precinct on Metropolitan Avenue. I'd recognized the driver, a kid named Bruce Lott, and even tossed a casual wave. Lott hadn't returned the greeting. Instead, his eyes had jumped to mine, held steady for a count of five, then casually turned away.

In my career, I'd known a female officer who had opened her locker to find a sperm-filled condom nestled in the cup of a spare brassiere, and a black cop who'd found a stuffed monkey sitting on the front seat of his car. A rat was no less a symbol because it was alive, and no more of a threat.

Threat or not, when I finally slowed for a light

220

and my brakes emitted a tiny squeal, I shivered like a wet puppy.

Nina Francisco was a loud woman – in her speech, in her general appearance, in her dress. She wore a flaming-red halter with a scoop neck that accentuated her cleavage, and purple jeans tight enough to constrict the circulation of her blood. Dyed to match her jeans, her short hair was heavily moussed into spikes the approximate thickness of drumsticks. Her voice was brassy enough to carry a salsa band.

'Wha' the fuck you want?' she demanded once I'd forced my way inside. She was standing with her fists pressed to her hips and her head cocked to the right. All five feet and ninety pounds of her.

I closed the door behind me and walked into the living room. 'Who else is in the apartment?'

'The baby.'

'Where?'

'In the bedroom. Asleep.'

'What about the other kids?'

'What the fuck do you care?'

'Where are they?'

Nina sneered, then smiled. 'They're on a play date, OK? Now why don' you tell me what the fuck you're doin' here.'

'I'm looking for Bucky.'

'Never heard of him.'

I took a couple of steps to the right and picked up a photograph clearly taken at a wedding. Nina was wearing a cobalt gown that swept to her feet, while the man who held her arm, the

221

man with the pronounced overbite, wore a white tuxedo.

'Listen here, Nina,' I said, holding out the photo for her inspection. 'I want Maximo Chavez and I want him right now. And don't lie to me any more. It's disrespectful.'

'I don't see why you wan' him so bad when you mos' likely the one who capped him.' Nina's lips pursed and her green eyes flashed defiance. There, now she'd shown me. I could have kissed her.

'Bucky's dead?'

When she didn't respond, I sat on one end of a long couch and leaned forward, laying my elbows on my knees so that I was looking up at her. Time for a curve ball.

'Nina, if I was a little rough before, well, I apologize. It seems like I woke up with a headache and it's been downhill from there.' I flashed my shield and ID for a second time, flipping the billfold open, snapping it shut. 'I'm not from the local precinct. I'm from internal affairs.'

The submissive posture and soothing tones caught Nina Francisco unprepared. I watched her eyes dart to the side and her weight shift from one leg to another as she processed the change of pace.

'We have good reason to believe,' I continued, 'that crooked cops are operating in Bushwick. Our goal is to get them off the street before they do any more damage. I'm not asking you to make a sworn statement, but ... Let's face it, Nina, cops don't testify against other cops. The only way to build a case is to go to the community.'

'Funny,' Nina finally replied, 'you ain't been here before now. Cause this shit's been goin' down, like, forever.'

I ignored the challenge in her voice and attempted to put her back on message. 'Tell me why you thought I might have killed Bucky,' I asked. 'Is he dead?'

'You already said it. The cops in Bushwick are dirty and everybody knows they're dirty.'

'Alright, we're agreed on that. Cops in Bushwick are dirty. But you haven't told me why you thought I might have killed Bucky.'

Forced, now, to make a direct response, Nina's facade cracked just enough to reveal the worry that lay beneath. Sure, Bucky was a scumbag, but he was Nina Francisco's scumbag. Family first, right?

'Bucky ain't been around,' she said, her tone considerably more subdued. 'He disappeared.'

'Has he ever disappeared before?'

'Not for no three weeks. He ain' even callin' his moms.'

I nodded and spread my hands, trying to reassure her. 'OK, so we're agreed on this, too. Bucky's nowhere to be found and you believe he might have been killed by cops. Now I need to know why the crooked cops wanted to kill Bucky Chavez. What was their motive?'

Again, I'd forced Nina to reply directly to a question and this time her response was more direct. Bucky had told her, as he'd told Paul Rakowitz, that he'd seen a cop walking into Paco Luna's headquarters unchallenged. What's more, he'd recognized the cop. The bad news was that he didn't know the cop's name and had made no effort to find out in the intervening months. Instead, Bucky had developed the story into an anecdote: 'Hey, bro, I ever tell you about the night I saw the cop go into Paco's house?'

By the time I asked Nina Francisco to name one dirty cop, I was berating myself for not choosing Greg Ianuzzi. Predictably, Nina was unable to name names, much less supply times and places. Though I hadn't been nursing unrealistic expectations, I'd hoped to come away with some tidbit I could use later on, maybe another Greenpoint Carton. The way it looked, I'd wasted the past two hours.

'So, whatta ya think?' Nina finally said.

'I think I'm gonna get outta here.'

'You don' wanna hear no more?'

'Is there any more to hear?'

Luck may be the residue of design, but dumb luck is just dumb. I was standing by the door when Nina finally got down to business. She smiled before she began to speak, a sly little-girl smile that I wouldn't have expected. 'Like, if I know a cop who, like, you know ... takes care of a girl, like a mistress ... does that count for dirty?'

'It could.'

'OK, I got this second cousin, Marissa. We went to school together and she was like my bes' girlfriend and shit, until she went behind my back. Marissa's got this cop pays her rent.'

'What's his name?'

She shook her head, but her tone remained

224

sincere. *'Mira*, what I'm tellin' you is the truth. Marissa has this cop, he comes over maybe three nights a week. I seen them together. It's true.'

'Fine, it's true. But so what? Do you even know if he's married?'

'Marissa said he wasn't.'

'Then you see my problem, sex between consenting adults not being a crime and all.'

'What about the money he gives her?'

Nina was becoming less sympathetic by the minute. 'If you're implying that your cousin is a whore, then you're way off-base. Prostitution involves the exchange of money in return for a specific sexual act. That's not what's happening here.'

'What if they had a baby together?'

'Then the money he gives her is called child support.'

I was halfway out the door when I remembered Dante Russo's photograph, tucked away in my jacket's inner pocket. Dutifully, I fished it out, unfolded it, then held it up for Nina's inspection.

'You know this—?'

'That's him. That's Marissa's boyfriend.' Suddenly, Nina's hands were back on her hips, her shoulders squared, her eyes defiant. We'd closed the circle. 'Yo, *maricon*, wha' the fuck you think you're doin' here? Askin' me shit when you know the answers.' She touched the tips of her fingers to her chest, daring me to make the first move. 'You disrespectin' me? You makin' fun of me? Cause I will kick your *gringo* ass. I don' care if you're ten fuckin' cops.'

TWENTY-NINE

Short, plump and submissive, Melissa Aubregon was her cousin's polar opposite. She let me into her apartment and answered the few questions I asked without hesitation, and without raising her voice. Only once did she demur, when I spotted a photo of Dante Russo on an end table. Even there, she compromised. Melissa was sitting on Dante's lap in the photo, staring up at him, her left arm draped around his neck.

'I need that photograph,' I told her. 'I want you to give it to me.'

'Dante will kill me.'

'Don't tell him.'

'He'll notice.'

'Say it got knocked over and the glass broke.'

Melissa shifted the baby she was cradling, from her right to her left arm, as she tried to come to a decision. Finally, she said, 'Would smaller be alright?'

The photo was an enlargement and Melissa still had the original snapshot. That was the compromise, a way to please me and please Dante at the same time. Melissa liked to please. When the baby began to fuss as she showed me to the door, she lifted him until his face was a few inches from hers and whispered, 'No, no, no, no, no. It's gonna be alright. Don't worry.'

When I got home, Adele had a surprise for me. New York State corporations, even privately held corporations, are required to file documents identifying their officers. That information is public knowledge and can be accessed through a number of online services that maintain databases of public information. Adele had used the largest of these to retrieve Greenpoint Carton Supply's filing. Three items stuck out. Greenpoint Carton had changed hands six months after the death of Clarence Spott. Anthony Szarek was the new president. Ellen Lodge was the new secretary-treasurer.

'Ellen, you fool,' I muttered.

'You feeling sorry for the widow, Corbin?'

Adele's question wasn't only sarcastic, though there was sarcasm aplenty in her tone. The whole business of interrogation requires that your emotions be put to one side. Though your approach may vary from threatening to soothing to consoling, the focus is always on manipulation. The little wedges are driven in wherever there's a chink in the armor; the emotions you project at any given moment are simply the right hammer applied to the right wedge. Later on, if you're successful and your subject is particularly odious, you experience an intense satisfaction. But that's for later on, when you're in the bar, when you've had a couple, when the bad guy is resting quietly in a cell. The feast comes after the hunt.

After recounting my activities that morning (including my encounter with the rat, to which my partner barely reacted), I produced the photo I'd taken from Marissa and passed it to Adele.

'What are you thinking, Corbin? That Ellen was in love with Russo?'

'Ellen Lodge had to find her way to the party somehow,' I finally replied. 'Why not love?'

'Are you going to ask that question when we visit her this afternoon?'

'No. Tomorrow, maybe, after I soften her up.' I looked at my watch. It was almost one and I had work to do. 'I need to use the computer, Adele.'

She got up and brushed by me. 'What are you going to do?'

'I'm going to make a record of everything we've accomplished so far and email it to Conrad Stehle. Just in case something happens to us.'

Adele nodded once. I'd mentioned Conrad many times in the course of the endless conversation that flows between partners. 'I've destroyed all the files: Russo's, Lodge's, Szarek's,' she announced, 'to protect my sources.'

'Good. We couldn't use them anyway.'

I turned to the computer, expecting Adele to go about her business, which in this case involved ordering lunch from a Chinese restaurant near Gramercy Park. But she lingered at the door long enough for me to look from the monitor into her eyes.

'I'm not going back to Mel,' she told me. 'Never again. I can't believe I've lived with him this long.'

'You wanna hang out here until you get your

head straight, it's alright.'

She reached out to stroke my face with the fingertips of her right hand. 'I was betting you wouldn't come back, that you'd choose the job. I was wrong and I'm sorry.'

I suppose I should have taken her in my arms at that point. Even if the signals she was sending weren't amorous, a comforting hug was certainly in order. But I lacked the courage to touch her, though I wanted her as badly as I'd ever wanted any woman, and I finally deflected the conversation with a pitiful attempt at humor.

'Tell 'em to make that Hunan pork extra spicy. If you don't mind.'

We got to Ellen Lodge's home at four o'clock, but I didn't approach the door immediately. First I loaded the four bags of garbage Ellen had left at the curb into my trunk while Adele remained in the Nissan. I was just closing the trunk when Ellen Lodge came through the door at a dead run.

'What do you think you're doing? I have neighbors, for Christ's sake.'

I said nothing for a moment. We were in the first day of New York's traditional January thaw. Though night had already fallen, the temperature was in the fifties, warm enough for me to brave the elements without an overcoat.

'When you put out your trash, Ellen, it ceases to be your property.'

'I'm not talkin' about callin' a lawyer. I'm talkin' about my neighbors. I been livin' here fifteen years.'

Adele chose that moment to emerge from the Nissan, making a spectacular entrance that brought Ellen Lodge's hand to her mouth.

'What happened to you?' she naturally asked.

'What happened to my partner,' I said, 'is that she got off lucky. Everybody else who crossed Dante Russo has ended up dead.' I gave it a few beats, my heart bursting with gratitude. All along, I'd been figuring Ellen for a dupe and her shock at Adele's appearance confirmed that suspicion. She wasn't there when the attack was planned and nobody had told her about it afterwards. 'Why don't we go inside and have this conversation in private?'

After a quick look up and down the block, she led us into the interior of the house, then up the stairs to the small sitting room where I'd conducted the last interview. Again, I was struck by the plush upholstery and vivid colors. The roses and peonies embroidered on the fabric covering the couch and chair were open and voluptuous, in stark contrast to the very guarded woman who'd chosen the pattern and who now took a seat across from me.

'My husband's killer is dead,' she declared, 'so I don't really see what you're doin' here stealin' my garbage.'

'There was a second man, Ellen, if you remember; a second assassin.'

'And you're lookin' for him in my trash?'

'I look for him everywhere, hoping to find him somewhere.'

'Spare me, please.' When I didn't respond, Ellen crossed her legs and leaned away from me.

'Fine, let's get it over with. What do you want?'

'We were wondering,' I said, 'if you've recovered any stray memories in the last week.' I watched her light a cigarette with a disposable lighter. As she drew the smoke down into her lungs, her eyes closed and I got the distinct feeling that she didn't want to open them. 'Something Davy might have said when you visited, or wrote in his letters.'

'As a matter of fact, I have. Davy told me that he worked in the prison shrink's office. He told me the shrink was crazy, that he was completely unreliable.'

Credit where credit is due. When I'd asked her about Nagy in our last interview, she'd denied all knowledge of his existence. Now she'd covered her ass.

'Was that something Davy said to you?'

'It was in his letters.'

'Anything else you can remember?'

The window behind Ellen was raised a few inches and a pair of red curtains fluttered in the draft, reaching to within a foot of her close-cropped hair. 'Why do you keep asking me these questions about Davy? If I remember right, he was the victim.'

The fact that she didn't claim victimhood for herself was encouraging. Not that I intended to respond to her questions. The subject never controls the interview.

'Do you remember I asked you about Tony Szarek last time I was here? The man they called the Broom?'

'Vaguely.'

231

'Well, you told me that you recognized the name, but that you'd never met him. I wonder if you want to reconsider that statement, if maybe some new memory has surfaced.'

Ellen Lodge's eyes flicked over to Adele. 'This ain't right,' she said.

If Ellen was looking for help from Adele, she'd come to the wrong source. Adele's gaze was absolutely ferocious, the gaze of someone who's been hit in the face with a bat and holds the individual before her responsible.

'I asked you a simple question, Ellen,' I said. 'You can always refuse to answer.'

'Alright, I could've run into him once or twice at Christmas parties in the precinct. Or at some other party. But I didn't actually know him.'

'Have you been in contact with him since he retired?'

'Do I need a lawyer here?'

'What you need to do is answer the very simple question I asked you.'

'I think I need a lawyer.'

I shook my head. Legal representation was not a place to which we could return over and over again.

'Face it, Ellen, this isn't *Law and Order* and you're not getting an attorney. And we're not leaving, either, not until we get some answers.' I kept my tone as non-confrontational as I could, allowing the words to speak for themselves. 'You were married to David Lodge, so you already know how it works. We're here to stay.

THIRTY

Ellen Lodge's eyes dropped to her hands and her shoulders slumped. For a moment I thought she was going to cave in, right then and there. I looked over at Adele, who gave me a surreptitious thumb's-up.

'You haven't even read me my rights,' Ellen finally announced without raising her head. 'Not even that.'

But I wasn't biting. 'Why don't we back up, Ellen, and not waste our breath. I asked you a simple question. Have you been in contact with Tony Szarek since he retired?'

As Ellen Lodge might have walked off earlier, she might have chosen, at that moment, to keep her mouth shut. I certainly wasn't prepared to force her to speak, despite my earlier refusal to leave, and I'm sure she knew it. But Ellen was a woefully inexperienced villain in a very tight spot. What did I know? What facts had I uncovered? How deep was the hole in which she now stood? She just had to find out.

'Why don't we skip the bullshit?' she suggested, finally raising her head to meet my eyes. 'Why don't we get to the bottom line?'

'Why won't you answer the question I asked? Have you had any contact with Tony Szarek

233

since he retired? It's so simple. All you have to say is yes or no.'

'Yes, then.' Having made the initial admission, Ellen couldn't slow her momentum, offering an explanation I hadn't requested. 'I just thought that it didn't really matter. I mean, it's not like we were friends. And Tony was dead, for God's sake. He couldn't have had anything to do with Davy's...' Though her lips continued to move, Ellen was unable to say the last word. Another good sign.

'Then you knew Szarek was dead?'

'Yeah, I knew.'

'Did you also know that he was murdered?'

'I still don't know that he was murdered.'

'Oh, he was murdered alright.' I placed my finger against my temple. 'When you shoot yourself from this position, two things happen. First, you get blood on your hand and wrist. This is called blowback. Second, the hand holding the gun becomes contaminated with the residue of the exploding primer and the gunpowder. Neither of these things happened to Szarek's hand. That means he didn't fire the gun himself.'

'The medical examiner called it suicide,' she insisted.

'You're clinging to a straw. The ME's finding of probable suicide was preliminary. Now that the lab reports are in, the case has been officially reopened.'

I watched Ellen react to the lies, her right knee taking a series of little hops before she brought herself under control. Momentarily, I considered firing off the best shots in my arsenal. But it was

234

still too early and I told her the story of DuWayne Spott instead, recounting the portrait drawn by my witnesses of a hapless addict clinging to the fringes of the criminal underworld. When I finished, I asked Ellen a series of questions.

'How do you think DuWayne Spott found out when Davy was being released from prison? How do you think he found out where Davy was going to stay? How do you think he found out when Davy was going to leave your house that morning?'

Though I paused between each question, Ellen didn't reply. Finally I asked, 'Can you see how thin it is? I'm talking about the whole business, Ellen. It can't hold up.'

'Is there a question here?'

In fact, there was, but as it was purely rhetorical, I simply continued on. 'That's three murders, Ellen. Tony Szarek, DuWayne Spott, David Lodge. And then there's that phone call you made just as Davy walked out the door. You said it went to a wrong number, that you were calling a friend. Who was the friend? What number did you intend to dial?'

'I don't even remember any more. That was weeks ago.'

'Is that what you're prepared to tell a jury? "I dialed the wrong number. I don't remember the number I meant to dial"?' I shook my head. 'One thing you might want to consider. Any lie told to the police can be used against you. That you didn't know Tony Szarek, for example. Or that you were kicked out of the great cop family.

235

Strange, isn't it, that you're now sharing a financial bed with Justin Whitlock and Dante Russo? And how about your insistence that Davy told you that he'd been targeted by Clarence Spott's crew, but somehow never spoke of his innocence? I've met the prison psychiatrist, by the way. I assure you that he'll make an excellent witness when the time comes.'

But the time hadn't come, a fact of life driven home when the doorbell rang downstairs. Ellen Lodge slid forward, preparing to rise. I reached out to stop her.

'That's my sister,' she announced. 'We're havin' dinner together.'

I'd been startled by the bell and was still a bit disoriented, even though I'd told myself, going in, that I wouldn't get the hours I needed to break Ellen Lodge, not on the first go-round. Nevertheless, the timing was all wrong. I wanted Ellen utterly vulnerable, a prey animal exhausted by the chase, but I knew she was feeling almost giddy. The weight was off. She'd escaped. No matter that the points I'd raised still hung above her head, sharp as daggers. For now, for this minute, she'd triumphed.

'Detective Bentibi,' I said, 'would you let Ellen's sister know that Ellen will be momentarily delayed?'

The bell rang for a second time, a steady clang that reminded me of the fire bell at PS 34 where I'd spent six miserable years. Adele rose without a word and left the room, the sound of her steps quickly fading as she negotiated the stairs.

'Am I under arrest?' Ellen finally asked.

236

'That's a little too dramatic, don't you think? I just have one more question, anyway. A question and a suggestion.'

'And which comes first?'

'The question.'

'Fire away.'

'How could you have been stupid enough to allow yourself to become an officer at Greenpoint Carton Supply? I mean, first you have Dante Russo, who was Davy's partner when Clarence Spott was killed. Then you have Justin Whitlock, who gave Dante an alibi. Then you have Tony Szarek, who put Davy alone with the prisoner. All of them involved in Greenpoint Carton? It makes sense, in a way. But you? Ellen Lodge? What the fuck are you doing there?'

I wasn't surprised when Ellen Lodge winced. Nor was I surprised when she recovered. Under ideal circumstances, she might have broken down at that point. By connecting her finances to the very people her husband blamed for his imprisonment, I'd saddled her with a motive for his murder.

'And what's the advice?' she asked after a minute. 'Make a full confession?'

'My advice is to start looking out for yourself before it's too late. In order to do that, you need to accept your vulnerability. I know Dante told you it was all over, that the case was closed. But that's not what's happening. No more than Tony Szarek's death is going down as a suicide.'

'That's it?'

'No, I want you to realize that you're in danger, that another murder doesn't mean anything

237

at this point, that you're the weakest link in the chain, that you can't protect yourself.'

'And the cops will protect me?' She waved off my confirming nod. 'Protect me in return for exactly what, detective? For a full confession? Well, excuse me if I point out that we're goin' around in circles.'

The breeze suddenly died out and the curtains dropped into place before the window. Ellen was running a finger over the raised edges of a small embroidered rose on the arm of her chair. Though she refused to look at me, I could feel the anger and resentment building again. I had maybe ten seconds before the dam burst.

'It all depends on how it happened,' I explained. 'If you didn't know Davy was gonna be clipped when you made that phone call, if maybe you thought he was just gonna be spoken to, then you're a double victim. You lost your husband and you were set up to take the heat for his murder. Hell, you might even escape prosecution altogether.'

Ellen shot to her feet and pushed past me. I let her go, satisfied that I'd done the best I could under difficult circumstances. I was still congratulating myself when she marched back across the room, stopping two feet away from my chest. Ellen was a small woman and she had to crane her head back to glare up at me. She wasn't intimidated, though. She was pissed.

'Tell me something, detective. You know what Davy was like on the street. You've listened to all the stories. So, do you think David Lodge kept his hands to himself when he came home at night?' She pointed at a small, crescent-shaped scar partially concealed by the hair covering her right temple. 'I got scars from Davy. I got a shoulder that dislocates once a month. I got fractured ribs. And don't tell me I should've walked out, not unless you know what the barrel of a gun tastes like.' She grinned, a parting of her lips not far removed from a snarl. 'Do you know what gun metal tastes like? Do you? It's sour, detective, and it makes your fillings tingle.'

By this time, she was jabbing me with her finger. I didn't protest. The interview was over and I knew the effort would cost her in the long run. Besides, I wasn't the good guy here. By targeting Ellen Lodge, I was definitely putting her life at risk.

'I was seventeen when I met Davy. He was twenty-three and already a cop. I felt so safe in his arms, like nothing bad could ever happen to me. Stupid, right? We weren't even married a year before he started hitting the bottle and hitting me, too. Answer me this, detective, what's the penalty for enslavement? What's the penalty for taking someone's whole life away from them? Wasn't I entitled to the same dreams as anybody else?'

She stopped there, her whole body quivering with tension. When I didn't respond, she said, 'As far as I'm concerned, David Lodge got exactly what he deserved. No matter who actually killed him.'

THIRTY-ONE

Adele waited patiently while I checked the car, smacking my palm against the windows, opening doors then jumping back. If she thought my display of anxiety amusing, she kept it to herself, entering the car without hesitation when I gave the all-clear. Though it was past dark, the temperature seemed to be rising and I kept the window lowered as I pulled away from the curb.

'You don't have to do this,' I said. 'You know that, right?'

'It was my suggestion.'

'True enough, but you still don't have to.'

She turned to face me, the smile on her face, as far as I could tell, entirely genuine. Adele was looking forward to the encounter and I wasn't really surprised. We were going to Sparkle's, to confront the lies being spread by the PBA. And though the odds against either of us gaining from the confrontation were very steep, Adele's need for combat was very strong.

Our grand entrance, ten minutes later, was electric. Every eye turned in Adele's direction; Sparkle, herself, appeared to pay homage. It was a little before six, prime time for cop bars, and Sparkle's was fairly crowded. Nydia Santiago was there, along with her main girlfriends, squeezed around a small table against the far wall. At the sight of Adele's damaged face, Nydia's expression hardened and she drew a breath sharp enough to hear across the room. Women cops are very sensitive to the physical dangers that go along with the job. Hardly shocking when they're the most likely to be among the injured if things get out of control on the street.

Far more numerous, the male cops reacted less dramatically. They appraised Adele, their looks vaguely suspicious, then turned to me with reproachful eyes. I was their friend and I'd not only thrown them a curve, I'd greased the ball.

Most human beings have a set of rules they hold dear and cops are no different. The first cop rule is silence. Thou shalt not speak ill of another cop, not to an outsider, not under any circumstances. Call it the blue wall of silence; call it *omerta*, NYPD style.

The silence rule, like all hard-and-fast rules, works better if you don't examine it too closely. By displaying Adele's injuries, we were forcing the cops in the room to open their eyes and they clearly didn't like what they saw.

I followed Adele to the end of the bar where five feet of rail miraculously cleared at our approach. Mike Blair, his expression grim, poured a Dewar's for me, then asked Adele what she was having.

'A screwdriver,' she announced, 'and a straw to drink it with.'

'The straw was overly dramatic,' I said as

241

Mike went off to make Adele's drink. 'You had a cup of coffee before we left the apartment. I don't remember anything about a straw.'

When Mike Blair returned with Adele's drink, I raised my glass to Sparkle, who beamed down approvingly, then let my eyes sweep the room. Everybody in the bar knew me, but nobody wanted to look in my direction. Not even my good buddy Jack Petro, who refused to make eye contact until I finally called his name and waved him over.

Jack came reluctantly, his conflicted loyalties apparent in his worried look. Which came first? Loyalty to the job? Or loyalty to your best cop buddy? A toughie, no doubt.

'Harry, Adele,' he said without offering his hand to either of us. 'How's it goin'?'

'Not too bad.' I finished my scotch and signaled for another. When Mike Blair carried the bottle to where we stood, I told him, 'Hang out for a minute, Mike. Adele's got something she wants to tell you.'

Adele launched into her statement before either man could object. 'David Lodge was a cop. A little on the rough side, but no worse than hundreds of cops who go out on the job every day. He was set up to take the fall for Clarence Spott's death and he was murdered upon discovering the truth.' She paused to sip at her drink, pulling the orange juice and vodka up through the straw before placing the glass on the bar. 'When you thought David Lodge's killer was a black pimp, you were ready to form a lynch mob. Now I'm telling you that his killers

242

are cops and you turn your backs, I think you are pathetic.'

As overkill was Adele's standard mode of communication, I wasn't surprised by the punch line. But Jack Petro flinched as though slapped, while Mike Blair stood open-mouthed, the Dewar's bottle cradled against his chest. Petro finally broke the silence.

'This ain't right,' he said to me, echoing Ellen Lodge.

'What isn't right, Jack? Taking down cop killers? Is that what's not right?' I was much taller than Jack, and in far better shape. When I stepped in close to him, though I hadn't meant to intimidate, he took a step back. 'The story's gonna come out, no matter what happens to me or my partner, and when it does the job's collective eyes are gonna be blacker than Adele's. That means that you, Jack Petro, when you're out on the street, are gonna feel the public's contempt, you and every other cop. But that's not my fault and it's not my partner's.'

'What are you telling me, Harry, that you suddenly got religion? Because me and you, we go back a long way and I don't recall you wearin' a halo in the past.'

The question caught me off-guard, a quick jab slipped beneath my glove. But Jack had it backwards. If I'd known what was coming when I got out of bed on the morning David Lodge was murdered, I'd have pulled up the covers and gone back to sleep. As it was, I'd been more than ready to pass the moral buck to my superiors. True, Adele hadn't put a gun to my head, but

243

she'd definitely set the example. I would never have found the courage to butt heads with the job if she hadn't been out there. Nor, truth to tell, would I have gotten very far without the files she'd gathered on her own.

I didn't explain any of that to Jack or Mike, but my attitude softened. 'Adele got lucky,' I said. 'Someone came out of her building as she was being attacked and her assailant ran away. But suppose he hadn't been interrupted? What do you think might have happened?' I shook my head. 'It won't work, Jack. Even if you truly believe the world is better off without the Spott brothers, you can't justify the attack on Adele, not unless you're prepared to stop thinking of yourself as a good guy.'

'The "good guy" was a little weak, Corbin,' Adele said as we crossed the bar and pushed through the door.

I took a quick glance over my shoulder. *Bye-bye, Sparkle*. 'I've known Jack for a long time. Trust me, once you get past the cynical attitude, he's a romantic. The rest of them, too. They think they're on the side of the angels.'

'Just like us?'

'That's the way I'm hoping it'll go. If we're all heroes, how can we be enemies?'

We came through the door to find Nydia Santiago waiting for us on the sidewalk. Nydia didn't even glance in my direction. She jerked her chin at the middle of Adele's face and said, 'Who did that?'

If Nydia's tone was demanding, Adele's was

244

uncompromising. 'Are there dirty cops in the Eight-Three?' she asked.

'What?'

'Because if there are dirty cops in the Eight-Three, they're the ones who did it. They punished me for picking up the rock they were hiding under.'

Over the last thirty years, police corruption scandals in New York have usually involved small groups of rogue officers who've been working together for years. They rip off dealers for drugs and money, put drugs back out on the street, sometimes even ride shotgun on large deals. Given the size of the NYPD and the latitude granted to ordinary patrol officers, the scandals have been relatively few and far between. But that wasn't the point Adele was making. Precincts in New York are quite small: Bushwick, for example, home to the 83rd, covers only two square miles and has well over a hundred officers working the streets. That's why it's impossible for rogue cops to operate anonymously. Other cops have to know.

Detective Nydia Santiago worked in the precinct, day after day, week after week, month after month. She had snitches of her own, naturally, snitches who'd undoubtedly repeated the same rumors Adele and I had so easily uncovered. I could see it in Nydia's eyes, that moment of reflection as she searched for a way to avoid the unpleasant truth.

I took out the small note pad I keep in my jacket pocket, wrote down the number of the cell phone I'd purchased earlier in the day, then tore off the sheet and offered it to Nydia.

'If you want to get in touch with me, it'd be best if you didn't use my home number.'

Nydia stared into my eyes, her expression defiant. Then she snatched the sheet of paper from my hand and jammed it into her pocket. For a moment, I was certain that she'd speak, but she finally turned on her heel and marched back into Sparkle's without saying a word.

THIRTY-TWO

I spotted the tail before I'd gone two blocks, not because I was especially alert, but because it's impossible to conduct a successful tail in a silver Jaguar. Not unless you want to be seen.

'We have company,' I told Adele.

Adele glanced in the outside mirror on her side of the car, then looked at me. 'Time to throw out the garbage.'

'What?'

'The garbage in the trunk, Corbin. Ellen Lodge's garbage. If you leave it where it is, the car will reek of it by tomorrow morning. And, of course, while you're disposing of the trash, you can take a closer look.'

We were on Wyckoff Avenue, a commercial street four lanes wide. I pulled to a stop, double-parking in front of an apartment building, then added the bags of trash in the Nissan's trunk to a

246

mound of similar bags stacked at the curb. We'd only taken them in order to shake up Ellen and I certainly didn't intend to sort through the coffee grinds in my apartment. The Jaguar stopped about thirty yards away. Its headlights remained on and I could feel the bass notes projected by its many speakers rumbling in my chest.

'Anything?' Adele said when I got back into the car.

'Two guys in the front for sure. I couldn't see into the rear. The headlights were too bright.'

When in doubt, confront. I led the Jaguar across Flushing Avenue, to a deserted street lined with warehouses. Halfway down the block, I slammed on the brakes, then jerked the Nissan into reverse before stomping on the gas pedal.

Brakes and tires screaming, Jaguar and Nissan came to a halt within six feet of each other. Adele was the first one out the door. Without my noticing, she'd removed her arm from the sling and now held the .40 caliber AMT in her right hand.

'Police,' she shouted. 'Police, police.'

I came up on the driver's side of the Jaguar, my immediate goal to prevent the situation from escalating. I needn't have bothered. The two men inside were sitting absolutely still, their expressions at the same time insolent and bored. If they even heard the rap music pouring from the Jaguar's high-end sound system, they gave no sign.

Adele tapped on the passenger's window and made a little rolling motion with her left hand.

Slowly, as though forcing his finger through increasing resistance, the man closest to her reached out to the controls on the door and let the window down. The music exploded onto the block, bouncing off the brick walls of the surrounding warehouses until it seemed to be coming from everywhere, so loud that I barely heard the trio of shots Adele fired into the dashboard, shutting down car and sound system both.

By the time the last echo died away, all eyes were on Adele and I felt the need to attract a bit of attention, just to remind the boys that I was still hanging around. So I kicked in the window on my side of the car, splattering the front seats and the men sitting on them with tiny shards of glass.

The man closest to me began to brush the glass off his lap. A Latino in his early twenties, he wore an Avirex leather jacket zipped to his throat. His soot-black hair was drawn into a pony tail that fell to his shoulder blades. The pony tail glistened as it moved, slivers of glass reflecting the pale amber light cast by a street lamp thirty feet away. 'Wha' the fuck you doin'? I ain' committed no crime.'

'How about driving while stupid?' Adele suggested.

'Yeah,' I continued, 'tailing somebody in a sixty-thousand-dollar car? You gotta be an idiot. Or did you want us to see you? Was that it? Were you disrespecting us? Because if I thought you were disrespecting us, I'd have to cuff you, take you into one of these alleys and teach you a
248

lesson.'

'We wasn't doin' nothin',' the man in the passenger seat declared. 'We was just drivin' around.' He was the older of the two, wearing a down coat that reached his ankles and a knit cap that clung to the contours of his narrow head. A tattooed spider's web ran from the corner of his left eye to his temple, leaving me to wonder if the spider was hiding in his hair.

We pulled both men out of the car, cuffed them with their hands behind their backs, finally conducted a quick search of their persons and of the vehicle, finding nothing of greater interest than a stack of porno magazines under the front seat.

'Take a message back to Paco Luna,' I said, as if the message sent by Adele wasn't already sufficient. 'Tell him it's time to cut his losses. What's happening here is between cops. If he gets in the middle, he's gonna be crushed.'

Only a few days before, I'd have been able to bring these scumbags into the house, to isolate them, to demand answers. As it was, I had two choices. I could drag one or the other into that convenient alleyway I'd mentioned earlier, then convince him to cooperate. Or I could let them go.

But Adele was already removing her man's cuffs and I quickly followed suit. In fact, neither man had committed any crime greater than contempt of cop, for which they'd been adequately punished. As I drove off, I watched them in the rear-view mirror. They were circling the crippled vehicle, their hands in their pockets. Wondering, perhaps, how they were going to explain why

249

they hadn't gone down with the car.

'Tell me something, partner,' I finally said as we drove back to Manhattan. 'Do you think it's possible that you overreacted? I mean by discharging your weapon into a defenseless automobile.'

'No,' she said after a moment, 'I don't. No more than I think either of those men would hesitate to kill me. Or you, for that matter.'

I drove down Flushing Avenue, then along Broadway under the El, and finally onto the Williamsburg Bridge. The moon was up and nearly full; I watched it flicker between the bridge's intersecting girders, winking on and off, lurid as a Delancey Street whore. On the Manhattan side of the river, the midtown office towers, so enticing from Woodward Avenue in Ridgewood, projected raw power from every lit window. I'd made this ride a thousand times, at sunrise and sunset, in every season, in every weather. I'd watched the twin towers burn and collapse from the center of the bridge, attempting to clear the traffic impeding a river of fire trucks, ambulances and police vehicles hurrying to the scene.

'Are you feeling better, Corbin?'

Adele's eyes were shadowed now, her fatigue evident. Without thinking about it, I reached out to stroke the side of her face, the backs of my fingers trailing along her cheek just beyond the dressings. Her eyes widened momentarily, then she smiled one of those unreadable female smiles that men dread.

'Are you thinking about Mel?' I asked.

250

'I am not, Corbin, thinking about Mel.'

'Then what?'

Her face sobered and she turned to look out through the windshield. 'I won't live a trivial life, Corbin,' she declared. 'I won't.'

Back in my apartment, I made a pot of coffee and got to work. I began with a detailed report of my interview with Ellen Lodge, which I emailed to Conrad Stehle. Then I opened my own emails, even the spam, but found nothing out of the ordinary. Vaguely disappointed, I shut the computer down, then punched Conrad's number into my new cell phone. When he answered on the second ring, I gave him my new number, explaining that I no longer trusted any phones listed in my name. Then I got down to business.

'Did you get my emails?' I asked.

'Yes, I did, Harry. And I say to you that they are very interesting.'

In his late sixties, Conrad had come to the United States from Germany shortly after Hitler's rise to power, his Marxist parents escaping hours ahead of a brown-shirt purge. Dieter and Loise Stehle never recovered from the experience, or so Conrad told me on more than one occasion. They pronounced themselves cowards for running; they convicted themselves of treason, of deserting the Fatherland in its moment of greatest peril. No matter that all of their comrades perished, and millions more besides. No matter that in saving themselves, they'd saved their two-year-old child. As far as Dieter and Loise were concerned, there were no mitigating circumstances. And no one left alive to forgive them.

The Stehles compensated, to a certain extent, by maintaining a strictly Germanic household. When Conrad walked into public school at age seven, he'd yet to speak a word of English. Sixty years later, he still retained a trace of his parent's tongue, not only in the sound of the words as he pronounced them, but also in his slightly stilted phrasing. The diffident tone, on the other hand, was pure affectation.

'Look, Conrad, anything happens to me, I want you to print two copies of my notes. Send one to a *New York Times* reporter named Albert Gruber. Send the other to Reverend Azuriah Donaldson at the Bedford Avenue Baptist Church. Then delete the original emails.'

After a slight hesitation, Conrad said, 'Don't allow your anger to cloud your judgment. Anger doesn't work here, any more than it worked in the pool.'

'I'm just being prudent.'

'Your request is prudent, yes. But you are still very angry. I can hear it in your voice. Your chest is tight and your esophagus constricted. If you were competing now, you would give out in the first hundred meters.'

The advice was well meant, but off-target. Conrad wasn't sensing anger, but keen anticipation. On one level, the trail we'd uncovered in Bushwick was no less than the stink of our enemy's fear. The sort of odor that might be given off by a rabbit inches away from the oncoming talons of a hawk.

252

THIRTY-THREE

An hour later, Adele and I shared an overcooked (in deference to Adele's injuries) pot of spaghetti and a Caesar salad. As we ate, we discussed what we'd done and what we hoped to do. The conversation held few surprises until Adele announced that she was preparing to avoid the NYPD altogether.

'I got David Lodge's file from an ADA named Ginnette Lansky.' She picked at her salad for a moment, then added, 'Ginnette heads the Major Crimes Bureau for the Queens DA.'

I shook my head. 'You're living in a fantasy. They'll never do it.'

'Do what?'

'You're thinking you can talk the District Attorney into taking over the investigation.'

'Which he has every right to do.'

Adele was correct. The DA, with his own staff of independent investigators, could open a grand jury investigation tomorrow. But why would the current holder of that office, Kenneth Alessio, want to go down that road? Most of his investigators were retired cops who'd be anything but eager to put heat on the job. Plus, he'd run a law-and-order campaign in the last election, where he was endorsed by the Patrolman's Benevolent

Association.

'You're playing an angle, right?' I finally asked. 'Something you haven't yet told me?'

Except for the swollen lips, Adele's grin might have been described as impish. 'Ginnette's father was murdered when she was fourteen, shot down in a robbery. She tells me that it changed her life.'

'Now she's a crusader?'

'You might say that Ginnette draws a sharp line between good and evil. You might say that outrage is her constant companion.'

'So, you think she can talk Alessio into embarrassing the NYPD?'

'I think she'll try.' Adele wiped her mouth, then folded her napkin and laid it beside her plate before looking up at me. 'And when it comes to questions of basic justice, Ginnette is a very convincing woman.'

'Does that mean she's been taking lessons from you?'

When my question produced nothing beyond a smile, I volunteered to clean up, and Adele announced that she was off to the shower. A few minutes later, I heard the water running. I knew she wouldn't be long. Rensselaer Village is cursed with a plumbing system that dates back to 1949 when the complex was built. In my apartment (and, I suspect, most apartments on the higher floors), it's simply impossible to maintain a constant water temperature in the shower, the water jumping from cold to scalding hot in a matter of seconds. This is not a condition that makes you want to linger and Adele didn't. Just as I finished clearing away the dinner things, I heard her scream. Whereupon the steady hiss of running water abruptly ceased.

Adele was still in the bathroom when my new cell phone began to ring. As the phone was still in my coat pocket, it took me a moment to retrieve it.

'That you, Conrad?' I asked without saying hello.

'Guess again, sport.'

'Nydia, how nice of you to call.'

'Lemme speak to Adele.'

'Adele's in the shower, but I'll give her your regards. What's up?'

Nydia's hesitation was accompanied by a slow, indrawn breath. I imagined her looking over both shoulders for an eavesdropper. Finally, I broke the silence.

'How'd you know Adele was here?'

'Everybody in the house knows.'

'Is the talk coming from Russo?'

'That's what I called about. Russo, he's a missing person. He hasn't been to work, hasn't answered the phone. Yesterday, two of his PBA buddies went to his house. They found newspapers on the lawn dating back to Saturday and the mail box stuffed with envelopes. Needless to say, Russo didn't answer the bell.'

'Did his PBA buddies go inside?'

'Yeah, through a window. The closets and bureaus were full, his passport was in a desk drawer, and a basement storage room contained a matched set of monogrammed luggage.'

When she stopped abruptly, I said, 'Thanks,

255

Nydia.'

'*De nada*, Harry. And that show you put on tonight? Well, I always knew you had balls. Only it's not gonna help you. The word in the house is that you and Adele are responsible for Russo's disappearance.'

'Then why hasn't anybody been to see us?'

'I don't know. Dante lived on Staten Island, in the One-Twenty, so it's not our case. Anyway, I gotta run. Just make sure to tell your partner I called. Tell her what she said tonight wasn't far off the mark. And tell her to watch her ass.'

'What about my ass, Nydia? I have an ass, too.'

'I know that, Harry. In fact, I've been watchin' it for a long time. The way I figure, if you keep on swimmin', you got another five years before it reaches the backs of your knees.'

Against all odds, the gambit Adele and I played in Sparkle's had paid off. If not for Nydia, it might have been days before we discovered that Russo was missing. As it now stood, Russo's disappearance could be used to harass Ellen Lodge and I dialed her number immediately.

'Hey, guess what,' she declared when I told her that Dante had vanished, 'I'm not the next of kin.'

The line was too good to be spontaneous, the news too important to be dismissed with a quip. What's more, Ellen had spoken without hesitation. That meant she'd had time to consider her response and how she'd deliver it. Still, I gave her credit for one thing. Feigning shock is be-

256

yond the scope of all but the most gifted actors. Ellen Lodge hadn't even tried.

'I called to give you a heads-up,' I said, 'but if you don't think you'll be next, there's nothing I can do. On the other hand, if you want out, I can put you in a safe place.'

My very predictable offer resulted in a pitifully theatrical hesitation. 'I gotta think about it.'

'Do you remember, Ellen, the first day I saw you, I gave you my card?'

'It's in my drawer.'

'Anytime, day or night.'

I now had two pieces of news to convey: Russo's disappearance and the widow's equanimity. Both were instantly forgotten, however, when the bathroom door opened to release a cloud of steam, shortly followed by Adele Bentibi in a white, terry-cloth robe. She was walking toward me, holding a roll of tape and a small pair of scissors in her right hand, a stack of gauze pads and a tube of antibiotic ointment in her left. Her arms were extended as she came, her face uncovered, her wounds clearly visible.

Adele's nose, once overly sharp, was now flattened in the center. There were two cuts beneath the lower orbits of her eyes, one on each cheek, and a vertical gash that ran from the inner corner of her left eye down along the side of her nose. These were not knife wounds. They were not clean and straight. Adele's cuts had been caused by the impact of a blunt object. They were jagged and irregular, their inflamed edges held together by dozens of micro-stitches that reminded me of ants swarming across slices of overripe fruit.

'The dressings came off easily, but I'm having a little trouble putting them back on.' She smiled as I continued to stare at her, then said, 'I've decided not to wear the splint over my nose. I only want to cover the cuts.'

I took her into the kitchen and positioned her beneath the overhead fluorescent light, far and away the brightest light in the apartment. Then I washed my hands thoroughly. Though I had a box of latex gloves (filched from the job), I worked with my fingers exposed, pressing a thin layer of antibiotic ointment into her wounds. I knew her wounds were still tender, but I felt no reluctance. I was far more aware of her eyes. With her chin tilted up, Adele was looking directly at me and for a moment I thought I could see all the way back to the twelfth century, that I could trace every voyage in the long wanderings of the Bentibi clan, that every calamity which befell them had also fallen across my shoulders.

It was the most intimate moment of my life. More intimate even than the sight of her naked when I undid her robe a few moments later. More intimate than when I entered her for the first time a short while later.

We didn't speak of Mel afterwards, though I remember thinking what a jerk he was to let Adele slip away and how I wasn't going to make the same mistake. That Adele was finished with him was obvious. I hadn't come between wife

258

and husband. If Adele were more religious, she'd already have chanted the prayer for the dead over his memory, abandoning him the way her family had abandoned Europe in 1948. So long, scumbag.

But if Mel was in her past, our future – Adele's and mine – was far from certain, a point she made as I was drifting off.

'I meant what I said, Corbin,' she told me. 'I won't live a trivial life.'

After careful consideration, I said, 'Do you think it's possible, in light of our changed relationship, for you to call me by my first name?'

'Alright, Harold.'

Thus comforted, I fell into a dreamless sleep.

I was up at six o'clock, online and retrieving my emails. Now that I was doing this chore every day, I had fewer messages to deal with, and my eye was immediately drawn to the one from B.ARNOLD@cyberlandcafe.net. I clicked on the little envelope and a text message appeared.

Harry, Harry, Harry. What am I going to do with you? Russo's picture is for Ridgewood; for the lady, not for Bushwick. Bushwick's a dead end.

And watch your back in the Eight-Three. The talk is that you and your girlfriend should be stopped before you bring down the whole precinct.

When I re-entered the bedroom, Adele was sitting up with the bedclothes gathered about her waist. For some inexplicable reason, my eyes fell to her breasts which were small and set high on her chest, the swollen aureoles surrounding her nipples as smooth as butter.

'Do I have to get dressed?' Adele finally asked.

I sat on the edge of the bed, looked into her eyes and saw that she was pleased. Everybody wants to be desired and Adele was no exception. Nor was I. As I recounted the phone calls from Nydia Santiago and our anonymous angel, she reached out with her uninjured arm to pull me down alongside her. The touch of her hand was so casually sensual that my eyes narrowed and I breathed in through my nose as though reaching for some un-nameable and ultimately intoxicating fragrance. When Adele laid her head on my shoulder, I remember thinking, *if this is what comes of acting virtuously, I'll be a good boy forever*. Then I looked down at Adele and realized that I wouldn't have all that much choice in the matter.

THIRTY-FOUR

Over breakfast the following morning, Adele and I settled on an unpleasant topic we might have discussed earlier. First, we had been tailed on the previous night by two mutts who we then humiliated. Second, the talk among the rank and file in the Bushwick Precinct was that Detectives

260

Corbin and Bentibi should be stopped before they brought down the house. That made for an awful lot of suspects if one of us (or both of us) should meet a violent end.

I buttered a piece of toast, dipping it into the yolk of my egg. That we would have to move fast went unsaid, and our conversation drifted to Ellen Lodge. If we were to accomplish anything in the short term, she would have to come clean. Nevertheless, there were difficulties and no guarantee that I could overcome them.

'Ellen Lodge?' I told Adele. 'If you asked me yesterday, I would have told you that she was easy meat, that I was playing her like a violin. Now I'm beginning to think it's the other way round.'

'Maybe someone convinced her that she was better off staying the course. Maybe the same person who told her that Russo disappeared.'

'And who would that person be?'

'Someone inside the conspiracy, someone she trusts. Maybe Justin Whitlock.'

'Then who told Justin?'

The large dressing that covered the center of Adele's face had been abandoned in favor of three smaller dressings. Her bruises were now the color of French mustard, the swelling, except around her nose, greatly reduced. Her breathing had improved as well, and she was beginning to use her right arm. Nevertheless, fifteen minutes later, I had to help her into the body armor I insisted she wear, then into her coat.

The phone rang as I was about to unlock the door. I answered to find Bill Sarney on the other

261

end of the line.

'Can you talk?' he asked.

'Better make it fast, Adele's in the bedroom. We're sleeping in this morning.'

'Tell me what happened last night. In Sparkle's.'

I ignored the suspicious tone, taking care to keep my own voice casual. 'It was my idea, Bill,' I explained, 'to let her blow off steam. Otherwise, she was going to call that reporter from the *Times*, what's his name...?'

'Albert Gruber.'

'Yeah, Gruber.'

'She wants to call him?'

'What could I say, the woman's pissed off. When I tried to tell her that her attack could have been a random mugging, I thought she was gonna shoot me.'

Sarney's breath hissed into the phone. 'You think she'll listen to reason?'

'Yeah, Boss, I do. And getting it off her chest helped a lot. You just give it a few more days, Bill, and I guarantee she'll come around.'

As Adele and I drove south along Avenue A toward the Williamsburg Bridge, I considered Dante Russo's fate. Was he dead? Or had he run without playing the last cards in his hand? When I put the question to Adele, she laughed at me.

'Russo's most likely crab food by now,' she declared.

The thing about bodies is that they sink to the bottom when immersed in water. The thing about New York is that there's water within a

262

few miles of almost any place you happen to commit a murder. True, bodies eventually rise when enough gas builds up in the abdominal cavity. But if Russo was in one of the rivers, or in the harbor, that wouldn't happen until next spring when the water temperature became high enough for bacteria to multiply.

We were on our way back to Ridgewood, to the homes surrounding Ellen Lodge's, to do another canvas. Our mission was simple: to connect Dante Russo and Ellen Lodge. It didn't take us long.

Twenty minutes after I parked the car, a chatty senior citizen named Emma Schmidt took one look at Dante Russo's photo and said, 'That's the boyfriend.'

Emma's apartment, on the second floor of a three-story row house, was a virtual shrine to the Virgin Mary. Statues on the tables, prints on the wall, candles and rosaries everywhere. The red stitches of a framed sampler next to the window conveyed a simple message: PURITY.

'Whose boyfriend?' Adele asked.

'*Mrs* Ellen Lodge's boyfriend.' Emma pressed her bony knuckles against her hips and blinked rapidly as she spoke. 'Her husband wasn't in jail yet when this one showed up. Brazen is what he was. Marchin' up to her door in the middle of the night.'

We'd interviewed Emma Schmidt during our initial canvas of the neighborhood, but had failed to ask the right question. Emma was one of those neighborhood guardians I mentioned earlier. In good weather, she spent much of her

263

time sitting on a lawn chair in front of her house, gossiping with friends. Ellen Lodge, she informed us, had been the subject of their collective ire for so long, she'd ceased to be news.

The January thaw was in full swing. The temperature was in the lower fifties, the sun sharp-edged and molten yellow, the sky a deep uniform blue punctuated by streaming ribbons of cloud. A soft breeze carried the odor of earth stirring, of roots come to life, a promise of spring no less welcome for being an illusion.

We were standing directly in front of Ellen's row house, making ourselves as conspicuous as possible. From behind us, the January sun flared in the windows and softened the buttery-yellow facade; it glistened on the feathers of a dozen pigeons taking their ease along the edge of the roof. Except for their heads, which swiveled back and forth, turning at impossible angles in search of danger, the pigeons lay so unmoving they might have been decoys.

'You ready, Corbin?' Adele finally said as we approached the door.

'Shouldn't I be asking you that question?'

News of Russo's disappearance had forced Adele and me to overhaul our strategy and we'd made a number of significant changes. The first was that Adele would conduct the interview, at least initially, playing the bad cop for all she was worth. It was a part, we both agreed, that came naturally.

'I see it's bad penny time,' Ellen Lodge said when she opened the door. Again, I was struck by the muddy circles beneath her eyes, by a distinct weariness in the way she held her jaw. Her tone was firm, though, echoing the sarcasm in her words, and she led us to her sitting room without protest, resuming her seat in the room's lone armchair. I slid out of my coat, helped Adele out of hers, then folded both coats before taking a seat at the far end of the couch.

Adele removed a small tape recorder from her coat pocket, started it up and laid it on a hassock midway between herself and her subject. Surprise number one and a big test. Plausible denial was now off the table. 'Mrs Lodge, before we start, I want to make you aware of your constitutional rights.'

Ellen listened to Adele read from a printed card, controlling her impatience until Adele reached the part about representation by counsel. 'What if I ask for a lawyer?' she demanded. 'Right this minute.'

'Then my partner and I will leave.' Adele's reply was the only one she could make. With the tape running, plausible denial was off the table for us as well. 'Now, do you understand these rights as I've read them to you?'

'Yeah, sure.'

'And are you willing to waive those rights?'

Ellen Lodge's smile was a mere parting of the lips that revealed gritted teeth. This wasn't the way it was supposed to go. 'Fine, let's just get it over with.'

'Get *what* over with, Mrs Lodge?'

'Whatever it is you're doing here.'

'But you know what we're doing here, right?'

265

'Why don't you tell me?'

'Because you already know. You knew when you set your husband up with that phone call.' Adele waved off Ellen's reply. 'Like you said, Ellen, let's just get it over with. Let's get your story on the record.'

THIRTY-FIVE

Removing and folding our coats was as much a signal as reading Ellen her rights. We were in control. We would proceed at a pace that we alone determined. The interrogation would be over when we said it was. This may seem absurd in light of our professed willingness to vacate the premises on demand, but I was almost certain that Ellen Lodge intended to stay the course, no matter how painful.

Adele began with the same general questions I'd asked on the days following Lodge's murder. The responses she drew echoed the party line. Ellen had offered her husband a pillow on which to lay his head, not because she loved, or even liked him, but out of the goodness of her heart. On the day of his release, she'd been too busy to talk when he showed up late in the afternoon and their dinner conversation had amounted to nothing more than chit-chat. On the next morning, she'd awakened him to answer the phone, after which he'd quit the house.

Adele's fingers drummed on the arm of the couch as she absorbed this recitation, occasionally shaking her head in disbelief. Ellen continued on, doggedly. From time to time, as she considered her answers, she focused on the turning spools of the little tape recorder as though to draw strength.

'OK,' Adele said when Ellen finally grew silent, 'now that we've got the bullshit over with, let's talk about the letters. Tell us what you did with them.'

'I threw them out, because—'

'I don't need a reason. Tell me what was in them. Tell me what your husband had to say.'

'He wrote me that Clarence Spott's people were out for revenge. He wrote me that he was scared.'

'Did he mention Spott by name?'

That brought a moment of hesitation. What had she said at that first interview? But then she recalled her lines. 'I don't remember exactly. I think he did. I can't be sure.'

'My partner went up to Attica, Mrs Lodge. He was there for maybe three whole hours. In that time, he met a corrections officer, a deputy warden and a prison psychiatrist who say that your husband left Attica believing he was innocent, that the only revenge he was concerned about was the revenge he expected to wreak on the people who framed him. Explain how your version and their versions can be so different.'

'What about Pete Jarazelsky? He'll tell you Davy was afraid for his life.'

'Oh, right, Jarazelsky. As it turns out, what you

267

told us – that Pete and your husband were good buddies – was an outright lie. Not only didn't they watch each other's backs, we have reason to believe that Davy beat Jarazelsky to a pulp.'

Adele was perched on the edge of the couch now, within six feet of Ellen Lodge who was pushed as far back in her chair as she could get. I didn't blame Ellen. Between the look in Adele's eye, her various wounds and the body armor, she seemed truly ferocious, even in profile.

'Explain it,' Adele again demanded. 'Explain how these versions can be so utterly different.'

'I can't.' Ellen's eyes dropped to the tape recorder.

'So, then it's just a question of who I should believe: three disinterested professionals or a woman whose finances are tied up with Tony Szarek's, Justin Whitlock's and Dante Russo's? Put yourself in my position, Ellen. Who would you believe, if you were me?'

Though it was clear that Ellen Lodge didn't want to answer the question, Adele forced a response by repeating herself twice more. 'If you were me, who would you believe?'

Finally, Ellen said, 'You can believe who you want, but I'm telling the truth.' This time her eyes never left the tape recorder. This was what she had to say, no more, no less. But the effort seemed to cost her as she began to pick at a loose thread in the arm of the couch.

Adele was silent for a moment. Then she turned to me and asked me to retrieve a notebook in her coat pocket. When I complied, she flicked through several pages before asking a series of specific questions, each beginning with the phrase, 'Did your husband ever mention...'

His plans for the future. His job prospects. Friends he wanted to look up. Friends who could help him find a job. Dante Russo. Tony Szarek. Justin Whitlock.

Ellen's responses were evasive throughout, every statement included a qualifier. 'I don't remember, exactly, but ... I'm not a hundred per cent sure, but...' They continued to be evasive when Adele shifted to Ellen's prison visit, asking the same questions she'd asked about his letters, snapping them out, one after another, her contempt even more obvious because she refused to challenge Ellen's lies. Of course, David Lodge had discussed his future plans as the date of his release approached. The future is all convicts have. But Adele's questions weren't designed to elicit relevant information. Stamina is one of the big advantages cops have in the wars euphemistically called interrogations. Not only do we know how to pace ourselves, our suspects' fatigue invigorates us. And Ellen Lodge was visibly wilting, the effort required to maintain the lies taking its toll.

'Alright,' Adele said, 'let's move on to a subject we haven't discussed before. Your phone conversations with your husband. How many times did you speak to your husband in the three months prior to his release?'

This was another of those weapons we'd been saving. State prisoners are allowed to make collect calls, a privilege that can be withdrawn for misbehavior. Ellen's phone records indicated that she'd received sixteen collect calls from Attica in the three months before Davy got out. As this was fourteen more than she'd received in the prior six and a half years, it had naturally caught Adele's attention.

Once again, Ellen began with a series of qualifiers, but this time Adele stopped her in her tracks. 'Sixteen times,' she said, 'between October fourteenth and January fourteenth. Does that refresh your memory?'

Ellen shrugged. 'I didn't keep track.'

'Sixteen times in three months. Tell me, did you speak to your husband that frequently throughout his incarceration?'

'I don't remember exactly.'

'Then let me refresh your memory again. For the first seventy-eight months of the eighty-four months your husband spent in prison, you spoke to him exactly twice.'

'I don't recall exactly.'

Adele exploded. 'Don't lie in my face. You spent a total of more than four hours talking directly to your husband in the last three months. I want you to tell me what those calls were about. In detail.'

But Ellen Lodge had no choice, not at that point, and she continued to equivocate, as Adele continued to browbeat, asking exactly the same questions she'd asked about the letters and visits, until I finally stepped in. By that time, we'd been at it for three hours.

I intervened because good guy was my role

270

and because Ellen Lodge asked to use the bathroom. Whether she knew it or not, she'd acknowledged her subservience with the request, as she would have with any request.

Adele and I exchanged smiles, but said nothing in the few moments we spent alone. Instead, we slipped into a little kitchen to have a drink of water, to splash water on our faces. By the time Ellen emerged from the bathroom, we were back in place.

'Are we almost done?' she asked as she sat down. 'Because I have a dentist's appointment later this afternoon.'

As before, Adele ignored the question. 'Tell me about Greenpoint Carton Supply.'

Ellen began by announcing that (so far as she knew, of course) Greenpoint Carton was 'wholly owned' by Tony Szarek, Dante Russo and Pete Jarazelsky. That brought a smile to my lips. According to Szarek's sister, Trina Zito, Szarek's shares had reverted to the corporation upon his death. If Russo was crab food, as Adele believed, Pete Jarazelsky would be the last man standing. Pete, of course, had the ultimate alibi.

I made a mental note to call Attica and speak to Deputy Warden Frank Beauchamp, the mighty hunter. To ask a question I might have asked a lot earlier.

'They took me in,' Ellen said after a moment, 'because they knew I got a raw deal and they wanted to look out for me. I get paid two thousand dollars a month. I'm the secretary-treasurer, but I got no interest in the business. I'm not a partner.'

271

'Tell us what you do for the two thousand,' Adele asked. 'What are your duties?'

'I don't have any.'

'They pay you two thousand dollars a month for nothing?'

'I sign papers once in a while. That's it.'

Adele shifted forward on the seat. 'When did you become secretary-treasurer?'

'I was there from the beginning.'

'When was that?'

'About six months after Davy killed the pimp.'

'Was Greenpoint Carton in existence at that time? Or did they start it from scratch?'

'They bought the business.'

'Who from?'

'I don't know.'

'How much did they pay for it?'

'That wasn't my business. Anyway, the deal was done before I was offered my ... position.'

'And who offered you that position?'

'Dante.'

'Not Tony Szarek or Pete Jarazelsky.'

'I barely knew Tony and Pete.'

'You didn't visit Jarazelsky when you went up to Attica? Or exchange letters with him?'

'Never.'

'But you knew Dante Russo?'

'We were lovers.'

THIRTY-SIX

'Give me a fucking break,' Adele snarled. 'You weren't Dante Russo's lover. You were his whore.'

Finally energized, Ellen Lodge came halfway out of her chair. 'You bitch!' she shouted back. 'What right do you have to judge me?'

'Cut the crap. You're knocking down twenty-four grand a year for a no-show job given to you by a man who rings your bell in the middle of the night. And, yeah, we already knew about your sugar daddy. But you probably figured that out, being as you're a girl who takes care of number one.'

They both stood at that point, facing off across the hassock that held the tape recorder, their bodies now three feet apart.

'Funny thing, Ellen, but you don't look like you're grieving, not for your husband or for Dante Russo. You look like you're worried. But don't be. If you're a good girl, if you accept Russo's death the way you accepted your husband's, I'm sure that you'll be well rewarded. Oh, by the way, Russo didn't spend last Friday night in your bed, did he? You didn't make one of those six-second phone calls just after he left? You didn't set up Dante the way you set up your

273

husband?'

Ellen Lodge was sucking on her cheeks, narrowing an already narrow face, and her lips were moving rapidly. I think she would eventually have spoken if I hadn't stepped in for the second time.

'Partner,' I said, rising to my feet, 'do you think I could speak to you for a minute?'

In the hallway, out of Ellen Lodge's sight, Adele shrugged her shoulders. 'How'd I do?'

I answered by leaning down and kissing her (very gently, of course) on the lips. She touched a finger to her lips, her expression quizzical, then reached out to lay her hand on my chest before turning abruptly. I watched her trip down the stairs and out the door, realizing that there might, in fact, be something I wanted more than to break this case. As I walked back into the sitting room, I found myself imagining ten days with Adele in Hawaii, a sort of honeymoon in the course of which neither sand nor surf would even be glimpsed.

Ellen was standing by the window. She'd pulled a curtain aside to look down at the street. I assumed she was watching Adele get into the Nissan.

'So,' she said without turning, 'I take it that you're the good cop.'

The tape recorder clicked off at that point and I replaced the cassette before answering. 'You'll have to excuse my partner. She's a bit on the self-righteous side.'

I sat on the couch, in Adele's place, and invited

274

Ellen to resume her seat. She looked at me for a moment, her expression hard. I endured the glare.

'Please, Ellen, bear with me for another few moments.'

But she wasn't ready, not yet. 'You think I don't know how this works? For Christ's sake, I was a cop's wife. First, the bitch pounds on my brain for hours, then you ride to the rescue. Excuse me if I say that you don't look like anybody's white knight.'

'And what do I look like?'

'You look like a hard-ass cop who'd cut off his grandfather's balls to get a confession.' Satisfied, she finally sat down, then lit a cigarette. 'Hope you don't mind if I smoke.'

I waved her on, then asked, 'When did Russo become your lover? Before or after Clarence Spott was killed?' My tone was as gentle as I could make it.

'Right before.' She took another pull on her cigarette then flicked imaginary ash into an ashtray on the table alongside her chair. 'And I'm not makin' any apologies. I already told you what Davy was like. I needed something in my life and Dante was there.'

'I understand that. You were stuck in a childless, abusive marriage and Davy wouldn't let you escape. It's natural to look for comfort under those circumstances.' I might have added that comfort takes many forms: an embrace, a kind word, a birthday gift ... or eliminating the discomfort at its source. Instead, I asked, 'How did you meet him?'

'Davy brought Dante around when they became partners.'

'They were friends?'

'Dante felt sorry for Davy. He was trying to help him.'

'Then you believe your husband murdered Clarence Spott?'

'Davy was convicted of manslaughter, not murder. If you remember.' Ellen settled back in her chair, noticeably more relaxed now. True, she knew about good cop/bad cop, as did virtually every mutt I interrogated. But that didn't mean she could resist its charms.

'I know we spoke about this before,' I said, 'but I want you to describe your husband's abuse.' I nodded at the tape recorder. 'For the record.' When she hesitated, I added, 'That's why we started from the beginning. We just want to get your story down once and for all.'

As I'd hoped, the question triggered a response Ellen was unable to control. She'd been rehearsing her grievances for many years. Her injuries were her drug of choice, her dope, and like any junkie, she couldn't get through the day without them. Even in her most relaxed moments, they hung just below the surface, ever ready to impede an attack of conscience.

I let her run on, nodding occasionally as she described a series of progressively gruesome incidents. Her husband, or so she told me, was given to sexual humiliation. By submitting, she was usually able to avoid his fists. But submission (and survival, too) had its own penalties.

276

Over time, she'd built up a reservoir of self-hatred deep enough to drown in. And drown she did, falling into a depression that marked every hour of every day.

'Suicidal ideation,' she declared, her voice by then as soft as my own, 'that's what the shrinks call it. You think "suicidal ideation" describes my state of mind, detective?'

'I think it lacks poetry.'

She looked at me, her gaze mild, and I had the distinct impression that she wanted to trust me, as she'd once trusted Davy Lodge, as she'd trusted Dante Russo. For just a moment, I felt hopeful. Maybe if I got past her anger, she'd finally come clean.

From suicide, Ellen Lodge again turned to her destroyed expectations. Everybody, she claimed, has a right to a life. Her husband had taken hers as surely as if he'd pulled the trigger when he'd jammed his gun into her mouth. She was no longer the person she'd been when she met David Lodge. She was not the person she would have become had she never met him. Instead, she was an embittered, childless, middle-aged woman scrabbling for economic survival. The two thousand a month she got from Greenpoint Carton didn't cover her mortgage and taxes.

I watched Ellen's reserves gradually ebb, watched her shoulders slump and her breathing slow, until the little hand on the dial finally pointed to empty and she came to a stop. By that time, I was ready.

'Betrayal,' I said, my voice so soft Ellen had to lean forward to catch my words, 'I know what it

277

is. My parents were junkies. They did coke, speed and whatever pills they could get their hands on. Percocets, Dilaudid, Codeine, Valium, Darvon, Ritalin, Demerol.' I paused long enough to take a breath. 'They got away with it because this was back in the Seventies when people were more tolerant of druggies, and because it's almost impossible to fire civil servants, which both of them were. They missed a few days of work? They came in late? They snorted coke twice an hour to get through the day? Well, I remember one time my father was suspended for a week, and another time my mother was forced into rehab, and there might have been other punishments as well. I wouldn't know about them because my parents mostly acted like I wasn't there.'

I shifted my weight slightly, and crossed my legs. My eyes drifted to my hands, as if my revelations were so intimate I couldn't look her in the face. 'You know, when you're a kid, you blame yourself for everything. That's because if you're not causing your own pain, you have no control at all. In some ways, it's like having a gun put to your head. I mean, where are you gonna run to when you're a five-year-old? To your relatives? My mother was from St Louis and my father's parents were living in Arizona. Plus, my parents' friends were druggies, too.'

When I finally raised my eyes to meet Ellen's, her gaze was intense, but not skeptical. Encouraged, I again spoke.

'OK, so you're a kid and your parents barely know you're alive and you blame yourself. What

278

do you do?'

'You try to become better.'

'Is that what you did with your husband?'

The question produced a short, choppy laugh devoid of mirth. 'Yeah, why not? I was only eighteen when I married Davy. I thought if I did better – if I cooked better, if I wore that lingerie he liked – things would improve. Ya wanna hear something really sad? I used to read sex manuals on how to please a man.'

'Well, I didn't go quite that far. But I started keeping my room clean, which was mostly what my parents complained about. I mean, by the time I was seven, my room would've passed a military inspection.'

'And your folks?'

'I got a couple of pats on the head, but then the novelty wore off and it was like it never happened. Ya gotta picture them here, Ellen. Most of the time, they used downers and I'd find them laid out like zombies on the couch. When they lucked into a few grams of cocaine, they'd suddenly come awake. I swear, it was like a resurrection. They'd pile the coke on a mirror, then place the mirror, dead center, on what was supposed to be the dining-room table. And that's exactly where they'd remain, staring down at that pile until it was fully consumed. I'm tellin' ya, I figured out, at a very early age, that the pile was a lot more important than I was. I wasn't allowed anywhere near it.'

THIRTY-SEVEN

Most of what I'd told Ellen, up to that point, was true, if greatly oversimplified. But the truth didn't matter to me, any more than I minded using my personal history to lure Ellen into making a statement against her penal interests. And, yes, Ellen Lodge was right about my grandfather. Which only put me on a par with any other good detective. The important thing was that I had Ellen's full attention as I began to play with the facts.

The long-term failure of my clean-bedroom strategy, I declared, hadn't discouraged me, not in the slightest. And why should it? A few pats are better than no pats at all. Just ask any dog.

I went on to describe how, in the course of about a year, I became a cleaning maniac, a master of the vacuum cleaner and the dust cloth, the mop and the broom. I was the scrubber of bathrooms, washer of windows, polisher of floors, king of the laundry. There was nothing I wouldn't do, no effort I wouldn't make, until the apartment was finally clean enough to withstand the scrutiny of a nineteenth century German housewife.

As I plunged into pure hyperbole, I became more and more animated. By degrees, my mouth expanded into the sort of comfortable smile that might be exchanged by two members of a support group over a post-session cup of coffee.

'One time,' I finally declared, 'I painted the entire living room while my parents watched reruns on Comedy Central.'

'You lie. There wasn't any Comedy Central thirty years ago.'

'No, I swear. It took me five hours, but you want to know the most amazing part? My parents' eyes never left the screen. And they never laughed, not once. They were too stoned.'

Ellen's smile was both amused and ironic. 'God,' she said, 'when you look back, you feel like such an idiot.'

'That's not the way it is for me. I don't blame myself, never. Hey, I haven't spoken to my mom in twenty years. When my father passed, I wasn't at his bedside and I didn't go to his funeral.'

I gave it a good five seconds, until the silence grew dense enough to notice, then went into the pocket of my jacket, removing the photo I'd taken from Marissa Aubregon's apartment, the one with Marissa perched on Dante Russo's lap. Working carefully, I unfolded the snapshot, smoothing the creases before leaning forward to lay it on Ellen's knees.

'Betrayal is what it was about, Ellen. That's why you don't have to blame yourself. You can hate the ones who hurt you instead.' I paused long enough to let the message sink in, then asked, 'You knew about this, didn't you?'

* * *

Ellen lit another cigarette with her disposable lighter, holding the end of the cigarette in the flame a moment too long as she weighed her options. I'd played my last card and we both knew it. She had to make up her mind now.

'Yeah,' she finally whispered, 'I did.' She dropped the cigarette into an ashtray and ran her fingers through her hair. 'Ya know how I said that I always wanted a kid?'

'I remember.'

'Well, I told Dante, "You don't have to marry me. You don't have to pay child support. I just want to have your child."'

'And what'd he say?'

'That he couldn't father a child and not take care of it. That he didn't think he'd be a good father. That he just wasn't prepared for the responsibility. Sometimes, when I brought it up, he'd get angry. Dante never raised a hand to me, not like Davy, but he could be very cold. And when he was really pissed, I just wouldn't hear from him, not until I called to apologize.'

'So, it must have been hard when you found out that he fathered Marissa's child.'

The look in Ellen Lodge's eyes was so wistful, I turned away. As I'd predicted, the outrage she'd marshaled in the face of Adele's onslaught had vanished. Now she was moving, not into a confessional mode, as I'd hoped, but into an attitude of resignation.

'She called me up. Marissa. I don't know how she found out about me and Dante, but she called and told me that Dante belonged to her, that she'd had his child.'

282

'And when did this happen?'

'Three weeks ago, maybe a month.'

'What did you do?'

Ellen's gaze dropped to the tape recorder. She watched the spools turn for a moment. 'Nothing,' she finally said. 'I didn't even confront the bastard. Davy was about to be released from Attica and I was already in over my head.'

The overall impression Ellen gave, as she told her story, was of a beaten-down woman upon whose back the last straw, Russo's infidelity, had been heaped. But the relief that naturally follows a true confession, whether it be made to a priest or a detective, was entirely absent. What I sensed was a grim surrender, bolstered by an unexpected measure of true grit. Ellen may have spent much of her time wallowing in her grievances, but there was a tougher part of her, a rational, calculating self that had done hard things in hard times.

And then there was the content of her remarks. At one point, I almost felt sorry for Dante Russo. He was at the center of every misdeed from the very beginning. It was Dante who'd convinced her that Davy killed Clarence Spott, and it was at Dante's request that she'd advised her husband to plead guilty.

'After he got sentenced, I hoped that would be the end of it,' she announced. 'Then Davy started writing to me, telling me how sorry he was. I mostly threw the letters in the garbage.'

'Mostly? Does that mean you answered some of them?'

'I told him to stop writing to me and that I didn't expect to see him after he got out. As far as I was concerned, we were through. One time I wrote that if he came around, I'd go to his parole officer. "The minute I see your face," I said, "I'm on the phone."'

That approach was jettisoned six months before Davy's release, when Dante Russo came calling. Far from his usually reserved self, Dante was extremely agitated. David Lodge, he explained, had become delusional and now believed he was innocent. Worse still, he was threatening bodily harm to all those who'd testified before the Grand Jury.

At this point, Ellen quoted Russo verbatim: '"We tried to talk to the jerk, but it was no good. When the guy gets a bug up his ass, it's like he becomes a maniac."'

Three weeks later, after submitting to a search of her bag and the scrutiny of a metal detector, Ellen had found herself seated across from her husband. A notice pasted on the yellowed Plexiglass screen separating them announced that visits were randomly monitored. Davy had pointed to his side of this notice when his wife mentioned Dante Russo, then had shaken his head.

Back home, Ellen began to write her husband and to accept his collect calls, only to find that the same principle applied. Letters and phone calls were also routinely monitored. Thus, the only facts Ellen had at her disposal were those supplied by Dante Russo. This was why she still believed her husband to be Clarence Spott's murderer on the morning of January 15th when she summoned him to the phone, then made a call of her own just after he left the house. The calls, of course, coming and going, were made and received by Dante Russo.

'I thought they were going to ... to confront him. Maybe even to threaten him. I never thought they were going to kill him.'

'Did Russo actually say he killed your husband?'

When she nodded, I pointed to the tape recorder. The words would have to be spoken aloud.

'Yeah,' she finally said, 'he did. I had to push him to the wall, but he finally told me that he'd been there, that he'd pulled the trigger.'

'Alright, now you said you thought "they" were going to confront Davy. Tell me who "they" are?'

But, alas, other than Tony Szarek, who was dead, and Pete Jarazelsky, who was incarcerated, Ellen didn't know the names of Dante's associates, any more than she knew her lover's fate. Dante, it seemed, like Davy Lodge, was a man who kept his own counsel.

'Ya know, he didn't even use my telephone. He made calls on his cell. I guess that should've told me something right there.'

I turned off the tape recorder and got on my own cell phone at that point, phoning down to Adele, summoning her back to the fray. When she was standing beside me, I compressed the bad news into a single sentence: 'Dante did it.'

'All by himself?'

'In the company of persons still to be named.'

'But not by Ellen Lodge?'

'Apparently not.'

We still had a couple of choices open to us. Adele might have taken another shot at playing the bad cop or I might have again appealed to Ellen's survival instincts by pointing out that the game was growing ever more dangerous. But it was nearly three o'clock and time was running short.

'You wanna hook her up?' Adele asked.

'Fine, but I'm leaving the frisk to you.'

'What's going on here?' Ellen demanded.

'We're placing you under arrest for conspiracy in the first degree.'

'What's that supposed to mean?'

'It means that you conspired to commit an A-One felony: the murder of your husband.'

'But I didn't. I didn't know what was going to happen.' When I failed to respond, she half-shouted, 'Yesterday, you said you were gonna protect me.'

Ellen's gaze dropped to the tape recorder and its unmoving spools. There was a record now and she would have to live with it. I watched her reactions carefully, hoping against hope that she'd revise her strategy. Instead, her eyes narrowed as she rose to her feet and placed her hands behind her back. 'Would it be alright,' she asked, 'if I brought along a little make-up? I wanna look my best when we do the perp walk.'

THIRTY-EIGHT

Despite the snow, I came up the block on foot, the closest parking space I could find two blocks away. It was much colder now and the wind was on the rise, pushing the heavy flakes in my direction, coating my head and shoulders before I covered fifteen feet. The snow screened me from view, so that I was almost on top of the One-Sixteen before the half-dozen cops huddled on the small porch fronting the entrance were aware of my presence. It was 3:45 p.m., a busy time in every precinct. The eight-to-four shift was coming in from the field, the four-to-midnight preparing to go out.

I was walking with Ellen Lodge to my left, holding onto her elbow. Though Ellen's coat was draped over her shoulders, hiding her cuffed wrists from view, I doubt that anybody was fooled into thinking she was a casual visitor. The chatter stopped dead when I was finally recognized, leaving only the soft wet sound of our footsteps in the slush and the steady moan of the wind.

Inside, the reception area was crowded with cops, male and female, waiting to be mustered out. They were beginning their night's toil and relatively energized, making small talk, joking,

287

laughing. I'd worked hard to establish a good working relationship with these folks, knew most of them by sight and four or five by name. In their collective eyes I now found the sort of forlorn shock I associated with news footage of ordinary citizens informed that the guy down the block is a serial killer.

And he seemed like such a nice man.

The desk officer, a lieutenant named Draper, found his voice as we approached the stairs leading to the squad room.

'Whatta ya got there, Harry?'

I led Ellen up a few steps before replying. All eyes were turned to me, which was what I'd hoped for and why I'd sought an elevated position in the first place.

'I've got Ellen Lodge,' I said evenly, 'under arrest for conspiring to murder her husband. His name is David Lodge, in case you haven't heard.'

'Hey, I don't need the sarcasm.' Draper turned to a patrol sergeant standing at his elbow. 'What a jerk,' he declared with a nod in my direction. 'He don't know who his friends are.'

But we were already moving up the stairs and into the squad room where we found Jack Petro and Bill Sarney, along with a trio of four-to-midnight tour detectives gathered around a bag of donuts. Petro was sitting behind his desk with his mouth open. Sarney was on the other side of the desk, his coat draped over his arm, his customary fedora already jammed over his naked scalp.

I watched Sarney's face redden, his hands

tighten into fists, his neck swell, his eyes bulge. Far from intimidated, it was all I could do to maintain a neutral expression as I repeated the message I'd offered to the desk officer: Ellen Lodge, wife of David Lodge, was under arrest for conspiring to murder her husband. Then I led Ellen Lodge to an interrogation room, removed her handcuffs, and told her to make herself comfortable. As I made my exit, she favored me with a string of curses, concluding her tirade with a demand that she be allowed to call her lawyer.

'You betrayed me.' Sarney's small dark eyes were glittery with rage, his forehead a mass of wrinkles all the way to the center of his scalp. We were alone now, in his office. 'You were on your way from nowhere to nowhere, running out the string on a nothing career, a step away from being a hairbag. I gave you homicide, Harry, and I got you promoted. Me, and nobody else. You hear what I'm sayin'? In your whole career, I'm the only one who recognized you for what you were. How is it that you can turn on me, now, when I really need you? For Christ's sake, you were at my kid's christening.'

I started to speak, but Sarney waved me off. 'And the worst part,' he told me, 'is that I personally vouched for you. I told Borough Command that you'd do the right thing. I took fucking responsibility. What am I supposed to say now?'

'Tell them what you just told me,' I suggested before he could go on. 'Tell them you gave it a

289

hundred per cent, but I played you anyway. I'm sure our conversations were recorded, just like Adele's phones were tapped, so you should come off believable.'

That brought him to a halt and he dropped down in his chair. 'You fucked me,' he warned, 'and I'm not gonna forget it. Sooner or later, I'll pay you back.'

I might have responded directly, but my mind was on other things. The case against Ellen Lodge, which I was going to have to justify, was flimsy. There was Ellen's recorded statement, complete with Miranda warning, and there was a documented call that might have been placed to anyone. Beyond that ... nothing.

'Do you think,' I asked, 'that we can get down to business? Because it's gonna be a long night, even without the lecture.'

Sarney's mouth twisted into a bitter smile. 'Yeah,' he said, 'by all means. And this better be good.'

But it wasn't good enough, that was obvious, and by the time I wound it up, Sarney's relief was apparent. 'This is garbage,' he finally declared. 'Lemme see that tape.'

'We're talking about tapes, boss, as in more than one. But I don't have them anyway. My partner has them.'

'You're sayin' you can't trust me with evidence, that maybe I'd flush those tapes down the toilet?' He might have come after me at that point, if he was just a little bigger, a little younger. As it was, he settled for pounding the side of his fist into the blotter on top of his desk. Then he did it again.

'If that's your only comment, Boss, I've got paperwork to do.'

'You got nothin'. I'm cutting her loose.'

'Why?'

'Show me one piece of physical evidence tying Dante Russo to the murder of David Lodge. Bring me an eyewitness. Better yet, prove that Ellen Lodge isn't telling the truth when she says she didn't know what was gonna happen to her husband.'

I countered with my best argument. 'Lodge admits she called Russo and she claims that Russo copped to the murder. Plus, she has a dual motive for wanting her husband dead. First, there was the money from Greenpoint Carton, which doesn't sound like a lot until you see how she was living. Second, there was the simple fact that she absolutely hated her husband. Ya know, Ellen was pretty much in control for the whole six hours. She only flipped out when she spoke about Davy. Believe me when I tell you, lieutenant, that the widow did not hold anything back.'

I sat down on the chair fronting his desk before continuing. 'And don't forget the lies. We did four interviews with Ellen Lodge. In the last interview she admits that every essential element of the first three interviews was untrue. So, why would a jury believe she's telling the truth about the one little item that exonerates her?'

When Sarney leaned forward to place his elbows on the desk, his swivel chair emitted a double screech that reminded me of a braying donkey. 'Take this to the bank, Corbin: a good defense attorney is gonna get this case dismissed before it goes to trial, even if a grand jury indicts her. And those lies she told don't mean shit. Everybody lies to the cops.'

We continued on for another few minutes, going back and forth, until I finally conceded that while the evidence against Ellen Lodge justified an arrest, a conviction might be difficult to obtain. The admission brought a faint smile from Sarney, but I quickly erased it when I said, 'But that's only because of the cover-up.'

Sarney looked out over my head. His office was little more than a glass-walled cubicle and I'd spoken loud enough for my words to be clear to anyone still remaining in the squad room.

'The evidence you're demanding is out there to be found,' I continued. 'I would have found it on my own, if I hadn't been pulled off the case. For example, the crime scene where DuWayne Spott overdosed? I admit that I didn't get much of a look at it before I was relieved, but what I did see was discarded garbage, soiled utensils, blankets and mattresses. We both know this evidence went into storage when the job decided that Spott's death resulted from an accidental overdose. Likewise for the evidence collected at the David Lodge scene. DuWayne killed David Lodge? There isn't going to be a trial because DuWayne is conveniently dead? Time to conserve our limited resources by packing the physical evidence into a box, then shipping it to the property clerk's office.'

Sarney attempted to interrupt, but I was well

into my act by then. 'Now take Ellen Lodge's phone records. Given that we know there were two shooters present when her husband was killed, and that we suspect she's covering for somebody by throwing all the blame on Dante Russo, it would be nice to run back through her phone records for the last six months. Just on the off-chance that she made contact with an unknown co-conspirator. But, of course, being as it's not my case, I have no way to get those records.'

I went on for some time, mentioning, along the way, Clarence Spott's vehicle, somehow unaccounted for on the night he was killed, the sad lack of scrutiny paid to the Broom's sudden demise, the failure to capitalize on Jarazelsky's parole status, and Ted Savio, the lawyer shared by David Lodge, Justin Whitlock, Pete Jarazelsky and Ellen Lodge.

'The finances,' I concluded, 'are the key. Russo's, Jarazelsky's, Szarek's, Ellen Lodge's, and most of all Greenpoint Carton's. Once we start tracing the money, the house of cards is gonna come crashing down.'

Sarney raised a finger, as if he expected to win on a technicality. 'Only a grand jury can subpoena financial records. And a grand jury can only be convened by the DA. You know that, right?'

'That's why Ellen Lodge has to be arrested. Look, David Lodge became a celebrity on the day he was charged with killing Clarence Spott. That's why his murder drew media scrutiny in the first place. So, what do you think's gonna

293

happen when the reporters find out his wife's been arrested for his murder?'

Sarney shuddered. 'If that were to happen,' he said, 'blood would flow.'

'Not necessarily.' I waited until Sarney's eyes rose to meet mine. 'If the job admits it made mistakes, then moves to clean house, the damage can be limited. There are bad apples in every barrel, right? On the other hand, if Ellen Lodge is released and some insider leaks it to the media after the fact? Think about it, lou. Think about what's gonna happen if Ellen Lodge is released on your authority. Think about what the job will do to protect itself. Think about what it feels like to be the official NYPD scapegoat.'

I expected Sarney to explode at that point, but he surprised me, perhaps because he'd already considered this outcome.

'Wait in the squad room,' he ordered, 'and see that Ellen Lodge gets to call her lawyer.'

Jack Petro and the four-to-midnight detectives were standing by the door when I came out. They fled at my appearance, which was fine by me. I knew they'd repeat the conversation they'd overheard to every cop they came across. That was all I wanted from them.

Ellen Lodge was considerably more subdued when I offered her my cell phone. She'd been contemplating her fate for an hour by this time.

'You still have options,' I explained, 'if you want to take them.'

She stared at the phone for a moment, her expression puzzled, as if she was having difficulty remembering what it was for. Then she said,

'You think I could use the bathroom?'

I accompanied her, but, of course, had to remain outside, risking the chance that she'd escape through the window. She didn't, emerging instead with her face scrubbed. Again, I made an attempt to reach her.

'Conspiracy in the first degree is an A-One felony,' I said. 'It carries a maximum penalty of life without parole, which you are very likely to get. We're looking at five murders here.'

Ellen shook her head. 'You're not supposed to talk to me without my lawyer present.'

'Well, that's just it, that lawyer. What you wanna do is instruct him to cut the best deal possible in return for your truthful testimony. It's the only way out.'

I could see it in her eyes, the message hitting home. She hadn't been expecting an arrest and was unprepared for the rigors to follow. Unless Sarney cut her loose, she'd be looking at a night on Rikers Island, then a very brief appearance before an arraignment judge who would remand her without bail, the fate of all accused murderers in New York City.

I led Ellen back to the interrogation room and left her with my cell phone. When I returned a few minutes later to retrieve the phone, I asked, 'You have any luck?'

'My lawyer will be here in an hour.'

'And what lawyer would that be?'

'Theodore Savio.'

Inspector Thaddeus Clark, accompanied by Sergeant Joe Flaherty, beat the lawyer by a good fifteen minutes. They barged into Sarney's office, without knocking and without so much as glancing in my direction. A few seconds later, the blinds came crashing down.

I recognized both men. From his office at Queens North Borough Command, Clark supervised the detective squads in six NYPD precincts. Flaherty was his driver.

When Theodore Savio arrived, he too went directly to Sarney's office, though he did pause long enough to knock before opening the door. Savio was tall, slender and well-dressed. He wore a Russian fur hat, undoubtedly sable, and a black overcoat, undoubtedly cashmere. Everything about the coat, from the fit of the shoulders to the ruler-straight drop from armpit to hem, was perfect.

Savio emerged less than a minute later. He crossed the room to a wooden coat rack near the stairwell, took off his hat and coat, finally hung them on hooks. 'Now,' he said, turning to me, 'if you'll kindly show me to my client.'

Though he maintained a polite smile throughout, Savio's overall intensity was apparent. He was young and hard-charging, with a long face, a square determined chin and the shoulders of a linebacker. If possible, his charcoal gray suit fit him even better than his coat.

I led him to his client, then walked back to my desk. For a short time, I fiddled with the five I'd eventually have to write, but then my thoughts began to wander.

The anger of my superiors, I decided, was nothing more than vanity. In their world, communication flowed in one direction only, from higher to lower. Pissant detectives, like myself, were supposed to take orders and keep their mouths shut. My failure to do so was not only a challenge to their authority but an affront to their dignity as well. The saddest part was that, if asked, each of these ranking officers would claim that their primary concern was to protect the Department. But what they were really protecting was their own asses. That was made clear ten minutes later when Flaherty summoned me into Sarney's office.

Inspector Clark cleared his throat as I entered. 'I want those tapes,' he said, 'and any copies you may have made.'

'What are you going to do with them?' I asked.

'None of your goddamned business.' Clark's hair was ghostly white and extremely fine. He wore it pasted flat against his skull, an affectation that drew attention to his shaggy eyebrows and oversized, horn-rimmed glasses. The rap on him was that he was a self-important ass who'd kill for a promotion to deputy chief.

'Did you hear what I said, detective?'

'Inspector,' I said, 'as I already told the lieutenant, I don't have the tapes. My partner has them.' I raised my arms. 'But if you wanna search me, I'm willing to give consent.'

'I don't need to hear that smart mouth. Where's your partner?'

'I'm not sure.'

Clark made an attempt to stare me down, but I simply absorbed the wrath pouring from his blue eyes. It was a little late in the game for intimidation. Finally, he said, 'I'm putting you on suspension. Place your badge and your weapon on the desk.'

'What's the charge?'

'Conduct unbecoming an officer.'

'And what conduct would that be?'

Clark leaned toward me, his little twisty mouth arranging itself in a smile. 'If you don't put your badge and weapon on that desk, and I mean right the fuck now, you're gonna find yourself in a cell next to Ellen Lodge.'

And what could I say to that? I took out the billfold holding my badge and ID, laid it on Sarney's desk, then followed the billfold with my Glock. Though I felt naked and exposed without the badge, surrendering the weapon didn't bother me at all. That was because I had a Smith & Wesson .38 snugged into a holster attached to my ankle. This was one outcome I'd been anticipating for days.

'It doesn't matter anyway,' I said. 'The investigating part is over. I've gone as far as I have to.'

'Is that supposed to be a threat?'

I responded by turning my back, then opening the door to reveal Ted Savio huddled with Adele Bentibi and Assistant District Attorney Ginnette Lansky. For a moment, I was as shocked as anybody in the room, but then Adele glanced up to flash a smile I knew well. She'd won again.

Lansky was well turned out in a brown leather coat that fell to mid-calf, a pair of suede boots and an orange scarf that hung open. She was

298

standing with her hands in the pockets of her coat when I opened the door, her lips moving rapidly as she communicated some urgent message to Theodore Savio.

'Mother of God,' Clark whispered, 'what have you done now?'

I was pretty certain the 'you' referred to Harry Corbin, but I didn't react. Ms. Lansky was walking directly toward me and I stepped aside to let her into the office before returning to my desk. Then Ted Savio went off to advise his client, leaving me alone with Adele. She took my hand and squeezed it. I returned the pressure before asking, 'Bad news for the widow?'

'Mixed news.'

'How so?'

'Well, she's going to be arrested, Corbin, and she'll have to spend the night in jail. But if she survives, the judge will release her tomorrow morning on her own recognizance. At the prosecution's request, of course.'

'Of course.' I was captivated by Adele's exuberance. She was as happy as I'd ever seen her.

'It was Ginnette's idea, but I have to admit it's brilliant.' Adele put her left hand on her hip. Her right was still cradled by the sling. 'Accused felons, if they're incarcerated, have to be indicted within a hundred and twenty hours of arrest. But if they're not incarcerated, the grand jury can investigate for months before delivering an indictment. And there's no limit on what the grand jury can investigate, either.'

The news was so good that my initial reaction

was to pick it apart. How, I wanted to know, could Adele be sure the DA, possibly in league with the NYPD, wouldn't bury the investigation? Especially in light of the fact that grand jury proceedings are secret.

The answer was simple enough. Ellen Lodge's arrest would be made public on the following morning. At the press conference, District Attorney Kenneth Alessio would announce that the grand jury charged with indicting Ellen Lodge would investigate every aspect of the case, from Clarence Spott's murder seven years before, to Dante Russo's disappearance. The only issue still to be resolved was whether the task force to be established would include NYPD personnel or be staffed entirely by the DA's own investigators.

Does it hurt *now*? Does it hurt *now*?

An hour later, when Bill Sarney returned my gun and badge, I was so high, I thought I'd explode.

THIRTY-NINE

If it weren't for the rat, Adele and I would have been inside the Nissan when the RAV-4, screened by the falling snow, pulled away from the curb with its headlights off. If it wasn't for the rat, I would certainly have been preoccupied – starting the Nissan in cold weather was a

300

challenge that required my complete attention. If it weren't for the rat, Adele would have been inside the car, facing forward, her view restricted by the wiper blades running across the windshield.

Trapped in a small enclosed space? With no warning? Time to sing your death song.

But we weren't inside the Nissan when the RAV-4 pulled away from the curb. Instead, having cleared the windows of snow and opened the door, I was circling the car, pounding on the roof, the hood and the windows. Just in case some mischievous co-worker had decided to play a little joke on me. The unattended Nissan had been parked a couple of blocks from the precinct for nearly four hours.

Adele was standing by the passenger's door when I finally got to the trunk, watching me with apparent amusement. Then she glanced over my shoulder toward the end of the block and her eyes narrowed.

'Heads up, Corbin,' she said as she slipped her right arm out of the sling. 'I think we're gonna have company.'

I spun around to find the silver SUV a half-block away, its tires spinning in several inches of frozen slush despite the four-wheel drive. On the passenger side, the head, shoulders and right arm of a man extended through the fully open window. Though the snow was falling pretty hard and I couldn't see his hand clearly, I was fairly certain the object he clutched was not a wallet. Nevertheless, though I drew my Glock and laid the sights on the center of his face, I did not fire my weapon until fired upon. Nor did I seek cover. I simply stood there, ignoring the wet, wind-driven snow in my face, muzzle flashes that lit the falling lines of snow with the intensity of a strobe, the SUV itself, which fishtailed back-and-forth, passing within a few feet of my body before describing a complete circle, then finally crashing into a mini-van parked near the corner.

The whole business took no more than a few seconds. I'd fired my weapon six times as the vehicle approached, then passed me, carefully re-sighting after each shot. All the while, I was aware of Adele's .40 caliber AMT firing behind me. That she continued to pull the trigger after the man shooting at us abruptly stopped was reassuring. True, the RAV-4 had been fishtailing from side to side, but there was still the chance that one of the bullets pegged in our general direction had found its mark.

'You hurt, Corbin?'

In fact, despite my inner calm, I'd somehow bitten deep enough into my lower lip to draw blood. 'Outside of a self-inflicted bite wound, I seem to have escaped without harm.' My weapon extended, I began to approach the RAV-4. 'And you?'

'Never better.'

I came up on the driver's side first. The RAV-4 was nosed almost vertically into the side of the mini-van and both its air bags had deployed upon impact. Though I couldn't know it at the time, the driver, foolish enough to pilot the vehicle without fastening his seat belt, had been killed by his air bag and not by any of the four bullets that passed through the windshield. I only knew that when I put my fingers to his throat, he had no pulse to take.

As for the second man, the shooter, he'd been hit twice in the face, once near his mouth, the other almost dead center in his forehead. I didn't bother to take his pulse, nor did I worry about making an identification. These were the same two men who'd trailed us in their boss's Jaguar on the previous night.

What a party we had. Internal Affairs, a shooting team, homicide and squad detectives, the Crime Scene Unit, the morgue wagon, a gaggle of overly caffeinated bosses, a pack of media jackals – everybody showed up. At one point, the job brought in a Winnebago outfitted as a command center. Since there was nothing to command, I assumed its function was to give the big dogs a private space in which to consume the coffee and donuts fetched for them by a series of fawning lieutenants.

Adele and I were separated, then subjected to thorough interrogations. But the shooting was justified and there was no getting past it. At one point, when we were alone, Inspector Clark whispered, 'You're a hero now, you hump, but trust me on this: unless you walk away from the job, there's gonna be a later on.'

I thanked him for his kind words, but held onto my shield nonetheless.

Adele had another problem, this one more immediate, but she managed to work her way past it. Somehow, she'd failed to register her AMT with the job, an oversight that could have resulted in departmental charges being filed against her. But Adele cleverly pointed out that she wasn't on duty, she was on vacation, plus as a police officer, she was legally entitled to possess the weapon in New York State. The bosses, she later told me, were grateful for the technicality. If we were to be presented as heroes, however briefly, tainting Adele would obviously be counter-productive.

It was approaching nine o'clock when a uniformed officer summoned me to the command center where I found Adele waiting alone. I wanted to put my arms around her, but settled for a wink. A moment later, Bill Sarney stepped inside and closed the door behind him.

'Congratulations,' he said, 'you won.'

'It's not a game,' Adele replied.

'Don't go there.'

But Adele was on a roll and she simply continued. 'It's not a football game, lieutenant, one side wins, the other side loses, next week we get to do it all over again. It's real people really getting killed and the NYPD acquiescing to an innocent man being framed for another man's crime.'

Far from losing his temper, Sarney folded his arms across his chest and completed his mission. It was over now, for better or for worse.

'You're being put on paid administrative leave until you're cleared to work by a department shrink,' he told us without addressing Adele's

304

accusation. 'Make the appointment whenever you're ready. You wanna take a month, fine. You wanna take a year, that's also fine.'

But Adele wasn't about to be bribed. She reached into her purse, withdrew the wallet holding her badge and ID, then tossed the wallet to Sarney. 'You're never going to get the message,' she declared. 'Never.'

Sarney looked down at the wallet in his hands, then slowly raised his eyes to meet mine. 'What about you, Harry? You wanna give up your shield?'

'Not me, boss. And I'm gonna make that appointment right away. I can't wait to get all this horrible killing off my chest so I can come back to work.'

FORTY

It was eleven o'clock before CSU cleared my vehicle, and another twenty minutes before Adele and I were able to clear the snow around it. I remained patient throughout the process. Not so Adele, who strode back and forth, her hands folded across her chest, watching the crime scene cops as if she believed they were aware of our plans and willfully delaying us.

I discovered the reason for her agitation only as we pulled away from the curb. 'We have another stop to make,' she told me. 'At Sparkle's.'

'Are you talking about Linus Potter?'

'Yes.'

Though I steered the Nissan toward the requested destination, I didn't reply for a moment. I'd been speculating on the identity of our anonymous informant from the beginning. Certainly, I'd suspected Linus Potter. I'd even called him by name in the course of our phone conversations, casting a bait to which he hadn't risen. But my suspicions were no more than a hunch based on our face-to-face talks. There was no evidence to connect him to any of the known co-conspirators.

I looked at Adele. She was staring out through the windshield, her expression set, a woman who knew exactly what she had to do and why she had to do it. There could be only one reason for her determination.

'It was Potter who attacked you,' I finally said, my tone more final than accusing.

'His face was covered, Corbin. But the tiny head, the shoulders, the gorilla chest – there's no doubt in my mind.'

'So, why didn't you tell me? Better yet, why did you say that you had no memory of what happened to you?'

Adele drew a breath, then turned far enough to look into my face. 'That night, when you came into my room in the hospital, I didn't know exactly where you stood. Later, after we made love, I was afraid that you'd go after him if I told you what really happened. There was other work to do first.'

The explanation only provoked another burst

of resentment, even though I knew she was right. Our methodical, step-by-step investigation had sealed the fate of all the conspirators, including Linus Potter. There was no escape for any of them. If I'd started with Linus, on the other hand, we might have lost everyone.

'That night,' Adele continued, 'I saw Potter as he came out from behind a parked SUV. He was carrying an aluminum baseball bat, holding it above his right shoulder with both hands. Somehow, I managed to raise an arm as I tried to duck into his body. I didn't get clear, of course, that's obvious. But I was able to move close enough to avoid the heavy part of the bat. Potter hit me with the thin part, the handle, which is the only reason I'm talking to you right now.'

I watched her eyes fill as she re-lived her attack, as the fear returned, and I had to wonder how many times the memories had swarmed, like bats from a cave, to invade her consciousness. In many ways, my own life had been an attempt to avoid the various terrors that propelled me through early adolescence, an attempt never entirely successful. Sure, I can hold them at bay, vampires before a cross, while I'm awake. But at night, in my dreams, they often come out to play.

'I know I'm not an easy person to live with,' Adele continued. 'I think that's why I stayed with Mel, even after I knew we were finished. A warm body on the other side of the bed? Better than nothing, right?'

'Are you saying that I'm just another warm body?'

'I'm saying that I love you, and I'm not used to that, either.'

Again, as when she asked me to bandage her wounds, I had the sense that Adele was opening herself up for my inspection. She was offering me a secret and the cost was obvious, in the tilt of her head, in the resigned tone. She held my gaze for a moment, then seemed to flinch as she fell back in the seat.

'Tell me what you want to do?' I asked. 'With Linus?'

'I need to pay him back, Corbin. Personally.'

'You need to be a lot more specific here, partner, because that part I already figured out.'

Adele smiled then. We were now thinking alike and my only fear, as we began to discuss strategy, was that Linus Potter, deterred by the weather, wouldn't be in Sparkle's when we got there.

I needn't have worried. When Adele and I stepped through the door a few minutes after midnight, Potter was sitting at his usual table, his back to the room, staring into an empty mug. Otherwise, the bar was deserted except for the boss, Mike Blair. Blair was standing in front of a small sink, washing and drying glasses. He looked up as we came through the door, then tossed the dish rag into the sink and pulled a bottle of Dewar's off the shelf. By the time I reached the bar, he'd poured me a double.

'You still drinkin' through a straw?' he asked Adele.

'I'd like a glass of whatever white wine you

308

have in the refrigerator.'

Blair shuddered, perhaps recalling a day when cops had simpler tastes, then ducked under the bar to fetch a half-empty bottle of Chardonnay. It even came with a cork.

I waited until Adele's wine was poured, then turned to Sparkle and raised my glass. 'To the job,' I said. For some reason, my ex-partner failed to echo the toast.

'I heard you had some trouble tonight.' Always nimble, always suspicious, Blair's eyes flicked from me to Adele. 'I heard you had a close call.'

I think Blair was searching for that line in the sand, the one you have to draw for yourself. True, Adele and I had brought disgrace on the job. But did that merit assassination? Perhaps there was some sort of technical exception that allowed the blue wall of silence to be momentarily breached. Or, perhaps, any hole in the dike would bring on a catastrophic flood.

'They were Paco Luna's men,' I said.

'You sure?'

'I'd be willing to bet my next six pay checks on it.'

'And you say there were cops involved in this?'

Adele finally spoke up. 'We were investigating cops and ex-cops, not Paco Luna. If Luna came after us, they sent him.'

That wasn't entirely true because I'd talked up Luna to my snitches, then again to Nina Francisco. But I didn't correct my partner. Instead, I picked up my drink, took a sip, then carried it to Linus Potter's table.

I sat down without asking, on the far side of the table with my back to the wall. Potter's eyes opened, but he didn't look up. Myself, I was in no hurry. I simply allowed the clock to run for several minutes as I carefully centered myself. Under no circumstances would I show Potter the rage boiling just beneath the surface. Under no circumstances would I let him know just how much I wanted to kill him. This was especially important because I'd already passed my back-up Smith & Wesson to Adele. My job was to provoke. The honor of killing him, if it came to that, was hers.

Finally, I asked, 'Back when you were still in uniform? What was your rep?'

Potter laughed, his eyes blinking rapidly. 'On the street, they called me Robocop. Tell ya the truth, Harry, I was flattered.' He hesitated for several seconds, his eyes still fixed on the mug resting between his fingers. 'What about you?'

'I was a "necessary force" kind of cop. It took a lot to get me pissed off.'

'But I somehow managed to accomplish the trick? I gotta say, Harry, I find that flattering, too.'

It was after twelve and detectives just coming off the four-to-midnight tour would ordinarily be stopping by to wet their whistles. But not to-night. Through a window in the front of the bar, I could see dark lines of snow silhouetted against a street light on Knickerbocker Avenue. If anything, Mike Blair was looking to close up and head home.

Potter broke the silence a few minutes later. 'You wired, Harry?'

'No need, Linus.'

Potter considered my response for a moment, then nodded. 'I knew you wouldn't stop. I knew you'd keep coming. I knew it from the first time you spoke to me. Dante thought you'd quit, but I knew you'd keep coming.'

'That's why you sent me Russo's photo. It's why you told me to connect Russo, Jarazelsky and Szarek. It's...' I paused when something flickered through Potter's eyes. He caught my hesitation and smiled, but chose not to speak. Perhaps I'd made one too many assumptions, a technical error, but we were both professionals. We knew that it wouldn't matter, in the short or the long run. Still, I changed the subject.

'Can I assume you're not connected to Greenpoint Carton?'

'Yeah, you can.'

I gave it a few beats, then shifted gears again, putting more distance between our conversation and my gaffe. 'We got a problem here. You want to know *why* and I want to know *what*. You can see how this creates a certain dilemma.'

'When,' Potter replied.

'When?'

'I want to know when, too.'

'When did I know for sure?' I asked.

'Yeah.'

Though I hadn't been certain of Potter's involvement until Adele identified him as her attacker, I straightened in my seat and assumed a positive tone as I got to work.

'Last Sunday, when I met Tony Szarek's girl-friend, that's when I knew. What was it you said about Tony? Something about traveling from a rented room to a bar stool all the days of his miserable life? That was very poetic, Linus, but it was complete bullshit. By all accounts, the Broom was a happy man. Now I admit, in and of itself, that wouldn't mean a whole lot. Maybe you and Tony were hardly acquainted, maybe you were just telling a good story. But you knew where Tony was buried. You said it right out, "Mount Olivet Cemetery." That indicates a closer relationship.'

Potter looked down at his mug for a moment, then carried it over to the bar. His jacket was unbuttoned far enough for me to catch a glimpse of the weapon snugged behind his hip as he got to his feet. But Potter's intent was not on may-hem, not at that moment. He waited patiently for his mug to be filled, then came back to the table without once looking at Adele.

'My mother,' he said as he sat down, 'was a very religious woman. One of the things she used to tell me was that I should live every day as if it was my last. Now I drink every beer as if it was my last. You think that's what she meant?'

He raised the mug to his mouth and drained it, his neck so muscular his Adam's apple was little more than a shadow moving beneath his skin. 'Fire away,' he said.

'If you remember, you told me you worked on the Clarence Spott case.'

'I was a fly on the wall.'

'Then you should have known about the car.

312

The one Clarence Spott was driving when Russo and Lodge pulled him over, the amazing vanishing car that was never heard about again.' When he grinned at that, I continued. 'Me, right from the first, I wanted to know what happened to that car. But you, Linus, you never even mentioned it.'

'Is there a question here?'

'I want to know what was in the car.'

'Seed money. Or a commodity that could be turned into seed money.'

'Seed money for what purpose?'

'To buy Greenpoint Carton. The owner was an old man named Epstein. His kids didn't want any part of the business and he was willing to sell cheap. It was an opportunity certain parties couldn't resist.'

'But not you?'

'Not me.'

'Glad to hear it. Now tell me what set off David Lodge. Tell me what he remembered. Being as you and Davy were such good friends, I'm sure he confided in you.'

'He didn't. The only story I got comes from Pete Jarazelsky, who I don't consider a reliable source.'

'Tell me anyway.'

'According to Pete, what Davy remembered was spotting two cops sitting in a cruiser as he drove away from the first confrontation with Clarence Spott, the one that took place on Knickerbocker Avenue. These cops were double-parked a block away from the scene, in full view of the scuffle, but they didn't back him up.

313

He thought this was strange.'

'I take it one of those cops was Pete Jarazel-sky?'

'Come to seize the loot, Harry, not rescue the drunk.'

'And the other one? The other cop?'

'If Davy even saw the other cop, he didn't remember. Just as well.'

I sipped at my scotch, then twirled the glass on the table as I watched Mike fidget behind the bar. 'I don't want any trouble here,' he declared.

Potter ignored the comment. 'Your turn to confess,' he said to me.

I looked up at Sparkle, at her pursed lips forever about to blow a kiss, and asked her for luck. What was apparent to me, by then, was that news of the grand jury investigation soon to begin had reached Linus Potter. He knew he was beaten, knew that it was only a matter of time before Pete Jarazelsky or Ellen Lodge gave him up.

'Those phone calls you made, they helped the bad guys, not me and Adele. The first one had us looking for DuWayne Spott when we should have been sweating Ellen Lodge. We wasted the whole afternoon on that search. The second call directed us to Spott's body, which of course, had to be found right away. The game plan called for the job to make a quick and easy decision. Du-Wayne Spott in close proximity to one of the TEC-9s that killed David Lodge? What could be simpler?'

'And it worked, too.'

314

'What can I say, Linus? You know your NYPD.'

Potter skillfully avoided the trap. 'Not me, Harry. I didn't say anything about me.' He turned to Mike Blair and shouted, 'Hey, you think I can get another Guinness here?' When Blair's only response was a narrowing of the eyes, Potter rose and did the job himself.

'Did I ever tell you,' he said, 'that me and Davy, we both had a little problem with alcohol?'

'Actually, you told me you kept him sober when you worked together.'

'God, I'm such a fibber.' He set down his mug, then raised his head. Potter's blue eyes were slanted at the corners, though not as sharply as Adele's. They'd appeared sad to me, the first time I'd looked into them, a quality now overshadowed by an unwavering stare that held whatever sorrow they revealed at a distance too great to be bridged. I saw anger, instead, and a trace of resignation. If he'd only been a little bit luckier. If only the first detectives to respond to David Lodge's murder had been other than Harry Corbin and Adele Bentibi. If only, if only, if only.

'If all you were after was the product in Clarence Spott's car,' I finally said, 'why did you have to kill him?'

'Excuse me, Harry, but you are once again employing the word *you* very freely. We're still talkin' theoretically here.'

'Answer the question, Linus.'

He flinched at my tone, his eyes hardening for

315

a moment. Then he smiled a smile that amounted to no more than a twitch of his upper lip. 'Do you think weasels are happy bein' weasels?' he asked.

'You talking about the little animals?'

'Yeah.'

'I figure they probably have a hard time imagining alternatives.'

'Good point, but that's not true for human weasels. Take Tony Szarek, for example. Now there's a guy, a weasel to his bones, who should have never come on the job. All he ever thought about was how to get over. Me, I'd rather cut my balls off than be a weasel, but Tony...' Potter shook his head, apparently in admiration. 'But you were right about Tony. He was a happy man.'

FORTY-ONE

What struck me, as Potter rambled on, was that responsibility for the taking of a human life was again being assigned to somebody who would never answer for the deed. The widow had blamed her husband's murder on the missing Dante Russo, who was probably dead. Now Clarence Spott's murder was being blamed on a man who was indisputably dead. Still, some elements of Potter's self-serving tale rang true.

According to Potter, Szarek had stolen David

Lodge's Fluugmann blackjack months before using it on Clarence Spott. He'd done this because he was a thief in his heart, a facet of his personality so well known that he was the only partner at Greenpoint Carton not allowed to sign checks.

'An asshole like that, you figure he deserves what he gets,' Potter explained, 'but the Broom, well, he was always lucky. Ya see, Dante made sure that Tony and Davy lawyered up right away, the idea being to use the extra time to get their stories together. Only problem: Davy Lodge, he didn't have a story. He didn't remember a fucking thing. Now Dante Russo, he was a born schemer, like Tony was a born thief. When he heard about Davy's blackout, he knew just what to do.'

'Frame David Lodge?'

'As Dante said at the time, "Never look a gift horse in the mouth."'

'What about Ted Savio?'

Potter showed surprise for the first time. 'Savio helped out when Clarence Spott was killed and Dante's been feeding him PBA business ever since. If there was something else goin' on, I never heard about it.'

If Potter's explanation of the events fit all the known facts, Szarek's motive remained obscure, even after all these years. Initially, the Broom told Russo that he'd been physically attacked by Spott and he was only defending himself. But after the autopsy proved that Spott was struck from behind, Szarek changed his story. The way

317

he then told it, Spott had attacked him psychologically by suggesting a physical relationship between Szarek's daughter and the family dog. Though Szarek had neither daughter, nor dog, he'd felt obliged to avenge this deadly insult. As would any other red-blooded cop.

A third version emerged several years later when Szarek admitted (over drinks, naturally) that he was so drunk at the time, the murder of Clarence Spott might have amounted to nothing more than a passing whim.

Potter rose at that point, to re-fill his mug. This time he didn't empty it in one gulp. He set it on the table and wrapped his fingers around the glass. 'Is that the works?' he asked. 'You finished tellin' me how bad I fucked up?'

'Well, there's the one item that'll eventually seal your fate. I'm saving that for last. But let me ask you this. Do you have an alibi for the time of David Lodge's murder? How about for the days leading up to DuWayne Spott's overdose in that hell-hole of a tenement? How about for last Saturday evening when my partner was attacked? You got an alibi for last Saturday?'

Potter laughed. 'You forgot Dante. I need an alibi for him, too.'

'Does that mean he's no longer among us?'

Again, Potter laughed. 'I think I'll wait for the punch line,' he said.

I finished my drink, looked over at the bar, finally set my glass on the table. The last thing I needed was more booze.

'You hooked up to the Internet, Linus?' I asked.

318

'Gimme a fuckin' break.'

'Hey, don't take that attitude. You can find out all kinds of interesting things on the web. For instance, I once stumbled across a CIA interrogation manual posted on this obscure bulletin board. Call it idle curiosity, but I printed the manual out and read it in one night. Interrogation has always been my strong point.'

'Mine, too. Only I got a suspicion we employ different methods.'

'That I wouldn't doubt. Anyway, the manual was pretty much a rehash of techniques you can read about in any textbook. But this one thing did catch my attention. The manual warned Agency de-briefers of a problem I'd never encountered. Terrorists and spies, it seems, are likely to have prepared fall-back stories to offer their interrogators if the pressure becomes intolerable. You understand, these fall-back stories are very elaborate and completely fabricated.'

'You talkin' about Ellen Lodge?'

'From the beginning, I thought I could break her.'

'And you couldn't?'

'Nope, Ellen had her fall-back story down pat: Dante Russo, Dante Russo, Dante Russo. She was so well prepared, I couldn't reach her. But I remembered this CIA manual as the interrogation went along, and that's how come I realized there was no way Ellen could've dreamed up this story on her own. It was too intricate, too complete. Somebody familiar with interrogation techniques had to provide the details and drill her until the words came automatically; somebody bold enough to insert himself into an investigation; a vain, narcissistic freak named Linus Potter.'

Potter wagged a finger in my direction. 'You could go too far, Harry.'

As that was my aim, I ignored the remark. 'You and Ellen Lodge, you wouldn't be an *item*, would you?'

At that, Adele snorted, a contemptuous honk that Potter ignored, though his eyes shifted as he considered the question. I knew there had to be a connection between them, and that the grand jury would eventually uncover that connection. Potter apparently knew it as well.

'Don't talk dirty about Ellen,' he cautioned. 'She's my cousin and we grew up in the same house. It was me who introduced her and Davy.'

'Well, I got some hot news for you, Linus. Your family ties are not gonna cut it.' I shook my head as I repeated the message I'd sent to Ellen Lodge. 'Conspiracy to commit murder carries a penalty of life without parole. Eventually, Ellen's gonna turn.'

But my news wasn't news at all. Linus had been all over this ground. 'She will,' he admitted without hesitation. 'Unless...'

'Unless some co-conspirator, in a moment of panic, decides to kill her? Me, I don't want that to happen.'

'So, you're here to protect Ellen? That's what you want me to believe?'

'I got a better question, Linus. Do you think freaks are happy bein' freaks? I'm asking you this because you're a freak, so you should know

320

the answer. And I'm not talking about your body. I'm talking about inside your head, where you live. You're so afraid someone's gonna see what's in there, you sit with your back to the room. But I'm lookin' directly at you now, so I can see the misshapen little freak hiding behind your eyes. He's a baby, that freak, an infant. Greed is what he knows, greed and envy, a kid who wants the tit every minute of every day. Are you gonna let the freak run the show, Linus? Are you gonna let the freak put you in a cell for the rest of your life? Are you that fucking stupid?'

Potter's eyes were shifting now, avoiding the unexpected onslaught. That I would challenge him this way in a public place had caught him by surprise.

'Christ, Harry, you're hell on wheels,' he finally muttered. 'Hell on wheels.' His eyes went flat as he completed the statement and I became unable to read anything in them.

'Tell me about Paco Luna,' I asked.

'The goose that laid the golden eggs.'

'The eggs that had to be laundered at Greenpoint Carton?'

'The very same eggs. Fact is, Harry, it was Luna who set up Clarence Spott seven years ago. Luna knew Spott would be transporting product because Luna sold the product to Spott in the first place. But you said something about an item that would seal my fate. I gotta admit, I'm anxious to hear what it is.'

I leaned back in the seat and allowed the air to fill with the hum of the refrigerator behind the bar and the faint buzz of a small neon sign in the front window. The sign's tubing was curled and twisted to form a tiny green leprechaun. Right eye closed in a leering wink, the leprechaun's head was tilted to one side. A line of script above his top hat announced: *HARP*.

Behind the bar, Mike was leaning forward, one elbow resting in a puddle. His eyes were hard-focused, his attention given over to our little drama. When Adele was the one to break the silence, Mike's head shot up as though he'd been punched.

'Have you ever had sex with a woman, Linus?' she asked. 'I don't mean a whore. I mean a woman who wanted to be in bed with you.'

Potter thought it over for a minute, his expression unchanging, then, without looking at Adele, said, 'You're pushin' the wrong buttons, Harry.'

Adele replied before I could speak. 'It was me who went to the DA. Don't blame Harry. I'm the one. If you have a complaint, you should direct it to me. That's assuming you have the balls to look a woman in the eye.'

When Linus didn't respond, I confirmed Adele's statement. 'Would ya believe, Linus, that in spite of everything we did, all our efforts, an Inspector named Thaddeus Clark told me that I should mind my own business? That's why Adele went around the job, why she used her connections to push the DA into convening a grand jury. That grand jury, it's gonna look at everything, from Clarence Spott to Dante Russo. And what they're gonna come up with, sooner or later, is you.'

'This I already know.'

I leaned forward over the table, my face gradually becoming more animated as I went on. 'Look, here's the way I see it unfolding. The memory David Lodge recovers leads him to Pete Jarazelsky, who is then persuaded to come across with additional details. Nobody's fool, Pete soon warns certain compromised parties back in New York. There isn't any rush, since Jarazelsky's beating occurs six months before Lodge is released.' I paused long enough to take a breath. I was going to run a bluff here. Though I'd made a mental note to ask Deputy Warden Beauchamp for a list of Jarazelsky's visitors, I hadn't actually done it.

'The first thing I asked myself was exactly who Jarazelsky contacted after the beating. The second thing was the means by which this communication took place. A phone call, a letter, or person-to-person. As it turned out, the right choice was door number three. The right choice was Linus Potter, who also visited Pete Jarazelsky whenever he went to see David Lodge, two good deeds for the price of one. Tell me, was Jarazelsky smart enough to hold something in reserve when David Lodge fell upon him? Like your name?'

Potter raised his mug and stared at the few inches of beer at the bottom. The beer was flat and he swirled the mug several times before drinking.

'Seems like the last one,' he declared, 'outta be better than that.'

He set down the mug and raised his eyes to

mine. They were as opaque as ever, but this time I was glad. If I'd been wrong, Potter would have been unable to conceal his triumph.

'When Davy cornered Pete down in the prison laundry,' he said, 'it was like a gorilla dropped out of a tree to land on a kitten. Pete had no defense whatsoever. Now, ya gotta figure Pete was terrified, what with the rumors that Davy killed a guy in Cayuga. But Pete was smart, too, and he'd been inside for a long time by then. He only gave up Szarek and Russo.'

'And that left you to play the good guy with David Lodge.'

'Me and Ellen.' Potter lapsed into a momentary silence, his eyes dropping to the table. Finally, he said, 'Davy couldn't be reasoned with.'

'Neither can Pete.' I waited a moment, but Potter had nothing to say. We were coming to the end and we both knew it. 'Being in Attica presents Jarazelsky with advantages and disadvantages. On the one hand, he's safe. Even if you kill them all, Ellen Lodge and whoever else is involved, you can't eliminate Jarazelsky. On the other hand, Pete's isolated. He has no idea what's going on down here. He'll find out, of course, and when he does, my bet is that he's on the phone to the DA within twenty-four hours. That'll be it for you, Linus, unless you move first.'

The phone rang at that moment. I think Mike Blair would have preferred to ignore it, but he finally stepped away from the bar after the fifth ring. When he did, Adele reached into her purse to withdraw the S&W revolver.

'You asked before, about *why*,' she said. 'About why Corbin didn't quit. Now, I'm going to tell you. Corbin would never admit this, but he takes crime personally.'

Mike Blair picked up the phone and muttered a few words into the mouthpiece. When he hung up and turned to find Adele pointing the .38 at Potter's head, he decided to remain where he was.

'When you commit a crime on Corbin's watch,' Adele continued, 'he sees it as an act of contempt. For him, it's like being challenged on the street. If you ignore the insult, your entire world implodes. This is a narrow view, and quite emotional at its base, but it's still a view that produces results. This was especially true in your case, Linus. In fact, your intrusion so upset my partner that he risked his career in order to bring you down. See, from Corbin's point of view, Linus Potter's decision to pit his intelligence and abilities against Harry Corbin's was more than a challenge. It was a calculated act of disrespect by a marked inferior. That's really why he came to Sparkle's in a blizzard. To show you that no pin-head freak can beat Harry Corbin at the game of policing. To show you face to face. Tell me something: how do you like it? Does it feel good? Does it feel as good, for instance, as hitting me in the face with a bat?'

Potter's mouth expanded into a tight and bitter smile. His eyes began to shift again, back and forth, from pure hate almost to the point of regret.

'You'll have to excuse my partner,' I said. 'She tends to over-analyze. But it does seem to me you have a pair of viable options, Linus. And one that's not viable. Let's take the last option first. You could walk out the door right now and hide behind your lawyer. That would buy you a couple of weeks of freedom. But you don't really want that, not after the way you've been humiliated tonight. You realize, of course, that once the story of what happened here gets around, you won't be able to leave your house. Knowing, as you will, that everybody else knows, too.'

Once again, Mike Blair spoke up. Again, he made a plea for calm. This time, Linus Potter responded first. 'Shut up, Mike,' he said. Then he jerked his chin in my direction. 'The viable options,' he said. 'Let's hear 'em.'

'The first one's called redemption. I'm not armed, Linus. The shooting board took my weapon. If you wanted to, you could show me the error of my ways right this minute. And when you think about it, killing me, killing my partner, even killing good old Mike – it wouldn't make all that much difference. You're already on the hook for life without parole. Plus, if you redeem your honor, it'll do wonders for your self-esteem.'

Potter shifted his weight to allow the right side of his unbuttoned jacket to fall to the side. 'And what's the downside?' he asked.

'The downside is that Adele's pointing a gun at the back of your head, so you're gonna have to be really quick.'

326

The information had no discernible effect on Linus Potter. 'What's my other option?'

'The freak's not gonna like this one, Linus, not one bit. The other option is confession, which is good for the soul, but not for the freak. Ellen's still holding out. Jarazelsky's in the dark. That gives you the option of being first. Now I know you've employed this line yourself, so I'm not gonna belabor the point. But if you want, we'll take you down to the DA, right now, and you can cut that good deal.'

'You and your partner, you want to take me to the DA?'

'Yeah.'

'Like I'm some kind of fucking trophy.'

'I told ya the freak wouldn't like it.'

Potter laughed. 'In my whole adult life,' he declared, 'nobody has ever talked to me like this. It takes some gettin' used to.' He settled back in his seat and called out, 'Hey, Mike, you think you could bring me that one last beer? The beer I been practicing all my life to drink?'

Blair waited for me to nod, then drew off a mug of Guinness. He brought it over to the table, careful to remain out of the line of fire, and set it down. Potter turned far enough to raise the mug in Sparkle's general direction, then drank it dry.

'Make up your mind, Linus. Which way do you wanna go?'

Linus answered by rising to his feet, then turning to face Adele and the gun she now held with both hands. Though he was seeing her weapon for the first time, his expression didn't change. 'You gonna shoot me, Adele?' He spread his own hands apart. 'I mean, I'm not threatening anyone here.'

After a moment, Potter took a step forward, then another, each step measured and deliberate. When they were ten feet apart, Adele cocked the revolver, the sharp click seeming almost obscene in my ears. Linus came to a stop at that point and I hastened to take myself out of the line of fire, circling to Potter's right. If Potter took another step, I was certain that Adele would kill him.

Potter let his hands drop to his sides as he looked past me to Mike Blair. On the way, our eyes met for just a moment. The rage and the hate were gone now, discarded like a Halloween mask. In their place, I registered layer upon layer of pain, a bone-deep sorrow that revealed everything the freak wanted to hide. Mike Blair stared directly into those eyes for several seconds. I don't know what he saw, or even if he recognized anything beyond the immediate threat. But Mike's tone, when he commented, was far from compassionate.

'If she blows your fucking brains out,' he declared, 'I'm gonna claim you made a try for your weapon.'

Potter flinched, the rebuke sharp enough to sting. He had no friends here. Slowly, he let his head come round far enough to face me.

'More than I don't wanna go to prison, I don't wanna die,' he explained with an apologetic shrug of his massive shoulders. 'Would ya believe that?'

'How about more than you want revenge?'

'Yeah,' he said, 'more than that, too.'

328

I came up behind him, then reached across his body to jerk his automatic out of its holster. As I backed away, I looked over at Adele. What I saw in her eyes was disappointment.

'Besides,' Potter said, 'I swear, I was hardly involved.'

'Just an innocent bystander?'

He winked. 'Harry, you're hell on wheels.'

FORTY-TWO

My first instinct was to put the whole business behind me. After all, the bad guys were knocking on the DA's door, each begging for an opportunity to testify against the others, and against Paco Luna whose operation was being systematically attacked by a task force that included the FBI and the DEA. About this outcome, I argued to myself, there was nothing not to like.

I made that rationalization last a couple of weeks, but it was like the first time you try to give up cigarettes. Somehow, the cravings just won't go away. In this case, what I craved was an answer, and not even the mini-honeymoon Adele and I were thoroughly enjoying was enough to sooth the itch.

'I have to do something about it,' I finally told Adele.

'Corbin,' she replied, 'are you taking this personally?'

I watched the knowing smile on her lips gradually expand, then came back at her with the wickedest shot in my arsenal. 'Ya know, Adele, if you weren't a girl, I'd hit you with this pillow.'

The proof was easy enough to gather, no more than the afternoon it took to track Justin Whitlock to an apartment on Avenue S, in Brooklyn. But I wasn't satisfied with the proof, not even close. I wanted to know why, and that took a while, forcing us once again to dip into Adele's old-girl network. As it turned out, we were well into the month of March by the time I fired up the Nissan and started out for Port Washington on the north shore of Long Island.

Bill Sarney was living the good life. His three-story colonial had wings at either end, one newly constructed, by the look of the still-raw brick, and a cobblestone driveway that swept up to the front of the house. Despite the fog, the paint job on an S-Class Mercedes parked in that driveway gleamed as though lit from within.

The money for all this high living came from Bill Sarney's wife, Rebecca, a senior partner at some Wall Street law firm with too many names to remember. I'd met Rebecca the few times I'd been out to the house, and I only had two memories of her. The first of her small and graceful hand, offered with the palm down, the second of her clear devotion to her husband and her two children.

The front door opened as I walked up the flagstone path, and Bill Sarney stepped onto the porch. He was wearing gray wool slacks, freshly pressed, and a pale blue shirt that fit tightly over the small bulge of his belly.

'Rebecca took the kids to her sister's,' he explained as I walked past him. 'We've got the place to ourselves.'

He closed and double-locked the door behind us, then led me through the living and dining rooms, to that newly built wing on the side of the house which he'd turned into a billiard room. I smiled appreciatively. The green felt on the table was so smooth it might have been combed fur.

'You want something to drink?' he asked. 'A beer, maybe?'

'Sure, a beer would be fine.'

Sarney opened a small refrigerator, removed two bottles of Bass Ale, poured them into a pair of tall glasses bearing unidentified crests. I got a shield on my glass, flanked by two standing lions who seemed about to break into song.

'So,' he asked, 'how're they treatin' ya, Harry?'

'No worse than expected.' I hesitated for a moment, then changed the subject. 'You hear about Tony Szarek?'

That caught his attention. His chin came up for a change and he looked directly into my eyes. 'No,' he admitted.

'Szarek was killed by his girlfriend's brother, a man named Ryszard Gierek. It was funny, Bill, how it went down. For reasons he took to the grave, Szarek told his lover that she was his sole heir when he didn't even have a will. Some kidder, that Tony.'

'How'd you know,' he asked, 'about the

331

Szarek arrest?'

'I got a pipeline into the task force, but that's not the point. What I'm talking about is the irony. When Szarek's death came up suspicious, me and Adele, we assumed that it was linked to the David Lodge killing. That got us trying to connect Lodge, Jarazelsky, Russo and Szarek, which we eventually did. Meanwhile, after drinking himself into unconsciousness, Tony was capped by a Polish immigrant who collects baseball memorabilia.'

Sarney smiled, drawing his thin lips into a crooked grimace that seemed more pained than happy. 'I take your point,' he conceded, 'but that's how it goes sometimes. You try your best to draw a straight line between where you are and where you want to be, only the world does not cooperate.'

I ignored the implications. 'And Bucky Chavez, that was another one,' I said. 'Another irony.'

Maximo 'Bucky' Chavez, who had us connecting dirty cops in the Eight-Three with Paco Luna's drug operation, had re-emerged a few days after my confrontation with Linus Potter. Subjected to an intense grilling, Bucky had finally admitted that he'd seen nothing more than a 'white man in a suit' enter Paco Luna's town house. The rest – the part about a cop from the Eight-Three – was the product of his naturally dishonest imagination. And there was nothing suspicious about Chavez's disappearing act, either. After a three-dollar hit on the number 437 netted him $1500, Bucky had quit Brooklyn to hang out with his 'outside woman' in Jersey City. Nina Francisco, he'd explained, would only have thrown the money away on something foolish. Like clothes for the kids.

'What's with the ironies?' Sarney asked. 'You and Bentibi writing a book?'

'Nope, in fact Adele got a job. She's starting on Monday.'

'What kind of job?'

'She's going to work for Alessio, the Queens DA, as an investigator for Major Cases.'

Again, I caught Sarney off guard. He turned away from me and walked to a window framed by pale yellow curtains. For a long moment, his gaze remained fixed on a slice of yard dominated by an ancient fruit tree. The tree was gnarled and twisted, its bark slick with dew, its every branch dotted with thick green buds that seemed about to explode.

'Well,' he said without turning, 'it looks as if Bentibi managed to land on her feet.'

'Yeah, she did. Just like you. But there's one more irony out there, and we need to discuss it.' I laid what remained of my beer on a coaster and took a few steps in Sarney's direction. I think by then he knew I had an agenda, and what that agenda was. One thing for sure, I hadn't come to beg forgiveness, which is what I'd told him in the course of a long phone call.

'When I first heard about Greenpoint Carton from Tony Szarek's sister,' I continued, 'I didn't think that much of it. A retired cop owns a little business? No big deal. But when I found out that Justin Whitlock was managing that business?

333

The same Justin Whitlock who alibied Russo in the Clarence Spott homicide? I tell ya, that got the old sap rising.'

Sarney finally turned around to face me. His features were composed, even relaxed, except for his eyes. They were focused on me with the intensity of a blow torch. 'When Justin Whitlock came up clean,' he admitted, 'it surprised everyone.'

But that, of course, was the irony. Justin Whitlock was exactly what he appeared to be: a hard-working manager who kept the inventory up and the deliveries flowing, who cashed his check at the end of the week and went home to his wife.

'Justin still works at Greenpoint Carton, making that commute from Gravesend every weekday. Personally, I don't see why he does it. Him and his wife, they own a nice little co-op, with no mortgage, in a nice little neighborhood. Plus they both have pensions and social security. Justin could just lay back and enjoy the remaining years, but...'

'Is there a point here?' Sarney finally interrupted.

'Only that Justin Whitlock told me, if I should run into you, to remember to say hello for him.' I smiled. 'Hello, Bill.'

When Sarney didn't reply, I turned to a cluster of photographs on the wall to the right of the window: Sarney shaking hands with Rudolph Giuliani, with Michael Bloomberg, with George Pataki, with Hillary Rodham Clinton, with two police commissioners, with a host of lesser lights. Arranged in what appeared to be a perfect rectangle, the tight grouping was impressive, even though I knew the photos had been snapped at expensive fund-raisers attended (and occasionally sponsored) by his wife's law firm.

'Where do you want to go, Bill?' I finally asked.

'What do you mean?'

'You're a captain, now, and there's no more civil service exams for you. If you're gonna move up, you're gonna have to do it by appointment. So my question is real simple. How big are your dreams? How high do you hope to rise? Inspector? Deputy Chief? Chief? How about Chief of Detectives? You stay another ten, fifteen years, it's not impossible.'

'Funny thing,' Sarney replied after a moment, 'but I somehow don't feel the slightest need to discuss the issue with Detective Harry Corbin.'

I nodded to myself, then turned and took a step in Sarney's direction. We were now standing a couple of yards apart. 'You remember those tips Adele and I received?' I asked. 'There were five of them in all.'

'Yeah, what about 'em?'

'Well, did you ever wonder who sent them?'

'My guess was Linus Potter, trying to control the investigation.'

'Potter sent the first two, but not the rest.'

'How do you know that?'

'Let's just say the fact was revealed to me when I mentioned receiving Russo's photo via email during my confrontation with Potter in Sparkle's. As it turns out, Linus Potter equates operating a computer with chemical castration. He wouldn't know an email attachment from a carrier pigeon.'

Though I'd promised Adele, going in, that I wouldn't lose my temper, some part of me hadn't been listening. 'You were really good, Bill. The way your face got all red and you pounded the desk when I walked into the precinct with Ellen Lodge. And that bit about how you rescued me, a nothing detective riding out the tail end of a nothing career? I tell ya, I didn't have a clue.'

I recalled Potter's story about David Lodge's confrontation with Justin Whitlock, how Lodge had intimidated Whitlock with a display of temper. Bill Sarney, I already knew, was of a different breed. 'I should've figured it out right away, of course. That first pair of tips – the one that had us looking for DuWayne Spott and the one that told us where to find him – they helped the bad guys. But the other three? They helped the good guys, Bill, meaning me and Adele. Now why would Linus Potter, or any of his buddies, want to aid the investigation? That was the logical question, but I was too busy, too focused on Russo and Szarek and Greenpoint Carton, to ask it.'

Sarney walked over to the pool table. He lifted one of the cues, hefted it for a minute, then put it back on the table.

'You made a lot of mistakes,' I told his back. 'First, whoever sent the last three tips must have known about the first two. That narrowed the

336

field to Bill Sarney or some higher-up who was following the investigation. Second, one of those tips advised me to stay out of Greenpoint; that Adele and I were wasting our time. Great advice, as it turned out, but it just raised more questions. Like, who knew we were working Greenpoint in the first place? And how did they know? That's when I ran down Justin Whitlock in his Sheepshead Bay co-op; that's when he told me he'd been visited by a ranking officer, a detective-lieutenant named William Sarney, on the day after I confronted him at Greenpoint Carton.'

Sarney finally put a little distance between us by walking over to the wet bar. 'You're pretty sharp, Harry, when it comes to judging other people, but the truth is that I didn't put a gun to your head. You made your own choices.'

'What about Russo's service photo? The one that turned up while I was still sitting on the fence.'

Sarney shook his head. 'Gimme a fuckin' break. You're a knight in shining armor, and you always have been. That's why I wanted to promote you and get you transferred to Homicide. The best detectives always take it personally; they're always out to right wrongs. Funny how Bentibi knows this and you don't.'

I watched him rinse his glass carefully, then dry it with a white bar towel. The towel was immaculate. It looked as if it had been ironed.

'Ask yourself,' he continued, setting the glass on the counter, 'why you went for the detectives in the first place. Ask yourself why, when it became obvious that you weren't going to be

337

promoted by the bosses, you didn't do what I did.'

'Which is what?'

'Which is pass the sergeant's exam, the lieutenant's exam, the captain's exam. Which is move up through the civil service, instead of waiting around for some arrogant jerk in Borough Command to decide you're worth promoting.'

I thought about it for a moment, then admitted, 'I was afraid, if I passed the sergeant's exam, I'd be transferred out of the Detective Bureau.'

'My point exactly.' Sarney turned to face me. As on the night I'd waltzed Ellen Lodge into the house, his act was very convincing. He tucked his chin down into his adam's apple, presenting me with a furrowed expanse of forehead, then stared up at me through his eyebrows. If he'd only remembered to blink, he would've been perfect. 'You're in love with that gold shield,' he continued, 'you and every other detective. But that's never been a crime. In fact, I'll even admit that seeking justice is an admirable way to pass a career.'

'But it's not Bill Sarney's way?'

'No, it's not.'

'True enough, but I did learn something from you, Bill. Tell me, what do you think would happen if I took what I have to Inspector Clark at Borough Command?'

'Look, Harry, I didn't arrange for David Lodge to get killed in the One-Sixteen, any more than I arranged for you and Bentibi to catch the case. It's just something that happened, one of those

338

random shit-storms life throws at you from time to time.' Sarney turned to face me before delivering the punch line. 'If you remember, right from the beginning, I advised you to cover your ass.'

'That doesn't answer the question. What would happen if I took what I have to Inspector Clark?'

Though Sarney looked as if he was ready to explode, he got the words out. 'Nothing. Nothing would happen.'

I nodded. 'See, that wasn't so hard. Now tell me why nothing would happen.'

Sarney stared at me, his dark eyes disbelieving. Here he was, a Captain, being pushed around by a nothing detective he'd consigned to the rubbish heap. I might have reminded him that life, as he'd been kind enough to explain, was full of nasty surprises, but I held my tongue.

'I wasn't alone,' he finally admitted. 'There were others who wanted Potter and his crew taken down.'

Cops on the job call NYPD headquarters, at 1 Police Plaza, the Puzzle Palace. Within its walls, or so the common mythology goes, the levels of intrigue rival those of a Byzantine court. Exactly who is doing what, and to whose benefit, and for what reason, is never entirely certain. I looked over at the collected photos on the wall, Commissioner Ray Kelly with his crooked nose, his square jaw, his jagged line of a mouth. Standing next to him, Sarney was grinning like a kid left alone in a candy store.

'We followed them for years,' Sarney continu-

339

ed, 'right through the killing of Clarence Spott, and the arrest of David Lodge. When Pete Jarazelsky was arrested for burglarizing that warehouse, I thought it was all over. I was sure Jarazelsky would flip. I still don't know why he didn't.'

'Maybe he was afraid, Bill, afraid of Linus Potter. Maybe you were afraid, too. Maybe that's why you didn't go after him yourself, why you sent Harry Corbin instead.'

Sarney absorbed the insult with a shrug of his shoulders. 'We knew about Greenpoint Carton,' he explained. 'That Jarazelsky, Szarek and Russo owned it, and we'd heard the rumors about Paco Luna, but we had no real proof. Then Szarek turned up dead. That got our attention, especially after we received word that David Lodge was going to be released.'

'Somebody called you from Attica?'

'Not me, Harry. And not anybody I'm willing to name.'

'But you knew Lodge was coming out.'

'Yeah.'

'And you knew he was claiming to be innocent.' I poked Sarney in the chest, but he held his ground. 'You knew there was going to be trouble and you did nothing to stop it.'

Now defiant, Sarney jammed his fists into his hips. 'Yes, I knew that blood would flow, Davy Lodge's or somebody else's, and I didn't give a shit. Potter and his little gang, they were a cancer growing on the job. We were determined to cut that cancer out, and we succeeded.'

'Didn't it bother you that some of that blood

might have flowed from innocent bystanders like Adele Bentibi and Harry Corbin? If you recall, Adele's features were permanently rearranged.'

'No,' he said, 'it didn't. Not before, and not afterwards.'

I hit him then, a right hand to the side of the face that drove him to the ground. When he didn't get up immediately, I took a step back and waited for him to climb to his feet before continuing. 'When you said nothing would happen if I took my case to the bosses, you were right. Being co-conspirators, they'd naturally have to protect you. But those tips you sent me? They're part of the case file, and how I received them is already being questioned. You gettin' this yet? Three days from now, Adele and I are going to meet with Ginnette Lansky to prepare our testimony before the grand jury. Ten days from now, Adele and I are going give that testimony. If we name you as the probable source of three of those tips, you will also be called to testify.'

I'd finally broken through. The anger dropped from Sarney's face, the smug superiority too, as his dilemma became clear. If called to testify, Sarney could not hide behind his Fifth Amendment rights because he wasn't being accused of any crime. That left him with a simple choice: he could swear that our conversation never took place, and expose himself to a charge of perjury, or he could name the bosses who'd conspired to bring down Linus Potter. Those bosses, they wouldn't be happy about that.

Sarney twisted for a few minutes, standing

before me on unsteady legs, one hand pressed to the side of his face. 'What do you want?' he finally asked.

'First, I want a pipeline into the Puzzle Palace. I want to be able to come to you when I need help, and I want you to be seen with me in public. I want you to make a commitment.'

'What else?'

'I want a transfer to Homicide, Bill, the place where white knights go to die.'

Sarney's laugh seemed genuinely amused, and perhaps a bit admiring, but his eyes had grown shrewd. 'Are you telling me you can deliver Bentibi?'

'I'm telling you those anonymous tips – all five of them – will remain anonymous. At least as far as we're concerned.'

We were almost at the end now. It was time to finish up and go home.

'You have to do your penance,' Sarney explained, 'and there's no getting around it. You can't shit on the bosses and expect to be rewarded.'

'Even if certain bosses wanted me to shit on them?'

Sarney ignored the sarcasm. 'And I can't stop the rumors going around about you and your girlfriend being IAB snitches. Those rumors are comin' from the PBA and that's a world unto itself.'

'Bill, are you telling me that you can't deliver?'

'No, I'm saying it's gonna take time, and that it's gonna be hard for you.'

342

The last part didn't interest me. 'How much time?' I asked.

'Nine months, a year.'

'And in the meantime?'

'In the meantime, we'll see about your rehabilitation.' He shifted his weight, nodding to himself. 'I'll tell you this,' he finally said, 'it's very good that you're cooperating here. Certain people will be impressed.'

'Well, let's make them doubly impressed. Ten days from now, the Holy Name Society is throwing its annual dinner-dance at the Sheraton. Adele and I are gonna be there.'

'And you want me to be there as well, to be seen with you?'

'That's right, Bill, and when I invite your wife to dance, I expect her to accept without hesitation.'

As Sarney considered the demand, his grin began to widen. Again, I sensed a degree of admiration, as if by playing his game, I was somehow flattering him.

'OK, I think I can make that dinner.' He reached out to touch my arm, a gesture as intimate as it was unwelcome. 'And if you wanna dance with Rebecca, it's fine, as long as you don't ask me to dance with Bentibi. That's one gesture I don't feel up to making.'

This time, when I hit Sarney, his eyes rolled up in his head and he went over backwards, crashing to the floor. I stood over him for a moment, half-hoping he'd make some attempt to rise, but the man lay as unmoving as a corpse. I thought of Adele, then, waiting for me back in Rens-

343

selaer Village. When we'd finally uncovered Sarney's contribution to the dramatics, her first instinct was to bury him. But she'd turned on a dime when I laid out my goal, and my plan to attain it. Her only moment of hesitation came after I announced my determination to confront Sarney alone.

'I'm afraid you'll lose control,' she'd announced. 'That you'll do something you can't take back.'

'Are you saying that I shouldn't lay a hand on him?'

'No, I'm saying you should hit him twice, once for each of us, then get the hell out of his house.'

Mission accomplished, I left without a backward glance.

FORTY-THREE

Though we continued to reside in Rensselaer Village, Adele and I were apart for days on end. Our hours were long, our working lives entirely separate. Adele was currently employed by the Queens District Attorney in the Major Crimes Bureau, while I'd been transferred to the 123rd Precinct on the southern tip of Staten Island and assigned to work the four-to-midnight tour. As often as not, by the time I returned home it was closing in on two o'clock in the morning and Adele was a shadow curled beneath the covers in a darkened room.

We'd compensated for our separate lives in a number of ways, one of which unfolded before me as I came out of the locker room at the Y on Twenty-Third Street. Adele had taken up swimming and she now stood at the edge of the pool, poised to make that initial leap. The idea (which had been presented to me as a done deal) was for us to spend more time in each other's company.

If Adele had asked me beforehand, I would have told her that swimming is a solitary pursuit, perhaps the most solitary of all sports. But I hadn't been asked and I now watched as Adele's knees bent, as she leaned toward the pool, as her arms swung back, as she sprang up and out, as the muscles in her thighs and buttocks flexed hard before releasing an instant after she hit the water.

After three months of co-habitation, I'd come to realize that I'd never penetrate Adele's essential reserve, that she would always be mysterious. This wasn't an impediment to our relationship; like most males, I have little interest in expressing my innermost feelings, assuming I have any worth expressing. For Adele, though, reticence was closely connected to her determination to avoid a trivial life. The idea, from her point of view, was not to restrict communication. She wished only that the messages we exchanged be non-verbal. It was more of a challenge that way.

I watched Adele swim a few laps, my eye now critical. She was in good shape and she had stamina, but even allowing for her inexperience,

I knew she'd never be a swimmer. For Adele, the water was an obstacle to be overcome through an effort of will. For born swimmers, on the other hand, there is no physical separation between flesh and water until the very end of a swim. And it's the flesh that fails.

My thoughts, when I finally got into the water that night, were not of whales and penguins. They were of my lover and her husband, Mel. I'd been wrong about Mel. He did have feelings, which he expressed in a series of phone calls that began while Adele and I were still working the David Lodge case. Of course he loved her. Of course he couldn't bear the pain of their separation. He would do anything, make any changes to his habits and personality, in order to recapture her affections. Of course.

Though utterly useless, Mel's pleadings were sincere enough. Losing Adele had carried him back to the very pain that had originally shut him down.

I remember raising the question of whether Mel's frequent calls had crossed the line and become harassment. Adele had responded with a sly smile and a toss of her hair.

'Soon enough,' she predicted, 'he will come back to himself.'

A week later, Mel announced (through his lawyer, Carolyn Bemis) that he not only planned to sue for divorce on the grounds of desertion, but to contest every item of communal property, from the electric toothbrush in the bathroom to the potted geraniums on the balcony.

My concern, as I cut through the water, was for Adele. There's nothing more trivial than an ugly divorce and Adele's first instinct was to avoid the matter, to turn her back and walk away. But she and her husband's financial affairs were completely interwoven, on top of which Mel had cleaned out their checking and savings accounts. Thus Adele had retained an attorney named William Melrose only a few days before. Melrose was urging her to counter-sue on the grounds of emotional cruelty.

'You need to take the offense here,' he'd counseled. 'You have to stay one step ahead of the game.'

One step ahead of the game. If that was all it took, Adele might not fare too badly after all. Certainly, she'd been one step ahead of the job throughout the Lodge investigation. Adele had barraged Ginnette Lansky with self-righteous descriptions of the NYPD's latest ethical failings, presenting a moral argument that acknowledged no blurring of the line between right and wrong. Her strategy was tailored to Lansky's rigid personality, a matter of telling the subject what the subject wanted to hear. This was a technique learned from Harry Corbin, a technique that finally inspired, in Ginnette Lansky, a desire to secure Adele's services far into the future.

It was a little past midnight when Adele and I stepped out onto Twenty-Third Street. Above us, a bank of low-hanging clouds played moon to Manhattan's sun, reflecting back the light from a million sources. Adele and I headed south,

347

toward a restaurant on Stuyvesant Street called Round the Clock. It was Saturday night, the sidewalks crowded, the mood on the street celebratory: a bitterly cold winter had finally been put to rest. In the distance a siren wailed, grew louder for a moment, then slowly receded without ever coming into view. Ahead, a pair of Latinos, short stocky men in white aprons, squatted outside the kitchen door of a Greek diner. They took quick puffs on their cigarettes, conversing in rapid-fire Spanish. As we passed, the younger of the two evaluated Adele with a searching, though not disrespectful, glance.

We were within a block of the restaurant when Adele turned to face me. She tugged at my lapels, pulling me down into a kiss. I think she was fearful. While life with Mel was far from fulfilling, it was certainly safe. If there was little to be gained, there was little at risk. But circumstances had now changed, and from time to time she looked to me for reassurance though it cut across the grain of her deepest instincts.

Once we had a table and cups of coffee before us, Adele put down her menu and tapped the edge of the table. *Listen up, Corbin.*

'Linus won the grand prize,' she told me.

'Who decided?'

'Kenneth Alessio, himself.' Adele shrugged. 'Potter had the most to offer.'

'And he was the most culpable as well.'

Adele didn't argue the point. After Potter came forward, the other conspirators had rushed to join him, including two previously unknown to us, Officers John Lacy and Judith Singer. As a

348

group, they'd worked the angles common to generations of rogue cops. Paco Luna was protected, for a price, but other dealers were fair game. And what a game they'd played with those unprotected dealers, inspiring by their own savagery a willingness on the part of their victims to surrender whatever cash and product they possessed. And to forget the incident ever occurred.

'I don't like the taste in my mouth,' Adele confessed. 'Potter's admitted to killing Dante Russo, then dumping his body into the East River. He'll plead guilty to manslaughter.'

'Just like David Lodge.'

'Linus Potter,' Adele countered, 'was involved in three homicides, while David Lodge was framed. Somehow it seems unjust that they should receive identical sentences. As if the state was simply balancing the scales.'

Not surprisingly, the stories offered by the various conspirators (in proffers that could not be used against them in a court of law) were entirely self-serving. While all agreed that Dante Russo, still missing, was one of the shooters at the Lodge scene, none admitted to being the other. Potter named John Lacy. John Lacy named Potter. Judith Singer claimed that she was in the clear, both shooters being male, and that's all she had to say on the subject. Jarazelsky might have cast the tie-breaking vote when he named Linus Potter, but Jarazelsky was too far removed from the actual events to be entirely credible.

Ellen Lodge was cursed with the same credibility problem. Once she realized that placing the blame on Dante Russo wouldn't earn her any consideration, she again reversed course. In the new version, Linus Potter, fiend incarnate, had masterminded the drama's every scene. He was author, producer, director, lead actor.

According to Adele, who'd interviewed Ellen Lodge in the company of her attorney, Ellen had told her story well enough, and she would have gotten the good deal if only she'd been consistent. But this was her third account and none of the ADAs working the Major Crimes Bureau believed she'd stand up to cross-examination if her testimony was placed before a jury.

That was good news for Detective Linus Potter, and might have been sufficient to put him in the winner's circle, even without his ace in the hole. Nevertheless, Linus played the card for everything it was worth. Of all the living conspirators, his lawyer pointed out, Linus was the only one who'd dealt face to face with Paco Luna. Even better, he'd surreptitiously taped many of their conversations.

'They all want Luna, Corbin,' Adele explained. 'The Brooklyn DA, the feds, the media and every civic group in Bushwick. If Alessio cuts a deal with Potter, he'll make a lot of friends.'

That the Queens District Attorney, Kenneth Alessio, aspired to loftier political heights was no secret. He'd all but declared for the mayoral primary to be held a year hence.

I knew that Adele was disappointed and I should have kept my mouth shut because the question I asked only made it worse. 'So, who's gonna take the weight?'

'Paco Luna.'

'Seriously?'

'The way it's shaping up, Ellen Lodge and Linus Potter will both plead to man-one. Ellen will be sentenced to fifteen years, Potter to seven. The other two, Lacy and Singer, will plead to extortion. They'll get two-and-a-third to seven.'

If the outcome was bittersweet, Adele's midnight snack – a waffle mounded with strawberries and whipped cream – more than made up for it. As it was my normal dinner hour, I'd ordered the chicken stir-fry, a healthy enough meal diminished only by my refusing the waiter's offer of brown rice.

In truth, Potter's good fortune didn't upset me. Everybody was being charged with something and that was enough. Besides, circumstances had moved me beyond Lodge and Russo and Potter and all the rest. My transfer to the boonies was strictly punitive, a point made early on when my new commander ignored me for three days. Equally cool, my peers generally observed a calculated silence when forced to work with me. At times, their eyes ran across my body as though searching for a wire. At times, the only thing that kept me going was the memory of that dance I'd danced with Bill Sarney's wife, and the promise it implied.

I watched Adele cut through the last bites of her waffle, her movements deft. Adele was a precise eater. If she'd ever allowed a morsel to drop from her fork to her blouse, I wasn't around to see it. I think this trait masked the size of her appetite – blessed from birth with the metabolism of a wolverine, most of the time she was trying to gain weight.

Smug as an overfed cat, Adele finally dropped her knife and fork on her plate, then wiped her mouth and laid her napkin on the table. 'When I eat whipped cream,' she told me, her expression studiously dead-pan, 'I commonly become multi-orgasmic.'

I acknowledged the straight line with a smile, then raised my hand. 'Waiter,' I called out. 'Check, please.'